THE WRECK

MARIE FORCE

The Wreck
By: Marie Force
Published by HTJB, Inc.
Copyright 2011. HTJB, Inc.
Cover by Hang Le
E-book Layout by E-book Formatting Fairies
ISBN: 978-1958035573

PART I
MAY 1995

*To every thing there is a season, and a time to every purpose under
the heaven: a time to be born, and
a time to die; a time to plant, and a time to pluck
up that which is planted.*

Ecclesiastes 3:1-2

CHAPTER 1

"*Tupelo Honey*" played on the jukebox. The scratchy drag of the needle over old vinyl, the cocoon of Brian's strong arms, the musty smell of mold in Toby's dark-paneled basement, the whispered giggles of the other three couples as they swayed to Van Morrison, and the easy comfort of doing what they had done forever filled Carly with contentment.

The seemingly endless New England winter had yielded to soft, fragrant spring days and long, lazy evenings. With her career as a high school cheerleader finished with the close of basketball season, Carly was free to relax and watch Brian play the game in which he truly shined. An imposing tight end and adequate point guard, he was a graceful, elegant pitcher with a fastball no one saw coming and few could actually hit.

Colleges interested in adding that smoking fastball to their bullpens had tried to recruit him, but the only thing Brian Westbury had ever really wanted—other than Carly Holbrook—was to be an attorney. So when they had both earned academic scholarships to the University of Michigan, he said no to the baseball offers so he could focus on securing the grades he would need in the prestigious undergraduate pre-law program to get into a top law school. He had his sights set on Harvard and had told only Carly that, lest he have to explain if he fell short of his goal. But he wouldn't. Carly, who planned to study elementary education, believed in him and was confident he could do anything he set his mind to. That was Brian.

Glancing up at him, she found his eyes closed and his soft dark hair still damp from the shower after his game. As if he could sense her watching him, he opened his hazel eyes and gazed down at her.

Anticipating being alone with him later sent a tremble rippling through her.

"Let's get out of here," he whispered in her ear.

"Not yet," she said breathlessly. "We can't be so obvious."

He smiled. "Like they don't know."

Across the room, Toby was wrapped around Michelle, while Brian's brother Sam, a year younger than the rest of them, made out with Jenny. Sarah held up Pete, who looked like he had fallen asleep to the gentle cadence of the song. Since the eight of them spent every possible minute together, the others had coupled up over the years out of convenience more than anything. But Carly and Brian were the real deal, and everyone knew it.

Michelle had been Carly's best friend since before they could remember, growing up as they had next door to each other. They had collected Jenny and Sarah in elementary school and added the boys in eighth grade. Brian and Carly had been a couple from the very beginning, despite their parents' worries about how serious they were at such a young age.

Yes, the eight of them were cliquey. Yes, they held the others in school at arm's length, which was why they worried

4

so much about Sam being all alone next year. But they made no apologies for friendships that transcended high school and caused others to look on in envy.

Carly returned her attention to Brian.

He sang along with the song, his lips close to her ear.

Filled with melancholy, she tightened her arms around him. Spring was usually her favorite time of year, with everything in bloom, the days growing longer, school winding down, and summer vacation looming on the horizon. This year was different, though. Soon they would graduate and go their separate ways. Toby had received an appointment to the Naval Academy and would be the first to leave home. Pete planned to take a year off from school to travel, Sarah was on her way to Smith, Jenny to cosmetology school, Michelle to the University of New Hampshire, and poor Sam faced one more lonely year of high school.

Carly and Brian had taken the money their parents had given them for college living expenses and rented an off-campus apartment in Ann Arbor, Michigan. It was the sneakiest thing either of them had ever done, and she lived in constant fear that they would get caught.

Even in 1995, a good Catholic girl didn't live with her boyfriend, at least not without a significant amount of guilt to cast a pall over the arrangement. But the thought of spending every night in his arms was worth all the worry and guilt. She had been saying a few extra Hail Mary's every week at confession, hoping the prayers would help to ease some of the guilt, because she had no plans to back out of plans they'd had for what felt like forever.

The phone rang, and Toby disentangled himself from Michelle to answer it. He returned a few minutes later to pull the plug on his father's vintage jukebox. "That was my sister. My parents just left her house."

The others sprang into action to get rid of any evidence

they had been there. Carly collected empty soda cans. They'd tried to score some beer earlier, but none of their older siblings had been around to buy it for them. That was fine with her since beer usually made her sick the next day.

"We can go to our house," Sam said, glancing at Brian for confirmation.

Brian nodded. "Our folks will be out late."

"Cool," Pete said with a big stretch and a yawn.

"Did you have a good nap?" Carly asked him with a teasing grin.

He rested his arm on Sarah's shoulders. "Sure did. Sarah is the *best* pillow."

Sarah poked his ribs, and Pete smiled at her.

"Let's get out of here," Toby said nervously. His mother had "issues" that made her unpredictable, and none of them wanted to be around when she got home.

"Thanks for indulging me, Tobe," Carly said.

"No problem. I know how much you love the jukebox."

"I think I'll miss it more than anything else next year," Carly said with a wistful glance at the vintage jukebox that had gone silent and dark.

"Gee, thanks a lot, Carly," Michelle joked. "I'm feeling the love."

They took a last look around to make sure they had left nothing behind and then followed Toby upstairs to the ranch house's cluttered kitchen. Outside, Brian tossed Sam the keys to the station wagon they shared. "We're going to walk," Brian said.

"Is that what it's called these days?" Sam asked with a snort. "*Walking?*"

"Shut up and unlock the car," Brian said to his brother.

As the others piled in, Brian grabbed his backpack from the front seat.

"Let's go get a pizza first," Pete said. "I'm starving."

"You're always starving," Jenny replied.

Indignant, Pete said, "So?"

"Save some for us," Brian said, taking Carly's hand.

Michelle tugged at Carly's free hand, trying to pull her into the car with them. "Come with us," Michelle said with a pout on her pretty face. "You can shag him anytime."

Carly blushed as Brian eased her out of Michelle's clutches and closed the door.

"We'll be right along," he called as Sam backed the car out of Toby's driveway.

"*Sure you will!*" came the loud chorus from inside the car.

Brian laughed as they watched the others drive away.

"So embarrassing," Carly muttered, hiding her blazing cheeks behind the curls that framed her face.

He laughed as he put his arm around her. "What? That they all know what we're going to do? Who cares?"

"I care." Despite significant effort on the part of the guys, none of the other couples had "gone all the way" yet, which was just another thing that set Brian and Carly apart. They had held out until the beginning of their junior year when love and hormones and rampant desire had finally won out over guilt and fear of pregnancy.

Raining soft kisses on her face, Brian said, "We don't have to. We can catch up to them at Ricardo's." He kissed her everywhere but where she wanted him most. "Just because I've been counting the minutes all day until I could get you alone doesn't mean—"

She reached up to anchor him in place and molded her lips to his until the sound of an approaching car compelled her to let him go.

He took her hand, and they dashed into the woods behind Toby's house just as his parents pulled into the driveway.

"That was too close," Brian said with a laugh.

"We are *so* going to get caught one of these days."

He led her along the well-worn path he had traveled since he was a kid. "We haven't yet."

"Our luck will run out eventually."

"Never," he said with the confidence of a young man who had known nothing but success in his brief life.

As daylight turned to dusk, anticipation propelled them along the path to their favorite spot by the lake, inside a huge weeping willow's waterfall of branches. The heat of the day clung to the soft ground under the blanket Brian pulled from his backpack.

He tugged the T-shirt over her head as her fingers flew over the buttons on his shirt. Unhooking her bra and pushing it out of his way, he gasped at the feel of her breasts against his chest.

She remembered that chest before the soft dusting of dark hair had appeared, before the strong pectorals and tight abs, before the boy had become a man. Carly reached for him, and they tumbled onto the blanket in a rush of passion that never failed to take her by surprise. They had gotten good at this. After fumbling through it at first, they had figured out how to bring each other the kind of pleasure that left them weak and panting and always, *always* wanting more.

When she pushed a hand into his shorts, he gasped against her lips. "Wait, Carly. Wait. Slow down."

She moaned in protest as he caressed her small but firm breasts.

He hovered above her, his eyes finding hers in the final golden burst of sunlight that filtered in through the curtain of willow branches. "I want to remember this."

Puzzlement turned to breathlessness when he nuzzled her breast.

"All day today," he said, making lazy circles around her nipple with his tongue, "I thought only about being here with you. Mr. Allen called on me in trig, and I had no idea what he'd been saying because I was already here, doing this to you." He drew her into his mouth, and her back arched off the blanket in response. "How am I ever going to concentrate on my classes at school when we'll have our own place and a real bed with no worries about being caught?"

Carly found it difficult to think about anything but the heat of his mouth on her breast. "Maybe it won't be as exciting when we don't have to think about getting caught," she managed to say.

His eyes had gone dark with desire when he glanced up at her. "It'll be every bit as exciting."

She wove her fingers into his hair. "Bri," she whispered. "I want you. Right now."

He moved fast to get rid of their shorts and wrapped the blanket tight around them.

Carly raised her hips, seeking him.

Brushing the curls back from her face, Brian leaned in to kiss her. "I love you." He filled her slowly and with more patience than he should have had after waiting all day.

"I love you, too. So much it hurts sometimes." She worked her legs farther apart in the tight confines of the blanket and took him deeper, so deep she couldn't say where she left off and he began.

"It's not supposed to hurt," he said with a smile as he kept his hips still, possessing her as only he could. Gazing down at her, he touched his lips to hers.

She squirmed under him, asking for more.

"Carly," he gasped. "I can't wait."

Clutching him to her, she said, "Don't. Don't wait."

With a moan, he flexed his hips and cried out. "Sorry," he whispered, still breathing hard as he lay on top of her.

She skimmed her hands over his back, which was slick with sweat. "For what?"

9

"You didn't, you know . . ."

"I don't care."

"Give me a minute, and I'll make it up to you."

"You don't need to."

His eyes danced with amusement. "Are you saying no to having an—"

"Stop!" With her fingers over his lips, she silenced him as her face heated with embarrassment. "Do *not* say it."

He laughed. "What am I going to do about you and your hang-ups?"

"Live with them?"

"How about I marry them instead? Will that make it better?"

Carly stared at him. "What did you say?"

"Let's get married. You're freaking out about living together, so let's make it legal. Then you won't have to spend the next four years worrying about getting caught."

"But, Brian," she sputtered. "Our parents will have a cow."

"We're going to do it eventually, so why not now? We're both eighteen. There's nothing they can say."

"They're helping us with school expenses," she reminded him. "What if they refuse to do that if we get married?"

"Do you really think they would? I think my parents would rather we get married than live together on the sneak for the next four years. And have you thought about the summers? We'll be back to doing it under the willow tree."

Carly nibbled on her lip as she thought it over. "Do you mean it? You really want to get married? Not just because of my so-called hang-ups?"

"I can't believe you'd ask me that. I *dream* about being married to you, Carly. I can't imagine waiting four more years until we can do it. We don't have to tell anyone that we're married if you don't want to."

She shook her head.

"You don't want to get married?"

"Of course I do. You know I do. But I don't want it to be a secret."

"Carly Holbrook, I love you more than anything, and I will for the rest of my life. Will you marry me?"

"Yes," she whispered. "Yes, I'll marry you, Brian."

He hugged her tightly. "We'll talk to Fr. Joe after mass on Sunday."

"We should tell our parents first."

"Probably," he agreed. "So does this mean we're officially engaged?"

"I guess it does."

He kissed her lips, her neck, and then her breasts. "Good because I want to give my fiancée an orgasm."

"*Brian!*"

His lips pressed against her belly, he laughed softly. "I can see that getting engaged didn't help with the hang-ups."

"It might take a while," she confessed.

"We've got the rest of our lives to work on it."

CHAPTER 2

The night had turned cooler and the moon had begun its ascent over the lake, but Brian and Carly made no move to leave their secret garden—the only place they were ever truly alone. On this momentous occasion, they were particularly reluctant to leave enchantment for reality.

Carly snuggled closer to Brian, pulling the blanket up over her shoulders against the chill. Usually they were fast to get dressed after their voracious desire had been sated, but not tonight. Caution had taken a back seat to the rare opportunity to linger.

"We should go," he said.

"Not yet. Ten more minutes."

"You're awfully frivolous tonight."

"I just got engaged, and the only place I want to be is right here with my fiancé."

He caressed her face and kissed her. "I'll get you a ring as soon as I can."

"I don't need one. Don't spend the money. We'll need it for more important things like food."

"I want you to have a ring," he insisted.

"As long as I have you, I have everything I need."

"You'll always have me." He stretched and yawned. "But we really should get going."

When he would've sat up, Carly tightened her hold on him.

"What are you doing?"

She slid her hand over his backside, making him groan. "I'm going to my grandmother's this weekend. Who knows when we'll get another chance?"

"We've never done it three times before."

"First time for everything."

"You'll be sore."

She urged him onto his back and straddled him. "I don't care."

"Carly," he whispered.

With a coy smile, she leaned forward to kiss him, showering his face with fragrant curls. "You aren't saying no, are you?"

Looping the curls around his fingers, he said, "I am definitely *not* saying no."

"That's good, because I don't want a husband who can't keep up with me."

The laughter that filled their secret garden faded to moans as she lowered herself down on him.

They had been gone almost two hours by the time they finally got dressed and began the mile-long walk to Brian's house to meet their friends. Above the lake, the moon cast a glow on the calm water, but the path they took was dark and shaded from the moonlight by the canopy of trees. The sound of crickets, another harbinger of spring, filled the air. When Carly tripped over a tree root, Brian's tight hold on her hand kept her from falling.

"We can slow down a bit. A few more minutes won't matter. We're already in for a serious ball busting."

She cringed at the idea of the teasing they would receive from their friends. "Can we tell them we're engaged?"

"Shouldn't we tell our parents first?"

After a moment of silence, they said, "Nah."

Carly giggled. "Like we could keep a secret like this from them anyway. Michelle will be able to tell something's up in two seconds—if it takes that long."

"True."

They were about a hundred yards from Tucker Road when the sickening screech of metal colliding with something hard and unyielding sliced through the peaceful night.

"What was *that*?" Carly asked as they broke into a run.

"Do you smell smoke?" he asked a few minutes later, panting from exertion.

"Yeah."

Running as fast as they dared on the dark path, Carly and Brian emerged from the thicket and stopped short at the sight of an inferno. A car had hit one of the big oaks that lined the road and was fully engulfed in flames.

"*Oh my God*," he gasped.

At the same moment the stench of burning flesh reached the side of the road where they looked on in horror, it registered with Brian that the car was his own station wagon. "*No!*" he shrieked, bending at the waist as if he had been punched. "*Sammy! Noooooooooo!*"

In an effort to break free of him, Carly tugged at the grip he had on her hand.

"*No, Carly!*" He lifted her off her feet to keep her from bolting across the street.

She struggled to break free. "*We can't just stand here!*" she shrieked. "*We have to do something!*"

Tears coursed down his cheeks as he turned her face into his heaving chest. "There's nothing we can do."

The initial blast of flame began to die down, making ghastly silhouettes of the bodies burning inside the car.

"Don't look," Brian said, choked by sobs and acrid smoke. "Please don't look."

Despite his pleas, Carly turned her face toward the heat and stiffened when realization set in. Her screams shattered the night.

~

STANDING by the side of the road, across from the smoldering remains of the car, his brother, and five of his best friends, Brian Westbury felt the fragile hold he had on his childhood give way to the stark, agonizing reality of adulthood. While the paramedics tended to Carly, who had screamed herself hoarse, the first cop on the scene focused on him.

"Do you know where your father is tonight?" asked Lieutenant Matt Collins, a man Brian knew well. Brian's father was the chief of police, and his officers would need his guidance as the full magnitude of the tragedy began to seep through the smoke. That the chief had lost the younger of his two sons maybe hadn't occurred to Matt yet.

Brian ran a trembling hand over his face. "They went to my aunt's in Cedarville."

"Do you know the number there?"

Brian's voice broke as he rattled off the number. "You aren't going to tell him it's Sam over the phone, are you?"

Lieutenant Collins put his arm around Brian's shoulders. "No, son." He barked out orders to the cops who had arrived after him, sending one of them to call in the chief's contact number to the dispatcher. When Brian's knees buckled, the lieutenant eased him to the ground and sat next to him.

"Is Carly all right?" Brian asked. He couldn't see her with the paramedics hovering over her, but her agonized shrieks continued unabated.

"They're taking good care of her. Don't worry." With his hand on Brian's shoulder, the lieutenant's voice was gentle. "I know this is awful for you, Brian, but can you tell me who was in the car with Sam?"

Brian took a deep breath and recited the names of five people who meant more to him than life itself. That they were all gone was simply unimaginable. The staggering weight of the tragedy settled over him, and sobs shook his body. Lieutenant Collins put his arms around Brian and held him until he had collected himself.

"I can ask the paramedics to give you something if you think you need it," the lieutenant offered. "There's no shame in taking the edge off after what you've just witnessed."

Brian shook his head and wiped his face. "I need to be clearheaded for my mother and Carly."

"Can you tell me what you saw?"

While they waited for the medical examiner to arrive, the other cops secured a perimeter around the wreck and held back the small group of onlookers that had gathered.

"We didn't see it happen. Carly and I were walking on the path from the lake when we heard the car hit the tree."

"What did it sound like?"

"A huge boom followed by the crunch of metal." If he lived forever, Brian would never forget that sound.

"Did it sound like an explosion?"

"Not really, but I can't be sure. It happened so fast." Brian swiped at the tears on his face and struggled to continue. "We ran as fast as we could, but we were still quite a ways from the road. By the time we got here, the car was burning." He began to cry again at the memory of the burning bodies and Carly's horrified screams. With a certainty he couldn't explain amid the thick fog of shock and disbelief, he knew he would also never forget the sight of the people he loved burning in the car, the sound of Carly's screams, or the horrific smell of death.

"You know I have to ask if Sam was drinking tonight," Lieutenant Collins said tentatively.

Brian shook his head. "We were together earlier at Toby's house, but there was no booze. They went out for pizza while Carly and I took a walk. You can check at Ricardo's to see what they had, but they don't serve us there. They know we're not legal."

"I appreciate you keeping it together, Brian. Your dad would be proud of you. I'm going to have someone take you home now to wait for your parents."

"I want to stay with Carly."

"Let me see what's going on with her. Stay here."

Brian rested his head on his knees and imagined his parents receiving the call every parent dreads. New tears filled his eyes at the thought of his mother hearing Sam was dead, that he had burned to death along with five other kids who had been in and out of their house for so many years his parents considered them their own.

Lieutenant Collins returned a few minutes later. "Carly is understandably in shock. They've sedated her and are taking her in as a precaution, but they don't think there's anything to worry about."

Brian stood. "I want to go with her."

"Her parents are on their way to the hospital." The lieutenant rested his hand on Brian's shoulder. "I'm not going to tell you what to do, but I think where you need to be right now is at home waiting for your parents. They're going to need you, Brian."

"Yeah, okay." Brian knew the lieutenant was right, but

with all his heart he wanted to stay with Carly. "Can I see her for a minute?"

"Of course." He led Brian over to where the paramedics had loaded her onto a gurney.

Brian leaned down to kiss her cheek and was startled by the vacant, empty look in her normally vibrant brown eyes. "Carly, it's Brian. I'm here." He took her cold hand and held it tightly. As tears blinded him, he wanted to assure her that she would be all right but couldn't bring himself to make such a promise just then. "They're going to take you to the hospital to make sure you're okay. Your parents will meet you there, so you won't be alone." He wiped the tears on his cheeks. "I'm going to go home to wait for my parents, but I'll be over to see you just as soon as I can."

She never looked at him or acknowledged she had heard him. Fear worked its way past the numbness and settled like a block of ice in his gut.

Lieutenant Collins rested his hand on Brian's shoulder. "Let the paramedics take care of her. She'll be okay after they get her to a doctor."

As Brian kissed her cheek and then her lips, he wondered if either of them would ever be okay again.

"Officer Beckett is going to give you a ride home and wait with you until your parents get there, all right?" Lieutenant Collins asked.

The medical examiner approached, but the lieutenant held up his hand to stop the other man until he had Brian settled.

Brian nodded and was led to one of the patrol cars. Since the road leading to his house was blocked, the emergency personnel cleared a path to allow the cruiser through. On the brief ride home, it occurred to Brian that this horrific night would come down to a matter of minutes. Had the others left the pizza place a minute or two later, maybe they would have arrived safely. Only two bends in the road separated the place where the lives of his brother and their friends had come to a fiery end and the split-level house where he and Sam lived with their parents.

If Brian and Carly had left the willow a few minutes earlier, they would've already been at his house and wouldn't have witnessed the aftermath. If Brian hadn't been worried about the teasing that seemed so ridiculous in hindsight, maybe he and Carly would have lingered at the willow a while longer and wouldn't have seen it. Minutes and seconds, making all the difference between life, death, and purgatory.

Because he had given his keys to Sam, Brian had no way to get in the house, so he and the patrolman sat in uneasy silence in the driveway.

While they waited, Brian continued to play the "what if" game as his mind raced with scenarios that somehow might've brought about a different end. If he and Carly hadn't been so anxious to be alone, they would've been in the car, too. Remembering how Sam had teased him about taking "a walk" with Carly had Brian sobbing again with the kind of helpless, massive grief from which there's no escape once it wraps itself with maddening finality around those who are left behind.

They were the last words he would ever hear his brother say. Ever. *Sammy.* The numbness began to wear off, and Brian cried the brokenhearted tears of a young man who'd lost his only sibling, the one person in the world who shared most of his memories, his very best friend. He had a lifetime to mourn the others. For right now, he could think only of Sam.

"Is there anything I can do?" Officer Beckett asked.

Brian shook his head but couldn't speak.

Thirty long minutes passed during which Brian wasn't sure what he wanted more—his parents to get there because he needed them or for them to stay away for that much longer, to be protected from what they would hear and how it would change them forever. He was grateful they would be coming from the other direction and wouldn't have to drive past the accident scene. By the time they finally pulled into the driveway behind the cruiser, Brian had decided that Sam had gotten the easier end of this deal.

His father came rushing out of the car.

Brian and Officer Beckett got out of the cruiser. The expressions on their faces stopped Chief Westbury in his tracks.

"What?" he whispered, touching Brian's face and then his chest, as if to confirm his son was safe. "They said there was an accident. What happened?"

"Dad," Brian said, his voice breaking. "It's Sammy."

From behind his father, his mother's scream was eerily reminiscent of Carly's. Before Brian could tell them that Sam hadn't died alone, his mother fainted.

CHAPTER 3

$\mathcal{T}$he small town of Granville is nestled in the rural northwest corner where Rhode Island comes together with Connecticut to the west and Massachusetts to the north. With an easy commute to Providence and Boston, Granville attracted executives looking to raise their families in a more bucolic setting. The "commuters" tended to gravitate to the fancy new subdivisions on the south side. Residents who could trace their roots back to the town's early nineteenth century origins clustered closer to a downtown made up of converted mills from Granville's glory days as an industrial hub.

In a town of just over fifteen thousand, the loss of six teenagers touched almost everyone in some way or another, uniting the commuters and the townies in a shared grief that brought the usual buzz of activity to a halt during the week following "the tragedy," as it came to be known.

Flags flew at half-mast, routine meetings were canceled, and the high school suspended classes but offered counseling to students who needed help making sense of something that made no sense. With an unexpected week off from school, young people gathered in subdued groups in the town common, at the beach by the lake, and in all their usual hangouts downtown.

Within two days, the scorched earth around the Tucker Road crash site was almost completely hidden by a makeshift shrine erected by the victims' classmates. Freshly painted white wooden crosses bearing the six names—Sam, Toby, Pete, Michelle, Jenny, and Sarah—were surrounded by flowers, candles, balloons, stuffed animals, letters, and drawings protected from the elements by plastic bags.

Thousands of people descended upon the town to pay their respects, to offer their support, and to satisfy the odd curiosity generated by epic tragedy. Recent Granville High School graduates flocked home from colleges around the country, and the story garnered national press coverage.

On Friday, one week to the day after the accident, Sam was the last to be laid to rest in the town cemetery where six fresh new graves dotted the landscape. Just two rows from his girlfriend Jenny and four rows from Pete, Sam's final resting place overlooked the town common where he had spent many an aimless afternoon. Standing with his parents at the gravesite after everyone else had left, Brian thought his brother would approve of the location.

He gave his parents credit for attending all six funerals, something many of the other parents had been unable to do. The lingering numbness from the other five funerals had no doubt helped the Westburys through this unimaginable day. *Was it really only a week ago that the eight of us were dancing in Toby's basement without a care in the world?* And now six of them were dead, Carly had yet to fully emerge from the stupor she'd descended into after the accident, and Brian was more alone than he'd ever been in his life.

His mother dabbed at her swollen eyes with a handkerchief grown sodden with tears.

Resting a hand on Brian's shoulder, his father asked, "Are you ready to go, son?"

Michael Westbury's broad shoulders were hunched, and his ruggedly handsome face had aged overnight. That his son had been driving the doomed car weighed heavily on the chief, as did the preliminary findings of the investigation.

"I'm going to take a walk over to check on Carly," Brian said, adding quickly, "If it's all right with you."

Mary Ann Westbury had clung to Brian over the last week, as if letting him out of her sight might bring about further disaster. He'd done his best to be patient with her, but he needed some distance, some time to process what had happened now that the protracted and agonizing ceremony of grieving had finally ended.

"What time will you be home?" his mother asked with an anxious frown. Mary Ann, a petite blonde with the hazel eyes she had passed to her sons, was first and foremost a mother. A full-time homemaker, she had devoted her life to her boys and their friends. More than anyone else touched by the tragedy, Brian worried about her. Well, he was desperately worried about Carly, too, but had yet to fully deal with that in the midst of all the other details and concerns of the past week.

"An hour, maybe two," he said in answer to his mother's question. "I'll call you if I'm going to be any later."

He knew she wanted him to come home with them to where their extended family waited to offer what comfort they could, and it seemed to cost her something to nod her approval. "Give Carly our love."

"I will." Brian wondered if it would matter to her.

They hugged him and left him standing at the top of the hill as they made their way to where the exhausted funeral director waited for them. Brian watched his father put an arm around his mother to guide her down the slope. He hoped they would somehow find a way to survive the crushing loss.

After they had driven off in the limo, Brian crouched down to run his fingers through the soft dirt that covered his brother. "What're we supposed to do without you?" he asked in a whisper as grief gave way to the anger that had simmered just below the surface all week. "What were you *thinking* driving like that? You didn't even *try* to slow down. They said there were no skid marks, that you just drove off the road into that tree. *You knew better, Sammy!* How many times has Dad told us we have to be better than everyone else because of who he is in this town? How could you do this to him?" Brian's throat closed, and tears filled eyes already raw and gritty. That there could be any tears left astounded him. His voice was once again a whisper when he added, "How could you do this to *me*? How could you leave me here all alone?"

He bent his head and cried the same way he had the night it happened, the same way he suspected he would cry for a long time to come. Over the last week Brian had discovered there was no escape from grief. If he was awake, it hung over every breath, every word, every corner of his life. Sporadic sleep provided no reprieve, haunted as it was by vivid dreams that forced him to relive the horror over and over again.

Wiping his face, he stood and took a long last look at his brother's grave before he turned and forced himself to walk away. He ambled down the hill and crossed the street to the sidewalk that wrapped around the town common. A group of boys he knew from school were in a circle playing hacky sack on the grass. They stopped their game to watch him walk by. Brian acknowledged them with a brief nod but didn't stop. He couldn't bear to listen to another awkward word of sympathy from peers so far out of their league they said only the wrong things.

As he left them to continue their game, it occurred to Brian that he didn't have any friends left. He had plenty of acquaintances but no one he could call to hang out with. He'd always had Sam and Toby, who'd been their friend since they were babies. Their mothers had been close before Mrs. Garrett's drinking had worsened right around the time the boys started high school.

They met Pete through Toby, and with the three of them always around, Brian hadn't felt the need for more close friends. Once he started going out with Carly, he'd had even less of a need for others. The eight of them hadn't set out to distance themselves from the rest of the kids, but they had nonetheless. Now Brian was left without a friend in the world and a girlfriend who either couldn't or wouldn't share her grief with him.

Wanting to avoid the accident site, he took the long way around downtown to Carly's house on South Road. They'd once counted the seven hundred and eighty steps between their houses.

The tulip border Mrs. Holbrook lovingly tended was in full bloom on either side of the sidewalk in front of the two-story white clapboard house. White wicker furniture with pretty floral pads decorated a wide front porch where Brian had whiled away many an hour with Carly. He closed the gate behind him and climbed the stairs. As he waited for someone to answer the door, he tugged his tie loose and took off his suit coat.

Mrs. Holbrook came to the door in the same dress she had worn to Sam's funeral. A headband contained her short auburn curls, and as she opened the screen door for him, he noticed her brown eyes, so much like Carly's, were still rimmed with red. "Brian," she said, welcoming him with a warm embrace. "How are you, honey?"

Mortified when his eyes filled again, he wondered if it would *ever* stop. "I'm okay."

She cradled his face in her hands. "Your eulogies for Sam and the others were just beautiful. I was so proud of you this week. How you ever managed to do what you did—"

Shrugging off her praise, he said, "Somebody had to." He glanced up the stairs. "How is she?"

"About the same." Mrs. Holbrook shook her head with dismay. "She let me feed her some soup earlier, so I guess that's something."

"Do you mind if I—"

"Go right ahead." With the wave of her hand, she invited him upstairs to Carly's room, which he had never even seen before this week. Everything was different now. Allowing their daughter's boyfriend into her bedroom was suddenly the least of her parents' worries.

Brian hung his suit coat on the newel post and started up the stairs.

CARLY PULLED a blanket around her and nestled deeper into the window seat. She'd had trouble staying warm over the last week, as if her blood had turned to ice or something. Maybe it had. She had spent most of the day staring out the window that overlooked Michelle's house. The police had come by again to see if she was able to talk with them about what she remembered from that night. She had heard her mother tell them she wasn't up to seeing them yet.

An hour or so ago, Michelle's mother had shuffled out to the mailbox. Mrs. Townsend wore an old housecoat and slippers. Her usually stylish hair had hung in ratty strings down her back. On her way inside, she had glanced up to find Carly watching her. She had attempted a smile for her daughter's best friend, but it had come out more like a grimace.

Carly wondered if Mrs. Townsend was mad at her for not dying with Michelle. She wouldn't blame her, because Carly felt the same way herself. If she and Brian hadn't been so anxious to have sex, they would have been in the car with the others. And Carly could say, without a shadow of a doubt, that she would rather be dead than have to live with the images of the others dying.

Over and over she remembered Michelle tugging at her hand. *"You can shag him anytime. You can shag him anytime."* Carly put her hands over her ears as if that could stop the relentless refrain.

Everyone was worried. She saw it on the faces of her parents and in Brian's eyes when he came by to see her. They wanted to know why she hadn't said anything since the accident. She had heard her parents talking about post-traumatic stress and shock and other terms she didn't recognize. Carly wasn't sure why she couldn't talk. She wanted to, mostly because she was desperate to help Brian through the loss of his brother. But she was afraid if she tried there would only be screams. So she didn't try.

"Hey," Brian said from the doorway, diverting her attention away from the window. He crossed the room, knelt before her, and wrapped his arms around her.

Carly ran her fingers through his thick dark hair. Wearing the shirt and tie they had chosen for homecoming what seemed now like a lifetime ago, he looked as she imagined he would someday when he was a successful attorney.

"It was nice," he said after a long period of silence. "Sam would've loved all the attention." He waited, as if he hoped she might say something. When she didn't, he continued. "My parents seem to be holding up okay."

Carly was relieved to hear that. She had thought of them constantly.

"But I'm worried about how my mother's going to be after her sisters leave and things go back to normal—or what's passing for normal now. I guess my Aunt Elaine is going to stick around for a week or two, which should help. Toby's parents were there today and Jenny's. I think Toby's mom was drunk, but I can't say I blame her. I would've liked to have been, too."

He looked up at her with heartbroken eyes. "Talk to me, Carly," he begged. "I need you."

Her eyes flooded with tears. Oh, how she wanted to! But the words just wouldn't come.

Scooping her up, blanket and all, he carried her to the double bed with the fluffy pink comforter. Kicking off his shoes, he lay down next to her and brought her into his arms.

Carly rested her head on his chest.

"This doesn't have to change everything for us. We'll have a quiet wedding and go to Michigan, just like we planned. That's what they would've wanted us to do. I know they would."

She shook with silent sobs.

Brian turned on his side and cupped her damp cheek in his hand. "We're still alive, Carly, and we have to find a way to go on. We have to live our lives the best way we can. We'll do it for them."

She pulled away from him and tried to sit up, but he stopped her.

"I'm sorry, honey." He guided her head back to his chest. "It's too soon to be talking about moving on. I know. I'm sorry." He exhaled a long deep breath full of the hitches that come after tears.

She hated that he was in so much pain, that he needed her so badly, and she had nothing to give him. Hanging heavily over her also was the guilt that came from thanking God over and over again for sparing Brian. If He'd had to take all the others, at least He had left behind the one she couldn't live without.

She glanced up at Brian and saw his eyes were closed.

Her mother came to the door. A week ago she would have freaked out at the sight of them snuggled together on the bed. Now, though, she came in and adjusted Carly's blanket to cover Brian, too. She brushed a hand over her daughter's hair and kissed her forehead. "He needs the rest," she whispered. "The poor guy has been a trouper this week. I'll call his mother to let her know he'll be here for a while."

After her mother left the room, Carly closed her eyes and wallowed in the comfort and safety of Brian's tight embrace. If she kept her eyes closed long enough, she could imagine they were married and resting in their bed in the small apartment they had rented in Michigan. She could pretend nothing bad had happened and they were right where they'd always planned to be. But then she remembered something bad *had* happened. Flashes of fire and that smell . . . It came rushing back like a nightmare that refused to end. Closing her eyes tighter to ward off the memories, it was all she could do not to scream.

MAY SLIPPED INTO JUNE, and somehow life went on. Brian forced himself to get up each day and go to school where he was treated with cautious but distant respect. Outside the main office, they had set up a memorial to the six students who had died. Once, when no one else was around, he stopped to study the portraits: Jenny and Sarah, both blond and blue-eyed; Michelle with her long dark hair and porcelain complexion; Pete's sandy curls and mischievous smile; Toby, dark-eyed and serious with the military bearing that made him a perfect fit for the Naval Academy.

And Sam. Brian and his brother had so often been mistaken for twins. Looking at Sam's smiling face was like looking in the mirror. How many times had he been called Sam? How many times had Sam jokingly complained about being mistaken for Brian? Realizing that would never, ever happen again was like losing his brother a second time. *There should be two more pictures up there,* Brian thought, *of the two whose lives had been ruined by the loss of the other six.* God, how he missed them—the ones who had died and the one who had checked out of life.

He sat through class in the mornings and left each day at lunchtime, something he wasn't allowed to do, but no one stopped him. By not showing up to practice, he quit a baseball team already crippled by the loss of the three starters who'd died. Brian simply couldn't bear to do anything that reminded him of that last day.

Every afternoon, he spent a couple of hours with Carly. She'd yet to leave her house or say a word, and had apparently developed a fear of cars, too. When her parents tried to take her to a post-traumatic stress disorder specialist, she had silently refused to get into the car. The doctor made an exception by coming to the house, but he had no success in getting through to her. The longer her silence persisted, the more frustrating it became for Brian, who had no one else to talk to.

Carly's father was equally frustrated, often ranting that she was refusing to talk on purpose. Her mother disagreed, and even though the Holbrook house was thick with tension, Brian preferred it to his own house where his mother rarely left the sofa.

Carly and Brian spent the night of their senior prom watching a movie in her basement family room. He had stopped pleading with her to talk to him and had given up on trying to get her to write notes to him, settling instead for her company, for the opportunity to hold her hand and be close to her. Final exams were done, graduation was just a week away, and the future that once seemed so assured was now filled with uncertainty.

After the movie, Brian took his time walking home. He went into the dark house where his father watched TV alone in the living room.

"Hey," Brian said.

"Hi, son. How's Carly?"

"About the same. How about Mom?"

"Same. She just went to bed." If things had been normal, she would've been waiting up for her boys to get home from the prom.

As Brian took a seat on the sofa, he and his father shared a sad smile, united in their concerns about the women they loved. "Is anything ever going to be the same again?" Brian asked.

"I don't think so."

Brian sighed.

"My father used to have a theory that there's one great tragedy in every lifetime. The good news is yours is behind you now, so you can rest easier. You won't have to worry as much about your own kids."

"Great," Brian said with a touch of sarcasm. "That's good to know."

Michael shrugged. "I know it doesn't bring much solace right now in light of all you've lost, but someday maybe it will."

Seeing that his father was struggling to help him, Brian

said, "I guess so." He hesitated and then took the plunge. "Dad? Can I talk to you about something?"

"Of course." Michael reached for the remote to turn off the TV. He flipped on a lamp and gave his eyes a moment to adjust to the light. "What's on your mind?"

"Well, ever since the accident, it's just . . ."

"What, son?"

"Sam didn't drive like that, Dad," Brian said in a rush of words. "I never once saw him be careless or reckless behind the wheel. And it wasn't just because I was in the car, either. I would've heard about it if he were being crazy. I know the investigation found he was speeding and lost control of the car, but I can't imagine that. I knew him, Dad. I *knew* him."

"There were no skid marks, no sign he did anything to try to stop or even slow down. That kind of evidence is hard to overlook, even for me as his father. If there was something else to be found, Brian, believe me, I would've found it."

"There *is* something else. I'm not sure if it matters, but—"

Michael sat up straighter. "What?"

"A couple of months before the accident, I was coming home from the library one night pretty late. I was on Tucker Road, right around the same place where the accident happened. Anyway, I came around that bend and there was someone standing in the road. I had to swerve to miss hitting him. It scared the shit out of me."

"Why haven't you said anything about this before?" Michael asked, speaking now in what his sons referred to as his chief-of-police voice.

"I'd forgotten all about it. The whole thing lasted less than ten seconds, and I never thought about it again until two days ago when I suddenly remembered it. Now it's all I can think about."

"You didn't see his face?"

"No, he was wearing a ball cap pulled down, but it was

like he was waiting for someone to come around that bend, you know? What if he was there again and Sam lost control of the car when he swerved to miss him?"

Michael rubbed at the stubble on his chin. "I like that explanation a whole lot better than any of the others."

"I do, too. I can't imagine Sam driving that fast, Dad. Especially with Jenny and the others in the car, and *especially* around those bends on Tucker Road. You were forever warning us about getting into trouble and how it would embarrass you. I'm not saying we were perfect, but we were always careful. Neither of us wanted to disappoint you."

Michael's eyes filled with tears. "Thank you," he said in a hushed tone. "Somehow that makes me feel better."

"Is there anything we can do about the other thing? The guy in the road?"

"I'll have someone look into it."

"Good," Brian said, relieved. "That's good. I'd hate to have Sam's name forever tied to this if it wasn't his fault."

"So would I, son."

CHAPTER 4

*T*he night before graduation, Brian found his mother in her favorite position since the accident —on the sofa, nursing a glass of what looked like whiskey. The drinking was new in the last month, and it just added to his already full plate of worries. He had seen what alcohol had done to Toby's mother and to their family. He'd wanted to go over to see Mr. and Mrs. Garrett but had been afraid of what he might find there, so he'd stayed away.

"Mom?"

"Oh, hi, honey. I ironed your shirt and hung it in your closet. Are you going to wear the maroon tie?"

"I guess so. Whatever you want."

"That would look nice with the black gown."

"You know, Mom, I'd understand if it was too much for you to go tomorrow night."

She pushed herself into a sitting position. "Don't be ridiculous. I wouldn't miss it for the world, Brian. I'm so very proud of you. Number *four* in your class." She shook her head with amazement and patted the cushion next to her.

He sat with her. "I've been thinking about deferring

Michigan for a year and staying closer to home next year. I'm sure one of the state schools would take me in light of everything that's happened—"

"No," she said firmly. "Absolutely not."

"How am I supposed to leave you and Dad and go halfway across the country? It won't matter if I wait a year. I'll still get the degree from Michigan."

"I won't have you changing your plans so you can babysit me. That's not going to happen. You're going to Michigan, and I don't want to hear another word about it."

"What about Carly, Mom? What's going to happen to her?"

Mary Ann reached for his hand. "I don't know, honey. But you can't put your life on hold until she bounces back. The two of you saw the same things, but for some reason it hit her harder. I wish I knew why."

"We were going to get married."

"*What? Married?*"

"I asked her the night of the accident."

"Oh, Brian."

"We used the money you guys and her parents gave us to rent an off-campus apartment in Ann Arbor so we could live together."

"I wondered if you would."

"Really?" Brian asked, amazed.

"I may be old, but I wasn't born yesterday," she said dryly.

"Wow," he said with a smile. "I really thought I was getting away with something, but I should've known you'd figure it out. Anyway, she was kind of freaking out about living together, and since we were going to get married someday anyhow, I just figured why not now?"

Mary Ann held his hand between both of hers.

He rested his head on her shoulder. "I don't know what

I'm supposed to do, Mom. She's my fiancée. Do I leave her here and go to school? How do I do that? I love her."

"Maybe she'll be better by the time August rolls around. It's only been a month. She might just need some more time."

"I'm not so sure. The Carly I know and love would never have let me go through the last month by myself, you know?"

"I know what you mean." She sniffed and wiped away the stray tear that rolled down her cheek. "Are you worried her condition might be permanent?"

"I'm starting to wonder," he said, giving voice to his greatest fear. "What am I supposed to *do*, Mom? This is *killing* me. I miss her so much. I miss them all, but having her here and unavailable is somehow worse. Is that awful for me to say?"

"No, baby, it isn't." She cradled his head on her chest. "It's not awful. All you can do is hope she'll come around."

He looked up at her. "And if she doesn't?"

"Then you have to find a way to go on. That's all you can do. You've got your whole life ahead of you, Brian, and you have to live every minute of it to the best of your ability. If you've learned nothing else from all this, I hope you've learned that."

"What will you do?"

"I've been thinking about getting a job."

"For real?" He had never known her to work.

"I've got to do something. I can't sit here drinking whiskey forever. It's time to pick myself up and figure out what's next."

"I'm glad to hear you say that. I've been worried about you."

She kissed his forehead. "I'm sorry you were worried."

"You'll really be okay if I go to Michigan?"

"I'll miss you like crazy, but I'll be fine. I promise."

BRIAN MADE two trips to the stage at graduation—one to collect the diploma the school board had voted to give Carly, even though she hadn't taken her final exams, and the other to pick up his own diploma. Both times his classmates stood and cheered. He'd declined the invitation to narrate a tribute to the five members of their class who had died in the accident. Their empty chairs, as well as Carly's, were decorated with photos, flowers, and balloons.

As he listened to the class president talk about each of his fallen friends, he felt all eyes on him as he struggled to maintain his composure. He managed to hold it together until they mentioned Sam. Tina West, a talented soprano in their class, concluded the tribute by singing "The Wind Beneath My Wings." Brian quit trying to control his tears when he realized there wasn't a dry eye in the big tent on the high school lawn.

After commencement, his parents invited his extended family back to the house for cake, and everyone made a tremendous effort to keep the mood celebratory. Brian opened gifts and ate the chocolate cake his mother had baked for him, but the forced sense of merriment was stifling. He kept waiting for Sam to appear, making wisecracks that Granville High would give a diploma to anyone. As soon as Brian could escape, he picked up Carly's diploma and walked over to her house.

She was sitting on the front porch, almost as if she had been waiting for him.

With a kiss to her cheek, he handed her the leather-bound piece of paper that declared her a high school graduate. "Congratulations."

She brushed a hand over the black leather.

"They did a nice tribute to the gang, and they included

Sam, too, which was cool. Tina sang that song from *Beaches*. I bawled my head off, but everyone did."

Reaching for his hand, she brought him down next to her on the porch swing.

After swinging in silence for several minutes, Brian said, "I can't believe we're high school graduates."

She replied with a small, sad smile.

Unable to resist the urge, he leaned in and kissed her. When she didn't pull back like he expected her to, he wrapped a hand around her neck and nudged at her lips with his tongue.

She turned her face away.

"Carly, honey, *please*. I miss you. I miss *us*. I miss making love with you. If you love me the way you always said you did, you'll talk to me. I *need* you."

Clutching his hand, she wept quietly as if even making the noise it took to cry was too much for her.

He pulled his hand free and stood up. "I can't do this anymore. I don't know how to help you, and you won't tell me. I'm not coming back again. When you're ready to talk to me, you know where to find me."

Her eyes beseeched him to stay, but he forced himself to turn away from her. He went down the stairs and out through the gate, letting it slam closed behind him.

THE WEEK after Brian left her was the worst of Carly's life, even worse than the week that followed the accident. Without his visits to look forward to, there was nothing left to live for. Except for occasional trips to the bathroom, she never got out of bed and refused to eat or shower.

"This is *bullshit*!" Her father's voice broke the silence one morning.

"Be quiet, Steve," her mother said. "She'll hear you."

"I don't care if she hears me! I've had enough of this! Apparently so has Brian."

"She's traumatized. She just needs some time to get over it."

"It's been five weeks, Carol! Brian saw the same things she did, but he's not refusing to talk or eat or get out of bed."

As Carly heard her mother speaking quietly in an attempt to pacify her father, she rolled her face into her pillow to keep from hearing any more. *Does he really think I* want *to live like this?* What she wanted was to be going to work at the coffee shop like she had every summer for years. She wanted to be meeting Brian after work to swim in the lake and make love under the willow. She wanted everything to be the way it used to be.

Carly heard her sisters talking as they got ready for work.

"She's doing it for attention," Caren said. She had recently finished her freshman year at the University of Connecticut.

"Why would she do that?" asked Cate, who'd just graduated from Boston College. "Brian's furious with her and so is Dad. Why would she be stirring up all this trouble on purpose? That's not Carly. Besides, you know how much she loves Brian. She'd never want to drive him away."

Thanks, Cate. Carly heard her father's car start and was relieved to realize he was leaving for work. Because they'd always been so close, Carly hated that she was upsetting him. As the youngest of the four Holbrook kids, she had loved being her daddy's little girl. The two most important men in her life were mad at her. She knew it was because they loved her so much and were frightened by her withdrawal from life, but knowing that didn't make it any easier.

Her mother came into the room and opened the drapes. "I drew you a bubble bath."

Carly winced from the sudden onset of light but didn't

39

resist when her mother pulled back the covers, tugged her out of bed, led her into the bathroom, and undressed her like she would a baby. Carly slipped into the tub and let the fragrant bubbles envelop her in their warmth.

As she worked the shampoo through Carly's long curls, her mother said, "Here's how this is going to go. You can have as much time as you need to get past what's happened, but you're going to get up every day, you're going to bathe, you're going to eat, and you're going to help out around here. Your father's right. This has gone on long enough. I know you're terribly sad. We all are, but enough is enough, Carly. Do you understand me?"

With tears rolling down her cheeks, Carly replied with a small nod.

Carol wiped away her daughter's tears. "Brian called to check on you."

Carly looked up at her mother to see if it was true.

"He loves you very much, but of course you know that. He told me you two got engaged the night of the accident. You never even got a chance to tell us, did you? You probably thought we'd be upset to see you getting married so young, right? Well, we probably would've been, but now . . ." As Carol rinsed Carly's hair she brushed at her own tears. "Don't you want to marry Brian and go to Michigan the way you planned? Isn't that what you want, honey?"

Again, Carly nodded.

"Then you have to talk to us. All those feelings you've got locked inside must be eating you up. You'll feel so much better if you let them out." She grasped Carly's chin, forcing her to make eye contact. "Will you try? Please?"

Carly opened her mouth, but nothing came out.

Carol kissed her cheek. "That's okay, love. We'll try again tomorrow."

∼

CARLY'S MOTHER invited Brian to their annual Fourth of July cookout. For days before the holiday, Carly was on pins and needles while she waited to see if he would come. She hadn't seen him in two weeks, the longest they'd ever gone without seeing each other in more than four years of dating. Every day without him had felt like a year to her.

On the morning of the Fourth, she spent extra time getting ready. She wore the white shorts she knew he loved and a red halter that made her feel sexy. For the first time since the accident, she felt a spark of interest in something and hoped that maybe she was finally beginning to recover.

Standing in front of the mirror, she was shocked by her pale face. Her once-vibrant brown eyes were now flat and sunken into her face.

Seeing herself looking so sickly spurred her to try to speak. *Just one word*, she thought. *Come on, no one will hear.* When nothing happened, she cleared her throat and tried again. Nothing. *I'm not doing it on purpose.* She was startled to realize it was true. Until that moment, she hadn't been entirely sure. *I want to talk, but I can't. I don't know why.*

Still absorbing the discovery she'd made in the bathroom, she spent the rest of the morning helping her mother in the kitchen. Her sisters were in and out with their friends, and her brother Craig was home from Boston with his wife Allison. The house was a beehive of activity, and for once Carly's father seemed to be relaxed. Perhaps he'd decided to take the day off from ranting.

Carly put the finishing touches on a huge bowl of potato salad and handed it to her mother.

With a grateful smile, Carol took the bowl from her and covered it with foil. "Thanks for the help, honey." In years past, Carly would have spent the morning at the lake with Brian and their friends, returning home just in time to eat.

By one o'clock, the preparations were done, so Carly wandered onto the front porch. The day was thick with humidity, and the electric wires that lined South Road buzzed in the heat. Across the street, the Durhams arrived home from the parade downtown and unloaded chairs and a cooler from the back of their van. Little David Durham, who Carly had babysat for years, waved to her. She waved back, wishing he'd wander over to see her the way he used to. But he turned away and followed his parents inside. Overwhelmed with sadness, Carly suspected he was afraid of her because she didn't talk anymore.

Her mother had invited Brian for one thirty, but he'd been noncommittal. By the time one forty-five rolled around, Carly was convinced he wasn't coming. The smoke from the barbeque wafted over the house, bringing with it the sounds of laughter and chatter from the backyard. As she got up to go inside, he appeared at the gate, looking hesitant and adorable. Her heart beating fast with excitement, Carly went down the stairs to open the gate for him.

With relief and maybe even joy in his eyes, he cradled her face in his hands and kissed her.

She wrapped her arms around his neck and fell into the kiss with the first bit of exuberance she'd felt since the accident.

Apparently, he felt it, too. "Carly," he whispered. "I've missed you so much." He kissed her more greedily the second time, as if he was afraid he wouldn't get another chance. "I'm sorry about what I said the last time I was here. I was frustrated."

She let him know she understood the only way she could, by reaching up to kiss him again.

"I can still see everything you feel in your eyes," he whispered against her lips. "That hasn't changed." They held each other for a long time, until Carly's mother came to the door.

"Oh, hi, Brian," Carol said with a smile. "I'm sorry, don't let me interrupt. You two take your time, and come on back when you're ready for something to eat."

"Thanks, Mrs. Holbrook." After her mother had left them alone, he smiled down at Carly. "Other things sure have changed, though, huh?"

She rewarded him with the first genuine smile she had given anyone since they left the willow tree and their innocence behind.

IN THE BACKYARD, picnic tables were covered with festive red-and-white-checkered tablecloths. Caren and Cate played croquet while Craig helped their father at the grill. Carly's sister-in-law Allison reclined on a lounge chair with a hand resting on her pregnant belly. Her first child was due in October.

"Craig, get Brian a drink, will you please?" Carol called to her son.

"Thanks," Brian said.

Craig pulled an icy can from the cooler. "Nice to see you, Brian." They shook hands. "I've been thinking about you. How're you doing?"

"Hanging in. How about you?"

"Can't complain." Craig glanced over at his wife and smiled. "I'm enjoying my last few months of relative freedom."

"How's the job at the law firm, Brian?" Steve Holbrook asked as he tended to the grill.

"Not bad. It's boring sometimes, but it's nice to have the chance to be in that environment and to see what goes on."

Carly hung on his every word, wanting to know everything he'd been up to since she last saw him.

"After a few months of delivering mail and fetching coffee for the partners, you'll be wondering why you ever wanted to be an ambulance chaser," Steve joked.

Brian smiled. "They haven't ruined it for me quite yet."

Carol chuckled and asked Carly to help her bring out the rest of the food.

She followed her mother inside and began taking covered bowls out of the refrigerator. Carly had made multiple trips to the picnic table by the time her father announced that the food on the grill was ready.

"Someone bring me a plate!" Steve called. "Hurry!"

Carol handed the platter to Carly, and she rushed outside with it. As she approached the stone patio, her father flipped a rack of ribs. The grease falling into the fire below caused the flames to flare up with a great roar.

Carly dropped the platter, and it shattered on the patio. Unable to tear her eyes off the licking flames, she began to tremble.

Brian rushed over to lead her away from the fire. "It's okay, baby." He sat with her in the shade and held her tight against him. "I've got you."

CHAPTER 5

The rest of the family hovered around Brian and Carly until Carol shooed them away. "Craig and Caren, please clean up the patio." After the others had stepped back, Carol squatted next to Carly. "Everything's all right, honey," she said in a soothing voice. "Everyone's safe."

Brian brushed his hand over Carly's curls and held her until the trembling subsided.

Carly was mortified that she had upset everyone and furious with herself for allowing a grill to resurrect memories she had worked so hard to push to the back of her mind. She'd been having the fire dream less and less often and had begun to think she might be getting past her fear. Now she knew that wasn't the case.

"Are you okay?" Brian asked, his face soft with concern and love.

With a small nod and a forced smile, she let him help her up. She hated that he was so worried about her. He'd lost his brother. She should be helping him through that, not giving him more cause for concern. Getting up, she brushed the grass off her shorts and took a seat at the picnic table.

Everyone else sat down and dug in.

Still feeling shaky, Carly pushed the food around on her plate while the others ate in subdued silence. She looked up to find her parents watching her with concern written all over faces that she could now see had aged since she had last looked closely. That, too, was her fault.

Brian reached for her hand under the table and gave it a reassuring squeeze.

Carly noticed Caren glaring at her from across the table.

"What's wrong, Caren?" their mother asked.

"Nothing."

"Clearly, something's on your mind," Carol said. "Why don't you spit it out so we can get back to enjoying our day?"

"Is that what we're doing? Enjoying our day?"

"Caren," Steve warned.

"It's okay for you to go on and on every day about what she's doing to our family?" Caren shot back at her father. "I thought maybe we'd get one day off from Carly and her *problems*, but I guess that's not going to happen."

"The fire scared her," Brian said in Carly's defense.

"*Everything* scares her!" Caren pushed her plate aside and stood. "I'm so sick and tired of having to tiptoe around her like she's made of glass and might break. No one in *our* family died! Why are we acting like someone did?" To Carly, she added, "Brian lost his *brother*, but you don't see him going around like the walking dead, wanting everyone to fall all over him."

"That's *enough*, Caren," Carol said in a tone that left no room for argument.

Carly got up and went inside. Before the screen door slammed closed behind her, she heard Craig say, "Way to go, Caren."

"Shut up, Craig! You don't live here. You don't know what it's been like."

Carly heard Brian following her as she went up to her room.

Sitting on the edge of the bed, he reached for her hand.

She propped her chin on her knees.

"Don't worry about Caren. She was blowing off steam."

From out in the street, the whir of bottle rockets filled the air, reminding Carly of another Fourth of July years earlier when Pete had shot off rockets at the lake.

"Remember Pete and the firecrackers?"

Carly's eyes widened with surprise as she nodded. She had forgotten how often they'd had the same thoughts.

Brian got up, went over to her desk, and picked up a pad. He grabbed a pen and returned to the bed. He plopped the pad down in front of her and held out the pen. "Talk to me."

She took the pen. Nibbling on the cap, she studied his handsome face. Usually by the beginning of July his skin was tanned to golden brown, but not this year. Leaning over the pad, she wrote the one thing she had missed saying to him the most: "Carly Holbrook loves Brian Westbury." She drew a heart around the words like she had for years on every note-book she owned.

He smiled. "Now tell me something I don't know."

She wrote, "I'm not doing this on purpose. I want to talk, but I can't."

"I know that, too, honey. I never thought for a minute that you were doing it on purpose."

"But you've been mad at me."

He shook his head. "I'm mad at life lately."

"Me, too."

He held her gaze for a long moment. "There's a new lead in the accident investigation."

Carly raised her eyebrows.

He told her about the man he had seen in the road a couple of months before the accident and how he had forgotten about it. "My dad started looking into it and found that two other drivers reported seeing someone lurking on the side of Tucker Road. He hasn't found anyone who saw him the night of the accident, but he's still digging around. I told my dad Sam never drove the way they said he must've been driving before the wreck."

"That's bothered me, too," Carly wrote. "I hope your dad can find a way to clear Sam's name."

"People in town are talking about us grasping at straws to clear Sam. They're saying my dad is abusing his position."

Carly shook her head.

"If there's a chance, even the *slightest* chance, it wasn't Sam's fault, don't we have to do all we can to get to the truth?"

"Of course you do," she wrote. "Don't worry about what anyone says."

Brian held out his arms to her.

She put down the pen and reached for him.

"Before everything happened, if you'd asked me when I was happiest with you, I would've said it was when we were doing this." He pulled back to kiss her and smiled when he added, "I would've said we were at our *very* best under the willow tree." He ran his lips over the pink blush on her cheeks, his voice going soft and thick with emotion. "But after not being able to talk to you during the worst two months of my life, I have a whole new perspective on what I love best about you. I can talk to you about anything and everything. I never realized how important that was to me until I didn't have it anymore."

Her eyes shimmered with tears as she caressed his face.

He held her close to him for a long time. "Do you feel like taking a walk?"

She shook her head.

"We won't go anywhere near Tucker Road."

Ashamed to admit that the only place she felt safe anymore was at home, the idea of leaving the house made her feel sick and panicky. Once she had made it as far as the gate, fully intending to walk around the block, but her heart had pounded so hard she'd thought she was having a heart attack. She'd had trouble breathing and had vomited right there in the front yard.

She'd felt like she was losing her mind, and it had scared her so badly she hadn't tried it again. Brian and her family had been so focused on her not talking, they hadn't figured out yet that she couldn't bring herself to leave the house. And after what had happened earlier, she wasn't prepared to add to the pile of "problems" her sister had referred to.

Brian sensed her hesitation. "Never mind. We'll do it another time."

After her sisters took off to meet their friends, Brian coaxed Carly out of her room. They spent the rest of the day with her parents, Craig, and Allison. Brian's parents stopped by to have a drink, and after sunset they left with the Holbrooks to watch the fireworks at the town common.

"You're *sure* you don't want to go see the fireworks?" Brian asked for the tenth time.

With a smile and the wave of her hand, she told him to go on ahead if he wanted to.

He pushed off the floor to get the porch swing moving again. "Not without you."

Carly could tell she surprised him when she turned and pressed her lips to his.

He wrapped his arms around her and kissed her with two months' worth of pent up desire and frustration. His tongue tangled with hers, reminding her of the passion they had shared from the first time his lips had tentatively touched hers at an eighth grade dance. Nothing, not time nor maturity nor even tragedy, could dampen it.

She drew back from him and wondered if she looked as dazed as she felt.

"I'm sorry, honey. I don't mean to push you."

Carly stood and held out a hand to him.

Startled, Brian laced his fingers through hers.

She tugged him to his feet.

"Carly?"

She led him inside and started up the stairs.

"Where are we going?"

She smiled over her shoulder. In her bedroom, she turned to him and slid her hands under his T-shirt.

He shuddered. "Carly, honey, this is *not* a good idea."

She raised an amused eyebrow and reached for the button on his shorts.

"What if your parents come back early?"

She crossed the room and flipped the lock on the door.

Brian groaned. "This is insane. We *can't*."

Returning to him, she backed him up to the bed and tugged the shirt over his head.

"Oh God," he said. "Are we really going to make love in a *bed*?"

Carly smiled as she nodded. They'd had that luxury only one other time, when they'd gone to Michigan to tour the campus and find a place to live. With just one night to spend in a hotel, they'd made the most of it.

He brought her down on top of him and untied her halter. Cupping her breasts, he said, "I love you, Carly. I love you forever and ever."

Carly wanted so badly to tell him she loved him just as much.

"I know, honey," he whispered. "I can see it in your eyes."

When she bent to capture his bottom lip between her teeth, he gasped.

He got rid of their shorts and held her tightly to him. "Are you still taking the pill?"

She nodded.

"Were you hoping we'd be together like this again?"

Her eyes shimmered as she nodded again.

Easing her legs apart, he slid into her. "No, don't close your eyes, Carly. I need you to look at me." He held her eyes for several long minutes before he dipped his head to graze his tongue over her nipple.

She came apart under him, silent even in the throes of passion.

He managed to hold on to his control long enough to urge her up and over again. This time he joined her.

"Carly," he gasped against her ear, sending a shiver through her. "You have no idea how often I've thought about that last time under the willow." He lifted his head so he could see her face. "You, too?"

She nodded and reached out to bring him back to her. With a soft, sweet kiss, she tried desperately to tell him everything she wished she could say. When he trembled, she knew he understood. She had forgotten how his body felt on top of hers, how it felt to take him inside of her, how his chest hair felt against her breasts, and the way the muscles in his back rippled under her hands when he loved her. He shifted to move onto his side, but she stopped him.

He raised a questioning eyebrow. "Again?"

She smiled in agreement.

"At some point we need to figure out where we're going from here," he said as they lay facing each other. "I mean, we're still engaged, right?"

With a finger to his lips, she told him this wasn't the time for serious business.

"We only have a month before freshman orientation starts," he reminded her.

Like she didn't know exactly how many weeks, days, and hours they had left. Soon enough she would have to tell him that she had written to Michigan to request a one-year deferment on her scholarship. She wouldn't be ready to move halfway across the country in just over a month, even if he would be right by her side every step of the way.

Somehow she had to find a way to tell him. And then she would have to find a way to get through the lonely weeks without him until he came home for Thanksgiving and then Christmas. But that was a conversation for another day. Today she just wanted to enjoy being with him after two long weeks of wondering if she would ever see him again.

"I forgot to tell you earlier I had lunch at Miss Molly's the other day. Mrs. Hanson asked me to pass along the message that you can come back to work whenever you're ready. She said you'll always have a job there. Nice, huh?"

With her head resting on his chest, Carly nodded.

Off in the distance they could hear the boom of the fireworks and waited until the rapid-fire finale had ended before they got up to get dressed.

As they were leaving her room, he stopped her. "Thank you for this. I've been so lost without you, Carly." She reached up to bring him down for another kiss.

By the time their parents returned, they were back on the porch swing.

THEY FELL into a routine after the holiday. He worked every day at the law firm in town and spent the evenings and weekends with her. Sometimes they "talked" using the pad and pen, other times they were content to just be together without the pressure to deal with all the loose ends that awaited resolution.

Two weeks after the Fourth of July, he asked her again to take a walk with him. "We don't have to go to the willow," he pleaded. "We can find a new place. I need to be with you, Carly. We never have a minute alone here."

She shook her head.

Making an effort to keep his cool, he asked, "You can't or you won't?"

She reached for the pad and wrote, "Can't."

Brian stared at the single word on the white page for several seconds before he looked up at her. "What are you saying?" Up until then he'd thought she was hiding out at home so she wouldn't have to face a world without their friends. Now, as he wondered if there was something more to it than that, the icy knot of fear that settled in his gut reminded him of the night of the accident when she'd had to be sedated to stop screaming. "Do you feel like you can't leave the house?"

With a hesitant nod, she confirmed his fear.

"Carly, honey, *come on*! What do you think will happen? I'd be right there with you." With his hand wrapped tightly around hers, he stood and headed for the porch stairs, determined to show her she was wrong.

Resisting him with everything she had, she fought wildly to get free.

He turned, and the terrified expression on her face stopped him cold. His heart started to beat faster as he studied her for an endless moment. "If you can't leave this house, how will you go to Michigan?"

She looked down at the floor.

And then suddenly he understood. "You're not going, are

you?" He pushed his hands through his hair as he struggled to absorb the blow. *"When were you going to tell me?"*

Picking up the pen that had fallen to the porch floor, she wrote, "Soon."

He was incredulous. *"Soon?* We're due to leave in *two weeks*, Carly!"

"Do you really think I can go like this?" she wrote frantically.

"Why not? You can get around and go to class and do everything anyone else can do."

"Except talk!" She underlined talk several times.

"You can write notes. I'll talk for you. We can do this, Carly. I *know* we can. There's nothing we can't get through as long as we're together."

"I can't."

He took a deep breath in an attempt to calm the burst of panic. "What about our engagement? You said you'd marry me."

"I still want to. That hasn't changed. It never will."

"So what? We get married and live in the house you won't leave for the rest of our lives? Is that really how you expect me to live?"

"I hope in time I'll feel differently."

"What if you never do? Where does that leave me?"

"I need some more time. I'm sorry."

He kneeled in front of her and took her hands. "Listen to me," he said, suddenly feeling as if his very life was on the line. "The best thing we can do for ourselves is get the hell out of this town and start a whole new life somewhere else, somewhere that isn't haunted by memories and ghosts."

Her eyes filled, and she turned her face away.

With a hand on her chin, he brought her back to him. "We have a chance to start all over. School is paid for, we have a place to live, and after everything that's happened, I guarantee you our parents would be thrilled to see us married and living together in Michigan. We can have everything we've ever dreamed of, but I can't do it by myself. You have to help me, Carly. You have to try." His voice broke, and tears filled his eyes. "Please."

Tears rolled down her cheeks as she tore her eyes away from his to write, "I'm not ready. Maybe next year I'll be stronger."

After he read what she'd written, he studied her for a long time. And then, without another word, he stood, went down the stairs and out the gate.

THE NEXT DAY he called to say he was having dinner with his parents and wouldn't be by to see Carly. The second day, he said he had to work late. By the third day, she was convinced she'd finally succeeded in pushing him away for good. However, he came that night and every night that followed, but he was quiet and withdrawn.

Carly could feel him pulling away from her, as if he was preparing himself for the long months of separation that loomed on the horizon. When they were down to just two days before his departure, she decided she couldn't stand his brooding silence for another minute. She wrote, "Talk to me."

After a long pause, he said, "I've made a decision." His face was set into a hard expression that frightened her.

"What?"

"When I leave here the day after tomorrow, I'm not coming back. Ever."

"WHY?"

"I need that fresh start we talked about. I need to get away from here, away from all the bad memories."

"Away from me?"

"No." He reached for her hand. "I want you to come with me. I've told you that every way I know how. Even if you don't go to school, you could live with me and be with me. You're choosing not to. Now I have to make my choices."

"What about your parents?" she asked as a feeling of desperation unlike anything she had ever experienced settled over her heart.

"They understand if I keep coming back here every few months I'll never get over what happened. So they'll come to me. They have no more desire to celebrate holidays in that house than I do. We'll go skiing for Christmas or take a cruise, maybe. I don't know. We haven't decided yet."

Carly forced herself to ask the only question that mattered. "What about us?"

He swallowed hard. "If you force me to leave here without you, if you do that to me, Carly, there is no more us."

She dissolved into deep but silent sobs that shook her body. The pad slipped off her lap and landed with a thump on the porch.

He gathered her into his arms. "I love you with all my heart, and I always will. But I can't put my life on hold until you work out whatever it is you've got going on. I lost my brother, Carly, and all my best friends except for you. I saw the same things you did—the same horrible things—yet I've managed to go on. I don't understand why you can't do that, too." He brushed away her tears and then his own. "I know you loved Sam, but he was *my* little brother. I loved him more than you did. I sound like a jerk for even saying that, because this certainly isn't a contest, but my loss was bigger than yours."

Carly was filled with shame, because she knew he was right. But knowing it didn't explain why her reaction was so disproportionate. There was no explanation. She caressed his face and tried to convey how she felt with the eyes he read so well.

"Think about what I said. I've got a ton of stuff to do tomorrow, so I won't see you, but I'll come by before I leave on Thursday morning. My parents are driving out with me and flying back. If you change your mind, there'll be room for you in the car." He kissed her cheek and then her lips. "It's time to step up, Carly. If you love me like you say you do, it's time to fight for us."

Filled with despair, she watched him go. He was doing what he needed to do to survive, and she understood that—better than anyone else possibly could. But after more than four years of loving him so desperately, how would she ever live without him? What kind of life did she have to look forward to if it didn't include him?

She lay awake for two nights trying to marshal the strength she needed to overcome her fears and regain control of her life. She tried to visualize herself walking through the gate and getting into the car with Brian and his parents. But then she would remember how the fire had consumed her friends, and she knew there was no way she could get into a car. As the sun rose on the day he was due to leave, she accepted that she couldn't do it, even for him. She wasn't ready. Maybe one day she would be but not today.

He came by at ten that morning as promised. Downstairs, she heard her mother talking to his parents as he trudged up the stairs to where she waited for him in her room.

His face fell with disappointment when he saw she hadn't packed anything. With his hands on his hips and his jaw tight with tension, he stood perfectly still and looked at her, as if to fill his heart and mind with enough to get him through a life without her. "I have no idea what I'm supposed to do right now," he finally said. "I never imagined we'd end up this way."

Carly handed him the note she'd written at five o'clock that morning. It said, "Every dream I've ever had begins and ends with you. No matter how much time passes, if you want to come home, I'll be here. I love you always. Only you."

Blinded by tears after reading it, he folded the note and put it in his shirt pocket. Then he reached for her.

With her arms around his waist, she rested her head on his chest.

He held her tight against him.

She wasn't sure if ten minutes had passed or only one when he whispered, "Brian Westbury loves Carly Holbrook." With a kiss to her forehead, he was gone.

Carly flew over to the window and held the curtain aside to watch her mother walk Brian and his parents to their car. At the gate, her mother hugged him and then reached up to wipe tears off his face. He said something, and Carol hugged him again.

He got into the car with his parents. With a last wave to Carly's mom, they drove away.

Carly stared out the window until long after the car was out of sight. Finally, she released the curtain and it fell back into place, cutting off her view of the outside world.

PART II
MAY 2010

A time to rend, and a time to sew; a time to keep silent, and a time to speak.

Ecclesiastes 3:7

CHAPTER 6

*M*ichael Westbury flipped on the radio and took the frozen dinner from the microwave, dropping it onto the stovetop with a muttered curse. He always forgot about the steam. Turning on the faucet, he let the cool water soothe the stinging burn on his hand. After waiting a safe amount of time, he peeled back the plastic and dug into the roasted turkey and potatoes.

While he ate, he pored over the files he had brought home from the station and nursed one of the two light beers he allowed himself every night after work. At the top of the hour, he tuned the radio to a news station in New York City. "We have a verdict," the announcer teased before launching into a commercial break that seemed to last forever.

Michael pushed the files aside and took a long drink from his beer bottle. "Come on," he whispered, his heart beating fast with anticipation while he waited through the interminable commercials.

"The jury has found New York socialite Barry Gooding *guilty* on all counts in the grizzly stabbing murder of his wife

Giselle in their Park Avenue penthouse just over two years ago."

"*Yes!*" Michael pumped his fist into the air. "Yes!"

"Assistant District Attorney Brian Westbury had this to say after the verdicts: 'It's a great day for the City of New York and for Giselle Gooding's loved ones. Justice has been served.'"

While Brian's tone was reserved and professional, Michael could hear the excitement in his son's voice.

"I'd like to thank everyone in my office who worked with me over the last two years to get this killer off the streets and to provide closure for the Goodings' two young children, whose bravery and courage has been an inspiration to us all. District Attorney Stein will hold a press conference later tonight. I'll let him take it from here. Thanks."

"Nice job, son," Michael whispered. "Nice job." He picked up the phone and dialed a number in Florida. "Did you hear?" he asked when Mary Ann answered.

"Just now on TV. How about that boy of ours?"

"I'm busting," Michael confessed.

Mary Ann laughed. "I can picture it. Has he called you yet?"

"Not yet. I'm sure he's bogged down with the media and a bottle of bubbly."

"You'll get a call before the night is over."

"I know." He stabbed his fork at what was left of his dinner. "How's the weather?"

"Gorgeous. I wish you were here."

"I'll be down next weekend."

"I guess I can wait that long."

He paused and then forced himself to ask, "You doing all right?"

"Define all right," she said with a laugh.

"I know. Me, too. Fifteen years. Impossible to believe."

"Life has some nerve going on like nothing happened, doesn't it?"

"Yeah." Tugging on the raised corner of the beer bottle label, Michael said, "I wonder what he'd be up to these days."

"With his good looks and smooth talk, he'd probably be a millionaire several times over by now."

Michael laughed. "Then I could finally retire, and we could live large in Florida year-round."

"That would work for me." Her voice softened. "You understand why I can't be there right now, don't you, Mike?"

"Of course I do."

"When you talk to Brian, ask him to call me when the dust settles."

"I'm sure you'll hear from him today or tomorrow."

"Will you take some flowers to the cemetery this week?"

"Sure."

"Tell him his mother is thinking of him."

Michael's throat tightened with emotion, but he managed to say, "You got it."

"Love you."

"You, too, babe."

Michael clicked off the phone and set it on the table. He attempted to return his attention to the files, but his concentration was blown. Pushing back the kitchen chair, he got up, dropped the plastic dinner tray into the recycling, and then wandered down the hallway. He rested his hand on the door-knob to Sam's room and worked up the wherewithal to open the door.

The room was just as Sam had left it: clothes in piles on the floor, three pairs of size twelve sneakers scattered about, scraps of paper on every surface, shelves of trophies and mementos, and a rumpled bed. For years after the accident, the room had smelled like him—an appealing combination of sweat, cologne, and youthful exuberance. Now, it was musty and lifeless.

At times, Michael could still hear his boys running through the house as toddlers, as Cub Scouts, as Little League standouts, and as high school stars. The two of them, looking so much alike that sometimes even he had to take a second look before he called them by name, were always together, always close, always a pair until one was gone.

During the chaotic years of working and raising a family, a man doesn't have time to prepare himself for the day when his house will once again fall silent. He doesn't know until it's too late that the quiet can break a father's heart.

When she was home, Mary Ann dusted in Sam's room once in a while, but otherwise they kept the door closed. They'd talked about cleaning out the room but had never gotten around to doing it. Michael suspected they might've moved if the specter of dealing with Sam's room hadn't hung over them.

Michael sat on the bed and reached for the photo on the bedside table. On one side of the double frame, Sam and Jenny were decked out for her junior prom. On the other side was a group shot of the eight friends in formal attire at the same prom. Tracing his fingers over the picture, he brushed away the dust that had settled on the glass. *Such beautiful kids*, Michael thought, *and such an awful waste*.

He and Mary Ann had set out to have four children but had been blessed with only two—one right after the other. They'd tried for years to have more, and when it didn't happen, they had thrown themselves into enjoying every minute with their two boys. The six others in the picture had become their extras, and they had mourned the loss of every one of them—and suffered through the added burden that came with being the parents of the one who'd been driving.

Fortunately, they'd never once felt an ounce of recrimination from any of the other parents. He suspected they had taken a "there but for the grace of God go I" philosophy, knowing that by the luck of the draw it'd been Sam Westbury behind the wheel that night when on any given night, it might've been one of their kids driving the doomed car.

Not a day had gone by in fifteen years that Michael hadn't thought of Sam and the lingering questions surrounding the accident—questions that had never been answered to Michael's satisfaction. But after more than thirty years in uniform, he knew the only thing that could clear his son's name was the one thing he didn't have: hard evidence.

Despite constant, relentless effort, he'd never found a shred of evidence to prove anything other than what they already knew: the car driven by his son had taken the curve on Tucker Road at a speed of at least forty miles per hour— fifteen miles above the speed limit—barreled into a massive oak tree, and burst into flames on impact.

Since the accident, two more rattled drivers had reported seeing a man standing in the middle of Tucker Road, but Michael and his officers hadn't been able to catch him. Years of beefed up patrols in the area had yielded nothing. Tired of seeing him defeated by the situation, Mary Ann had encouraged him to let it go, but he never would. As long as he had a breath left in him, he would work to clear his boy's name.

Michael returned the photo to Sam's bedside table and left the room, closing the door behind him. In the room that used to be Brian's, Mary Ann had set up her sewing machine and Michael had installed a computer. He chuckled at the dichotomy—a shrine to the boy who'd died and nothing in Brian's old room to remind them of the boy who had lived. Not that he would care. True to his word, Brian had never come home again after he left for college.

The phone rang, and Michael dashed into the kitchen to answer it.

"Hello?"

"Hey, Dad, did you hear the news?"

Michael smiled at the rare sound of euphoria in his son's voice and a party going on in the background. "I sure did. Congratulations, Bri."

"Thanks. It's a huge relief. That bastard was guilty as sin, but he had one hell of a defense attorney. I was sweating this one big-time."

"You did a great job." Michael had read every word written about the trial and knew Brian had left nothing to chance.

"My eyes are burning from the champagne they sprayed at me when I got back to the office."

"Enjoy the celebration. You've certainly earned it."

"You've just got to wonder how a guy can do what he did in front of his kids."

"He's a monster, and thanks to you, he's exactly where he belongs tonight. Where are the kids now?"

"Living with Giselle's sister in Missouri, and I hear they're doing a lot better. They were amazing during the trial."

"I read about them in the paper."

"Their testimony definitely sealed the deal. Hopefully, they can move past it now and have relatively normal lives."

"With luck, they won't remember much of it," Michael said, even though he was skeptical. Some things could never be forgotten. "Mom sends her congratulations, too."

"I'll call her when we hang up." Brian paused before he asked, "How's she doing?"

"She seems to be hanging in there."

"And you?"

"I'm okay. Tough time of year for all of us."

"Yeah. I could come up if you don't want to be alone that day."

"What's this?" Michael joked. "You? Come home?"

"I would if you needed me."

"I know, son." His good boy had grown up to be a nice man. "But it's not necessary. We'll plan a weekend in New York soon. Mom will fly up to meet us."

"Saul's been making noise about me taking a vacation now that the trial is over."

"When was the last time you had one? A real one?"

"He says six years, but I think it's more like three."

"I believe him."

Brian laughed. "What the hell am I going to do with a vacation?"

"Oh, I don't know, relax maybe? Read a book? Get laid?"

"Christ, Dad," Brian huffed. "Is that necessary?"

"Absolutely necessary to your health and well-being."

"All right, this conversation is over. I'm calling my mother who would never dream of saying such a thing to me."

Laughing, Michael said, "You need to get yourself a life outside of that office."

"I tried that—twice, in fact—and as you well know, I discovered I'm a much better workaholic than I am a husband."

Michael grimaced. "I'm sorry. I was out of line."

"Don't go all serious on me, Dad. I like you better when you're busting my balls, even if it's embarrassing."

A knock on the back door brought Michael to his feet. "It's open," he called. To Brian, he said, "Congratulations again. I couldn't be more proud of you."

"Thanks, Dad."

"Give your mother a call."

"Will do."

"Talk to you soon."

He ended the call as his deputy chief, Matt Collins, came into the kitchen still in uniform.

"Sorry to interrupt," Matt said. "I brought those files you called about."

"No interruption. Thanks for the files." Michael added them to his pile on the table. "That was Brian. Did you hear he won?"

"It's already on the radio. You must be thrilled."

"I'm thrilled *and* relieved," Michael admitted. "Beer?"

"Sure, I'm off duty."

Michael opened two bottles and handed one to Matt. "Back in the swing after your vacation?"

"Give me another day, and I will be."

"How's everyone in Milwaukee?"

"Good. My parents are enjoying the hell out of retirement, and my sister's kids are getting big. It was nice to be home."

"Glad you had a good time."

"So big win for Brian, huh?"

"Yeah. He sounded really happy just now."

"With good reason." Matt followed Michael to the living room. "That was quite a trial. He'll be in hot demand after a win like that."

"He gets recruited all the time, but he loves what he's doing in New York. Plus he works for a decent guy who gives him a lot of leeway. He's got a good thing going there."

"I'm glad to hear he's happy and doing well. He surely deserves it."

"You know it." Michael took a drink from his bottle. He had never forgotten the gentle care this man had shown his son at the darkest moment of Brian's young life. Matt Collins was much more than a colleague to Michael. "Anything going on?"

"Not here. Quiet shift." Matt set his bottle on the coffee table. "But we got word an hour ago there's been another rape. This time in Smithfield."

"Son of a bitch," Michael hissed. "Another kid?"

"Sixteen."

"Same M.O.?"

Matt nodded. "Tied her up and left her stark naked in the woods. She was there all night." His expression was grim when he added, "He did some nasty shit to her. Another clean job, though. Not a trace of DNA."

"Let me guess—a popular cheerleader type?"

"You got it."

Michael rubbed a weary hand over his face. "One here, one in Smithfield, one in Cranston. Without the DNA, though, all we have is the M.O. to tie them together."

"It's got to be the same guy."

"We've got a serial sex offender on our hands here. Tomorrow I'll get with the other chiefs to form a task force."

"I'll take the lead on behalf of Granville, if you want," Matt offered.

"I'd appreciate that."

"I did some digging around on the computer earlier. I put a few parameters into the unsolved statewide files and got an interesting hit. Remember the young couple in Pawtucket that was murdered about five years ago?"

"Carjacking?"

"That's the one."

"What about it?"

"Both were tied up and raped. No DNA. Not a hair, not a fiber, nada."

"How old were the victims?"

"She was nineteen, and he was twenty-one. I called up the coverage that was in the *Providence Journal*. Before she graduated, she was the captain of the cheerleading squad at Shea High School."

"Jesus," Michael whispered.

"There might be others. Do you want me to keep digging?"

"Yeah, but keep it quiet. We don't want to set off a panic until we know more."

"I agree. I'll keep you in the loop."

"I don't like the feel of this."

"Neither do I."

MICHAEL LEFT the station at noon the next day. After a brief stop at the florist, he drove on to the cemetery and parked his town-issued sedan at the foot of the hill. Carrying a vase of pastel tulips, he started up the hill to the large granite stone bearing the name WESTBURY. Engraved beneath were the words "Samuel Michael, April 5, 1978 – May 19, 1995, Beloved Son, Grandson, Brother & Friend." Michael crouched to tug some weeds from around the stone and placed the tulips on the base.

Every time he came here, he was struck by the wrongness of it all. People were right when they said parents shouldn't have to bury their children. It was unnatural, and the pain of it didn't lessen with time the way those same people said it did. Rather, you somehow learned to live with it and to accept that it was a permanent part of you now, something you carried like a heavy suitcase every moment of your life.

"Mom says hi," he whispered, feeling somewhat foolish. He didn't really believe Sam could hear him. With all his heart, he wanted to think it was possible, but the practical side of him didn't buy it. However, since he had promised Mary Ann . . .

"She's at the house in Florida, but she wanted me to tell you she loves you and she's thinking of you—always, but this week in particular. You would've liked the place in Florida,

Sammy. There's a pool in the complex and a beach nearby. We'll probably move down there permanently if I ever decide to retire. We'll see. Brian won his big trial, and they interviewed him on TV last night. It's pretty amazing to turn on the tube and see your own boy talking with so much authority and expertise." He brushed at some dirt on the stone. "Well, I just wanted to come by and say hello, and to let you know . . ." His eyes filled. "I miss you every day, and I love you."

Standing, he stared at the stone for a long time before he turned to leave. He was startled to find Jenny's mother, Jean Randall, waiting for him.

She walked over to him. "I'm sorry, Mike. I didn't mean to intrude."

"You didn't." He kissed her cheek. "How are you, Jean?"

Her face lifted into a sad smile. "Oh, you know."

"It's always tougher this week."

"Even after fifteen years."

He nodded in agreement and gestured to the paper she held in her hand. "What've you got there?"

"Just some trash I found on Jenny's grave. Honestly, I don't know what makes people do the stuff they do in cemeteries."

"Why? What is it?"

She held up the piece of paper with the words "CHEER-LEADER WHORE" written in vivid red ink.

Michael's breath got stuck in his throat, and he worked at keeping his expression neutral. "You found that on her grave?"

"Right at the base of the stone."

"Do you mind if I take it? I'd like to have it worked up. We might be able to figure out where it came from."

"I'd hate to start something over litter."

"I'd hate for that to go unpunished."

She handed the paper to him. "You're right."

He pinched his fingers around a corner and took it from her. "I'll let you know if anything comes of it."

"How's Mary Ann?"

"Good. She's enjoying Florida." Michael forced himself to make conversation when all he wanted was to get that piece of paper into an evidence bag and then scour the cemetery for anything else that might be waiting to be discovered.

"Do you get down at all?"

"Every couple of weeks for two or three days. Whenever I can."

"Be sure to tell her I was asking for her."

"I'll do that. I haven't seen Bob at the Lodge lately. I've been meaning to give him a call."

"He's been under the weather, so he's sticking closer to home these days."

"Nothing serious, I hope."

"Just this time of year," she said with a shrug. "I saw Brian on TV last night. He looks wonderful, all handsome and grown up. You must be so proud."

"I am. He's done okay for himself."

She glanced at Sam's grave and then quickly brought her eyes back to Michael. "I'm sure you need to get back to work." Squeezing his arm, she added, "Take care of yourself, Mike."

"You, too. Tell Bob to give me a ring if he's up for a visit."

"I will."

He waited until she had walked down the hill and crossed the street to the town common before he reached for his cell phone. "Hey, Matt, it's Michael. Can you meet me at the cemetery? Now?"

CHAPTER 7

*T*he day after the verdict, Brian went to his office to do battle with the mess that had accumulated during the two-month trial. He dropped into his desk chair and contemplated the towering stacks of mail and trade publications. If he fired up his computer, he'd no doubt find the same pile up in his e-mail in-box. He reached for the trashcan under his desk and began weeding through the first of three foot-high piles.

Colleagues who had been out of the office the day before poked their heads in to say congratulations.

"Thank you," he said each time.

When he quickly filled up the trashcan, he ventured out to find some garbage bags and made eye contact with District Attorney Saul Stein across the wide-open space.

"Crap," Brian muttered, hightailing it back to his office.

Saul made a beeline for him. "What are you doing here?"

"I'm not officially here." Brian pointed to his jeans and polo shirt. "No tie."

Saul's eyes narrowed. "I believe I was quite explicit

yesterday when I told you I didn't want to see you for at least two weeks."

"Look at this disaster area. When am I supposed to deal with it?"

"In two weeks."

"I'm starting to get a complex. Don't you like me, Saul?"

"Don't be cheeky with me, Westbury. I told you to take a vacation. You've got so much time racked up that if you were to quit, paying you for it would throw the city into receivership."

"I'm not going to quit, but I'll take a vacation day to clean my office." Brian tossed one paper after another into the trash. "Happy?"

With a withering look for Brian, Saul wandered over to the credenza under the window and picked up one of the three photos Brian kept there. "Is this you?"

"Yeah, I framed a picture of myself in case you work me so hard I forget what I look like." Brian laughed at Saul's nasty scowl. "That's my brother."

"Oh! So you *weren't* spawned. You *do* have a family! Why don't you go visit him?" Saul put the photo back and turned to Brian.

A surprising stab of pain cut through him. That it still could hurt so much . . . "He's, ah, not available right now." In more than eight years at the D.A.'s office, he had never told anyone he worked with about the brother he had lost.

"What about your parents?" Saul persisted. "Don't they like to see your ugly mug once in a while?"

"They saw me on TV last night. They're good for now."

Exasperated, Saul flopped down into the chair in front of Brian's desk and looped his thumbs under his blue suspenders. "You're pissing me off, Westbury."

"What're you going to do? Fire me?" When most of the first stack had landed in the trash, Brian turned to the next one. He set aside the cell phone bill with the bright red "OVERDUE" stamp on it and reached for a folded, stapled yellow flyer. His heart skipped a beat when he saw the Granville return address. He tore it open. "GHS Class of 1995 Fifteen-Year Reunion. Come home to Granville to reconnect with old friends and remember good times!" The reunion was set for Fourth of July weekend, beginning with a cookout at the lake. As Brian studied the flyer, he was swamped with longing—for his hometown, for the old friends, and the good times that ended far too abruptly.

"What's that?" Saul asked.

Consumed by memories, Brian had forgotten his boss was there. "Nothing." He tossed the flyer into the pile of overdue bills.

"All kidding aside," Saul said, "I want you to take some time off." When Brian began to protest, Saul held up a hand to stop him. "You did an outstanding job with the Gooding trial—masterful, in fact. But you'll be no good to the people of this city—or to me—if you don't take a break and recharge."

"I've got nothing else I want to do."

"That's pathetic on so many levels I'm not even going to list them all. You're still a young guy, and I imagine the women don't find you totally repulsive. There's got to be someone out there dying to spend some time with the celebrated attorney who put away that scumbag Gooding."

"There isn't."

"You remind me a lot of myself when I was your age," Saul confessed. "I have five kids who went and grew up on me while I was hiding out in this office."

"I'm not hiding out."

Saul continued as if Brian hadn't spoken. "I hardly ever hear from them, and my ex-wife is now married to my ex-best friend."

The story was well known, but Brian hadn't seen the pain before.

"You're a good kid, Brian, and a damned fine prosecutor. I don't want you to end up old and alone like me." He stood. "So no new cases until you take a vacation."

"But—"

"Two weeks. Not one minute in this office—and I have spies who *will* report to me if you show your face. They may like you better, but I'm the boss." On his way out the door, he added, "The two weeks start when you leave today."

After Saul had walked away, Brian sat back and fumed. *What the hell am I going to do for two weeks if I can't work?* The idea of filling all that time—and having all that time to think —left him feeling panicked.

Reaching for the reunion flyer, he read it again. The longings had been striking at odd times lately, like in the middle of a trial that had taken over his life the way nothing else ever had. Maybe it was the anniversary of the accident causing the melancholy. Whatever it was, it was starting to get on his nerves. He crumpled up the flyer and tossed it into the trash.

At the bottom of the second pile, he unearthed a crushed Chinese food carton. "Ugh," he muttered, grossed out by the smell as he pushed it into the bag. Stuck to the desk calendar under the carton was the business card of the psychologist who had worked with the Gooding children to prepare them to testify against their father. The younger of the two kids, Christian, had been just five years old when he watched his father stab the life out of his mother.

Brian pried the card free of the paper calendar. Thomas Pellingrino, Ph.D., specialized in children who'd been traumatized by abuse, neglect, and violence. He had worked miracles with Christian Gooding, who'd been transformed from an uncommunicative child to an articulate witness under Dr. Pellingrino's care. As Brian held the card in his hand, he wondered—and not for the first time—if Dr. Pellingrino might be able to help Carly.

Carly.

He didn't think about her every day anymore. To function properly in a job that required his complete attention, he simply couldn't allow thoughts of her to occupy his mind. While other memories from that time in his life had faded somewhat, he remembered her with a vividness that was almost disturbing. Her scent, the way her curls had wrapped around his fingers, the smoothness of her skin, her laughter, those soft brown eyes that could hide nothing from him, and the connection he'd spent half a lifetime looking for in others but had never found again. Oh yes, he remembered her.

He went out of his way not to ask his parents about her, so he had no idea what her life was like today. Even as he told himself he didn't want to know, he knew he was lying. He wanted to know everything, and that desire to know had been growing stronger over the last few months. *Why now? After all these years, why has the longing set in now?*

Tossing Dr. Pellingrino's business card into the drawer that served as his Rolodex, Brian stood and went over to the credenza. He picked up the picture of Sam on the rope swing at the lake. Taken in by his brother's laughing face, Brian wondered if anyone ever thought as they smiled for a photograph that someday a particular instant caught on film would be all that was left of them. Between the picture of Sam and the one of Brian with his parents at his law school graduation was the group photo from the junior prom. Putting Sam down, he picked up the other one and studied it for a long time, for once giving himself permission to remember, to feel, to wish, and to regret.

For the first time in years, he slid the back off the frame and removed a second picture, the one he had hidden under the group shot. These two and the picture of Sam were the only photos he had taken with him when he left home. Brian's arms were around Carly from behind. Her hands rested on his, the corsage he had given her decorated her wrist, and her auburn curls fell over shoulders left bare by a peach dress. Her pleased, contented smile said there was nowhere in the world she'd rather be than in his arms.

He missed her. The feeling came over him like a tidal wave, leaving him stupid and weak with need. Yesterday, in the courtroom, when the jury foreman had said the word he had waited months to hear—*guilty*—the first person he'd wanted to tell was Carly. He had tried hundreds of cases and heard that word many, many times before, but this was the first time he had wanted—no, *needed*—to share it with her. *Why? Why now?*

It's got to be the anniversary of the accident, he reasoned, taking a long last look at the picture before he returned it to its hiding place and put the frame back together. *There've been fifteen anniversaries. Why should this one be so different?* He couldn't answer that question nor could he explain the sudden overwhelming yearning for what used to be.

He pulled his wallet from his pocket. As he eased the piece of paper from the compartment where he kept it, he told himself that doing this—especially in his current state of mind—was a mistake. The vellum had grown soft with age, the folds sharp and pronounced. He opened it carefully, afraid not just of what it said but what it still had the power to make him feel. *Every dream I've ever had begins and ends with you. No matter how much time passes, if you want to come home, I'll be here. I love you always. Only you.* Her voice, her essence filled him so completely it was as if he had last seen her only five minutes ago.

"Pointless," he said out loud as he put the paper away. "This is pointless." As he returned the wallet to his back pocket, he vowed to carry on as he had for fifteen years and to keep the past where it belonged. His determination to move forward, to continue putting one foot in front of the other, had gotten him this far, and it couldn't fail him now.

Like a man on a mission, he quickly disposed of the third stack of paper. He wrote checks for the overdue bills and dug around in his top drawer until he found some stamps. It took another hour to go through his e-mail. When there was nothing left to clean, he collected the huge assortment of discarded clothes that were piled on the sofa where he had spent many a recent night, jammed them into his gym bag, and set the posted bills with the bag by the door.

Returning to his desk, he picked up his cell phone and was almost surprised to find he still had service after not paying the bill in months. "Hi, Mom," he said when she answered.

"Hey! This is a surprise. Twice in two days?"

"Don't get used to it," he joked.

"All my friends down here are buzzing about you being on TV."

"I did a phone interview with MSNBC earlier. That might be on by now."

"I'll watch for it. Did you get some sleep last night?"

"Not much. I was still kind of keyed up."

"That's a big high to come down from."

"No kidding. Listen, Mom, I was wondering . . ."

"What, honey?"

"Do you think I could come see you for a week or so? Saul is kicking me out."

"Are you *serious*? I would *love* that!"

He smiled. "You can't fuss over me like I'm six, you hear?"

"I make no promises. When are you coming?"

"Would tonight be too soon?"

She paused, and he swore he heard tears in her voice when she said, "No, Brian, tonight would *not* be too soon."

LATE ON HIS last afternoon in Florida, Brian lay on a lounge chair next to his mother's and watched two young boys toss a Frisbee back and forth. After a busy day, the beach had cleared out, leaving just a few groups scattered along the wide expanse of sand. For the first time in longer than he could remember, Brian was completely relaxed. He hated to admit Saul might've been right.

"What do you feel like doing for dinner?" Mary Ann asked.

"I thought you were snoozing."

"I was. Now I'm thinking about a drink and some food."

Brian smiled. They'd had a great time together, and despite his vociferous protests, he had enjoyed being mothered. "I wouldn't mind going back to that Mexican place we went to the other night."

"I should cook for you on your last night."

"That would take far too much energy."

"I'm never this lazy. You've completely ruined me."

"I was just thinking that *you* had ruined *me*. How am I supposed to go back to work after this?"

"If I know you, you'll be back in work mode so fast you'll forget you ever had a vacation." She reached for his hand. "I'm so glad you came, especially since Dad had to cancel his trip."

"I wonder what's got him so tied up that he missed the chance to hang out with us."

"Whatever it is, he's not saying much about it." She released his hand to run her fingers through her short mop of blonde hair. Even in her late fifties, Mary Ann Westbury was still an attractive woman.

"I'll call him when I get back and see if I can get it out of him," Brian said.

"If you do, tell me."

"You know I can't do that. Those of us in law enforcement—"

"Have to stick together," she said in a long-suffering tone. "You know where you two can stick that."

Brian laughed.

"You know he's crazy proud of you. We both are."

"That means a lot to me." All at once Brian realized he was running out of time to ask the question he'd been trying to work up the nerve to ask all week. "Mom?"

"Hmm?"

"Can I ask you something?"

Something in his voice had her turning to look at him. "Of course you can."

He hesitated, knowing he was about to open the door to a past he might not be ready to face, even now.

"What is it, honey?" she asked with concern on her face and in her voice.

With a deep breath, he asked, "Do you ever see Carly when you're home?"

Startled by the question, Mary Ann studied him for a long moment before she replied. "All the time."

"Is she, you know, still at her parents' house?"

"No."

Brian's heart beat hard as he waited for her to continue.

"She works at Miss Molly's," Mary Ann said.

"Then she must be talking, too."

Mary Ann shook her head.

"But how does she waitress if she can't talk?"

"Everyone in town knows her. They tell her what they want, and she brings it to them. It's pretty simple."

Suddenly he needed more. He needed everything. "How long ago did she leave the house? How did it happen?"

"From what Carol told me, about a year after you left for school, Steve reached his limit. He told Carly she could either get a job or go to school, but she wasn't spending one more minute locked up in that house. He told her if she didn't do it, he would kick her out of the house."

Hungry for more and filled with questions, Brian forced himself to stay quiet and listen.

"Until then, I guess Carol had been running interference between Carly and Steve. But Carol had reached her limit, too, and couldn't stand another minute of watching that beautiful young girl wasting away in her room. So she stood by her husband. She said it was one of the worst moments of her life. The next day, Carly came downstairs in her uniform and walked out the door like she'd been doing it every day."

"Wow," Brian said, exhaling a long deep breath. He couldn't help but wonder what might have been different for Carly—for both of them—if Mr. Holbrook had made his stand a year earlier.

"She'd been back to work a couple of years when she rented the apartment above Carson's."

Brian conjured up a picture of the general store in downtown Granville.

"She still lives there."

He said nothing as he watched the sunset and tried to imagine Carly's life.

"She walks everywhere. I see her all over town. She's always happy to see me, always has a hug for me and your dad, too."

"She still won't get in a car?"

"No." Mary Ann shook her head as she raised her lounge

chair a notch. "You've never asked about her before, so I didn't tell you any of this when it happened. I figured you wouldn't want to know."

"It wasn't that I didn't *want* to know. It just seemed better to make a clean break."

"So what's changed?"

He shrugged. "I've been thinking a lot about home lately. I'm not sure why. I suspect it's the anniversary of the accident and all that."

"If you're thinking about home then it's only natural you're thinking about Carly, too."

"I guess."

She raised an eyebrow. "Bri? What's going on?"

He knew he shouldn't be surprised that her mother's intuition had kicked in. "I miss her."

Mary Ann's eyes went soft with emotion. "Of course you do."

"I've always missed her, but I haven't let myself dwell on it, you know? I had to stay focused on school and then work. But lately I miss her more than ever. I don't get why it's happening now."

"Maybe it's finally taking too much energy to run from the past."

"I haven't been doing that," he said hotly.

"Sure you have."

"What was I supposed to do?"

"There was nothing else you *could* do."

"You're confusing me."

"When you left for school and said you wouldn't be back, we didn't believe you. Dad gave you until Thanksgiving. I said Christmas."

"You must've been disappointed when you were wrong."

"No. We were amazed, Brian. You don't often see that kind of strength in someone so young."

"It didn't feel like strength. It felt like cowardice."

"Why would you say that?"

"I was wrong to leave her the way I did, to walk away from her at the lowest point in her life. Leaving was easy. Staying would've been the courageous thing."

Mary Ann was incredulous. "How can you say that? Leaving took everything you had and then some. Your courage was awe-inspiring."

"Really, Mom," Brian said with disdain. "That's kind of overstating it a bit, isn't it?"

"No, it's not. You didn't let losing Sam and the others derail you. If that's not courage, I don't know what is. You didn't let what happened ruin your life."

"Didn't it, though?"

Her eyebrows knitted with confusion.

"My life is my job. When Saul forced me to take a vacation, I panicked. Fortunately, my mom was up for hanging out with me for a week. I have no idea what I'll do with next week."

"Brian," she said, her eyes bright with tears.

"I've been satisfied with living the way I do for a long time. Why should I suddenly be so dissatisfied?"

"You've had your share of disappointments."

"You mean Beth and Jane?"

"To start with."

"They didn't disappoint me. By the time Beth told me she'd met someone else, I was relieved."

"She was so sweet. I wish you could've made it work with her."

"I didn't love her. I married her because I liked hanging out with her. She deserved more than that, and she found it with Joe. I'm glad for her."

"I *know* you didn't love Jane," Mary Ann said with distaste.

"Jane and I had an understanding. We had the same job,

the same crazy hours, the same kind of ambition, and we were both tired of being alone all the time."

"You would've been better off alone. There wasn't an ounce of warmth in that woman."

"I didn't marry her for her warmth," Brian said with a lascivious grin.

"*Ugh*, don't say any more." Mary Ann groaned. "So if you had an 'understanding,' what went wrong? Not that I was heartbroken when you two broke up, but I've wondered what happened."

"She changed the rules by wanting more."

"And that didn't disappoint you?"

"Not like you think it did. If you aren't in love, what does it matter?" He paused and then added, "You know what she said to me before she left?"

"I have a feeling I'm not going to like this . . ."

"She said being with me was like biting into an Easter bunny, and instead of finding rich chocolate, you discover the bunny's hollow and the chocolate's fake."

"That's *outrageous*!" Mary Ann huffed. "You're a kind, wonderful man who was far too good for the likes of her."

"She was right, Mom." He looked out at the ocean for several minutes. "Do you know that since I left home, I've never told anyone, and I mean *anyone*, about what happened on May 19, 1995? Not Beth, not Jane, not anyone."

Startled, Mary Ann stared at him. "What do you say about Sam?"

"That he died in a car accident."

"Oh, Brian," she said with a sigh. "No wonder you're so homesick. It's all catching up to you." For a long while they were quiet as they watched the sky turn to vivid pinks and oranges. Finally she said, "You know, sometimes you have to go back before you can go forward."

"I'm beginning to think you might be right."

CHAPTER 8

*G*ood Golly Miss Molly's was rocking and rolling for a Monday morning. The coffee shop was right out of the 1950s with its black-and-white-checkered floor, chrome stools, and tables topped in red, yellow, and black Formica and tiny jukeboxes. With two waitresses out with the stomach flu, Carly had twice as many tables as usual.

Looking as fresh in her yellow uniform dress as the bright spring day outside, Carly brought a full pot of coffee around, stopping at a table where three guys she had known since elementary school gathered on most weekday mornings if they were working in town. Tony Russo, Luke McInnis, and Tommy Spellman worked for Tony's father's construction company and always sat in Carly's section.

"Crazy morning, Carly," Tommy commented as she refilled their coffee cups.

She rolled her eyes in agreement and moved on to the next table. Returning the pot to the warmer, she pulled her pad from her pocket and approached a table where an older couple was studying the menu. An unwritten rule in the shop made it so Carly never waited on people she didn't know, but since they were shorthanded today, she had no choice.

With a friendly smile, she positioned her pen over her pad, ready to take the couple's order.

The man looked up at her with a scowl. "Are you gonna just stand there, girl?" he asked gruffly.

Carly tapped her pen against her pad, hoping to spur the man into giving his order and shutting his mouth.

"What's wrong with you?"

Her heart began to beat hard. This didn't happen very often. She pointed to her throat.

"What kind of place hires a girl who don't talk?" he asked his wife in a booming voice.

Carly often encountered people who assumed because she couldn't talk, she couldn't hear, either.

"That's enough, Paul," the wife said sharply. To Carly, she said, "I'll have a blueberry muffin and a coffee, please."

Carly sent her a grateful smile.

"Are you mocking me, girl?"

Rigid with shock, Carly felt heat creep into her cheeks. "Paul!"

From behind Carly, Luke McInnis said, "Is there a problem here?"

"Mind your own damned business," the man snapped at Luke.

As she realized the shop had fallen silent and all eyes were on her, Carly's embarrassment kicked into overdrive.

Luke leaned down from his considerable height until he was an inch from the man's face. "No one talks to Carly like that, do you hear me?"

Molly Hanson, the grandmotherly woman who owned the shop, eased Carly aside. "I think you folks had better be moving along," she said in a bright singsong voice. Her eyes, however, were hard and unyielding.

"Well," the man huffed. "I don't know what kind of business you're running here—"

"The kind where you're not welcome."

The wife got up, grabbed her purse and, with an apologetic glance at Carly, walked out the door. Her husband pushed past Molly and Luke on his way to the door.

After they were gone, Molly patted Carly's shoulder and went back to work behind the counter.

"Are you all right?" Luke asked Carly. His dark hair was mussed from the ball cap he had worn earlier, his blue eyes filled with concern.

Carly nodded. The other customers had gone back to their meals, and the conversation level returned to normal.

"Are you sure?" Luke asked.

Carly forced a smile and nodded again. When he began to walk away, she reached out to squeeze his arm.

He looked down at her hand and then up at her eyes. "You're welcome."

CARLY'S SHIFT ended at two. Still trying to shake off the ugly incident from earlier, she left Miss Molly's and walked slowly along Main Street, nodding hello to the people who greeted her. Flower boxes full of colorful, fragrant blooms sat outside the wide variety of shops that faced the town common. She climbed the stairs to her second-floor apartment over Carson's. On the small deck at the top of the stairs, she noticed her impatiens needed water.

Inside her eclectically furnished apartment, she peeled off the yellow dress, dropped it into the hamper, and stretched out the aches and pains that came from spending eight hours on her feet. Now that she was thirty-three, the aches and pains were more pronounced and longer lasting than they used to be. She tugged her long hair free of the ponytail she had worn to work, ran a brush through the riot of curls, and tamed them into a new ponytail. Her sofa beckoned, but Carly resisted, changing into denim shorts and an old T-shirt. She watered her geraniums and impatiens, plucked a few blooms from another of her ceramic pots, and took them inside to find a vase.

Grabbing her tote bag of gardening tools and a bottle of water from the refrigerator, she set off down the stairs. As much as she would love a nap, she couldn't resist the warm spring day. She'd had lots of time to be lazy in April when day after day of rain had kept her inside on too many afternoons.

She wound her way through downtown and took a right onto Tucker Road. It had taken her three years and multiple attempts to return to the accident site. When she had finally worked up the nerve to walk around that last bend in the road, she'd been appalled to find the site overgrown with weeds that all but obscured the six crosses bearing the faded names of her friends. That first time, she had also been surprised to find no sign of the fire and vegetation almost completely masking the place where her friends' lives had come to such a horrifying end.

The white paint had been chipping from crosses covered with slimy moss. Over the next month, Carly had made multiple trips to the site, once carrying paint and brushes, another time bringing clippers and a trash bag.

Today she was pleased that the wildflowers she'd planted before the April rains had exploded into colorful blooms. She pulled the weeds from around the crosses and trimmed back the snapdragons and cosmos so they wouldn't block the view of the crosses from the road.

Maintaining this place had been therapeutic for Carly. She saw it as something she could do for the friends she had lost, a way to honor their memories. Only when she was here did she allow herself to dwell on the events of that long-ago spring. She wondered what they would all be doing if they had lived. Would Toby still be in the Navy? Would Pete have ever honored the promise he had made to his parents to return from his travels and go to college? Would Jenny work at the fancy new hair salon that had opened downtown last year? Or would she have her own salon by now?

Carly wondered if she and Michelle might have raised their children together, the way their mothers had raised them. She suspected Sam would've followed his father into the police department and Sarah might've been a doctor. Envisioning how their lives might be today was a source of comfort to Carly since it allowed her to briefly entertain the fantasy that they were out there living their lives somewhere. She didn't spend a lot of time wondering how her own life would have turned out, because she knew. She'd be married to Brian, and they would have at least three children by now.

All over town last week and especially at Miss Molly's, people had been abuzz about his big win. Carly had recorded his interview on TV and replayed it again and again. She had seen photos of him in the newspaper over the years, but it had been so startling to hear the new deeper timbre of his voice. He had matured into rugged good looks that reminded her of his father as a younger man.

She was so proud of Brian. He'd done exactly what he had set out to do and was obviously an amazing attorney. She wasn't surprised he had chosen to be a prosecutor. It was just like him to want to help people, and public service *was* in his genes, after all.

When she finished pulling the weeds and collected a few pieces of trash, Carly stepped back to take a critical look at her work. She wished she could tell them all how much she loved and missed them, but she suspected they knew. She liked to picture them together in heaven, doing the same things they'd always done, going on like nothing had ever happened. She knew what it felt like to be alone, so imagining her friends still had each other took the edge off her sadness.

As she was getting ready to walk away, one last piece of paper poking out of the wildflowers caught her eye. She reached down to pick up a white scrap with vivid red words that said, "WHORES AND ASSHOLES." Shocked and repulsed, she quickly pushed the paper into the trash bag. Who would leave such a thing here, of all places?

A ripple of fear went through her when she suddenly had the overwhelming feeling she was being watched. Looking left and then right, she saw no one anywhere in sight. Telling herself she was being ridiculous, Carly gathered up her gardening tools, grabbed the garbage bag, and set off down Tucker Road. Adrenaline had her walking faster than usual, until she finally broke into a jog on the way to her parents' house.

To get to South Road, she had to pass Brian's parents' house. Seven hundred and eighty-six steps later, she stood at the front gate to the house where she had grown up. Anytime Carly made that walk, she remembered the night she and Brian had counted the steps between their two houses. Filled with nostalgia that was less sad than it used to be, she used her key in the front door.

Even though the windows were open, the house was musty, since her parents had left for Europe a week earlier. They would be gone another three weeks, and while Carly was thrilled they were finally retired and able to enjoy themselves, she missed them. Her mother was the only person in Carly's life—other than her nieces and nephews—who could communicate effortlessly with her without the need for words.

Carly watered her mother's plants and added some junk mail to the garbage bag she had brought with her. She unlocked the deadbolt on the back door and took the bag to the trashcan in the yard. Lifting the rubber lid, she gasped when she found another note sitting on top of the bag already in the can. This one said, "WHORE" in the same vivid red ink as the note from the accident site. Carly dropped the lid and the bag she was holding and ran into the house. She flipped the deadbolt on the door. Her hands shaking, she reached for the phone and dialed 911.

"911, please state your emergency."

Carly was paralyzed with fear and furious that when she tried to speak nothing came out.

"911, please state your emergency." Carly didn't answer, so the operator said, "Please stay on the line. I'm dispatching the police to 22 South Road. If you're able to answer the door, please press the pound key."

Carly did as the operator asked.

"Hang on just a minute. Police are on their way."

She could hear the sirens, and taking the portable phone with her, she went to the front window to watch for them. Two cruisers pulled up to the curb. Carly opened the front door to Deputy Chief Matt Collins and a patrolman.

"Carly?" Matt said. "What's wrong?"

Carly led them to the kitchen where her parents kept a small dry-erase board for her use. She quickly told the officers about the notes she had found and the sensation she'd had earlier that she was being watched. As she finished writing, she looked up to find a somber expression on Matt's face.

He called for crime scene backup and asked Carly to show him the notes.

The house and yard were soon overrun with police. Chief Westbury arrived ten minutes after Matt called in the initial report. Something about the grave way the police handled the collection of evidence frightened Carly and led her to suspect this wasn't the first they had seen of these notes.

"What's going on?" she wrote to Chief Westbury.

"We're not sure. Are you all right, Carly? You're ghostly pale."

"I'm okay. Rattled but okay."

He sat next to her on the sofa while his officers continued their work. "You didn't see anyone at the accident site?"

She shook her head. "I just felt like I was being watched."

"That hasn't happened before?" It was no secret in town that Carly maintained the memorial at the crash site.

"No." They sat in silence for several minutes before she took a deep breath and wrote, "You must be so proud of him."

Michael studied her words for a long moment before he glanced up at her. "Yes," he said almost in a whisper. "Very."

After a moment's hesitation, she wrote, "How is he?" She had never once asked that question of either of Brian's parents in all the years since he left home.

"He's good. He works too hard, but he just spent a week with Mary Ann in Florida. They had a great time."

Carly nodded and resisted the overwhelming urge to ask more.

"You know," Michael said tentatively, "I'm sure he'd love to hear from you if you wanted to write him a letter or something. I'd be happy to give you his address."

Sending him a sad smile, she shook her head. "It's better this way."

"Carly—"

Matt Collins came into the room. "Chief, we found a partial footprint on the path from the side yard gate to the trashcans."

Michael's eyes lit up. "Let me see." He squeezed Carly's hand and got up to follow his deputy outside.

～

THE POLICE SPENT another two hours scouring every inch of the yard without discovering anything else. The crime scene officers left to do a perfunctory investigation at the accident site, which had been compromised by the work Carly had done there earlier. But Michael instructed them to check anyway.

After they left, he came into the house through the back door. They had taken a sample of Carly's fingerprints to rule out hers on the note she had picked from the wildflowers on Tucker Road.

"Do you have a number where I can reach your parents?"

"A call from you will terrify them," she wrote. "I'll ask Caren to call them, if you don't mind."

"Of course. That's fine. It's getting dark. Where are you headed from here?"

"Just to Caren's." Her sister's house was less than a mile from their parents' home.

"I'll walk you."

"That's not necessary," Carly protested.

"I *said* I'll walk you." His face was set in a stern expression that made her smile.

"Thank you." Carly hated to admit she was grateful for his insistence. If someone was in fact watching her, it wouldn't hurt to have the chief of police serving as her escort.

Michael checked the deadbolt on the back door one last

time. He waited while Carly locked the front door and then extended his arm to her. "Madame?"

With a grateful smile for the man who, in another life, would've been her father-in-law, Carly hooked her hand through his arm and let him walk her the short distance to her sister's house.

CHAPTER 9

*M*ichael sat in the police station conference room that had become the command post for the unfolding investigation. Photocopies of each piece of evidence were tacked up on a bulletin board. A large map of Rhode Island, Connecticut, and Massachusetts occupied most of one wall. Four red pushpins indicated where each of the recent sexual assaults had occurred.

Five smaller blue tacks marked the locations where the notes had been found—three in the cemetery and the two discovered by Carly. A yellow pin marked the unsolved carjacking in Pawtucket, which had characteristics that mirrored the recent attacks with one distinct difference—the carjacking victims had been murdered.

Since most of the pins were clustered around tiny Granville, Michael, the other chiefs, and the state police officers on the task force had concluded a sexual predator, who was also possibly a murderer, was living among the citizens of his town. The conclusion infuriated the man charged with keeping Granville safe. That someone he knew could be capable of these crimes was unimaginable to him.

The fourth red pushpin was located just over the border in Connecticut. Since the case now involved multiple states and jurisdictions, the task force members had agreed to call in the FBI. They were meeting with federal agents in the morning.

Matt Collins came into the room. "Mike? I thought you had left."

"Oh, hey," Michael said. "What's up?"

"We got the labs back on the new notes."

"Let me guess? Nothing?"

Matt's expression was grim when he said, "Right. Just Carly's prints on the one from Tucker Road." He used blue pins to add copies of the latest notes to the board. "They're still working on the partial footprint."

"I hate to admit I'm actually relieved the feds are on their way." Under normal circumstances, he would resent the intrusion.

"We're out of our league here," Matt agreed.

"It's someone we know," Michael said, feeling the need to say it out loud.

Matt sat down on the other side of the conference table. "Yes."

Michael studied the map intently.

"What's on your mind, Mike?"

"I just wonder . . ."

"What?"

Michael finally took his eyes off the map and focused on his friend. "This is between you and me."

"Of course."

"I also want to be clear that I'm speaking as a police officer and not a grieving father."

"You're thinking there's a connection between our perp and the accident, aren't you?"

"Hear me out on this," Michael insisted. "A few weeks

before the accident, Brian sees a man standing in the road at the exact place where the accident later occurs. He has to swerve to avoid hitting him but is able to maintain control of the car. Now factor in that our perp clearly has an ax to grind with popular kids."

Matt nodded in agreement.

"You've got a group of cheerleaders and athletes in a car that travels up and down Tucker Road every day. How hard would it be in this town to track the whereabouts of kids who do everything together?"

As he thought about it, Matt rubbed at the blond stubble on his chin.

"Isn't it *possible*?" Michael hated the desperation he heard in his own voice.

"I know you want it to be."

"But?"

"A guy standing in the road doesn't discount the fact that Sam was driving too fast."

Michael sat back in his chair. "Granted, but maybe he doesn't lose control of the car if he's not trying to avoid hitting someone who was waiting for one of the Westbury boys to drive by."

"For the sake of argument, let's say it happened just the way you think." Matt stood, picked up a dry-erase marker, and wrote "May 19, 1995: Accident on Tucker Road" on the board. "The next incident is on July 6, 2000," Matt said as he added the carjacking to the list under the accident.

"That's the next *known* incident."

"Work with me here."

Michael scowled and forced himself to stay quiet.

"Five years after he allegedly orchestrates a car accident that kills six popular teenagers, he carjacks a young couple, rapes and sodomizes both of them, and then strangles them. Are we in agreement on the facts?"

"Yes."

"The M.O.s don't match." Matt raised his hands to make his point. "In five years he goes from standing in the middle of a road to kidnapping, raping, and murdering?"

"I'll admit it's a leap," Michael conceded as he studied the dry-erase board. Suddenly he froze.

"What?"

Michael got up and walked over to the board. "Remember studying investigation tactics in the academy?"

"Yeah, so?"

Michael never took his eyes off the board when he said, "They told us to look for patterns, right?"

"Where you going with this, Mike?"

"Look at the years—1995, 2000." He reached for the pen and added 2010 to the list, leaving a space between the carjacking and the recent spate of attacks. In the space he wrote "2005" with a question mark after it. He turned to Matt. "Until you put the dates on the board, I didn't see it."

"An anniversary perp?"

The two men looked at each other for a long moment.

"I'll pull a statewide list of unsolved cases from 2005," Matt finally said.

"Check 1990, too. Maybe this didn't start with the accident."

On his way to the door, Matt stopped and turned around to face his friend. "If we run with this, Mike, you need to be prepared for what people will say about your motives."

"Let them say whatever they want. If I'm right and we can clear Sam's name, it'll be worth it."

Desperate to get through the second half of his forced vacation, Brian took long walks through his Tribeca neighborhood and ventured north to SoHo, Chinatown, and Little Italy. One day he set out for Battery Park, the southernmost point in Manhattan where the Hudson and East Rivers come together. Watching the ferries running back and forth from Manhattan to the Statue of Liberty and Ellis Island, Brian thought about taking a trip out there, but somehow it seemed like it would require too much effort.

Another day he wandered through the gentrified Lower East Side and across the Brooklyn Bridge, stopping on the Brooklyn side for a cup of coffee in a diner that reminded him of Miss Molly's and Carly. Like he'd done all week, he pushed the thought from his head and set out back across the bridge to Manhattan. Another day he wandered into a few of the galleries in SoHo. It was the most time he'd ever spent playing tourist in more than eight years of living in the city.

When he wasn't out walking, he caught up on his laundry, picked up a ton of dry cleaning, and puttered around the small loft he had bought his first year in New York. At the time, he'd considered the purchase price a small fortune, but the place had appreciated significantly and was now worth an actual fortune.

While he was doing nothing more than killing time until he could go back to work, Brian was also making an effort not to think about his recent longings for home or his desire to see Carly again. After talking it over with his mother in Florida, he'd decided to chalk up his odd feelings to the emotional anniversary of the accident and the roller-coaster ride of the trial. The idea of going home and confronting the past filled him with the kind of anxiety he seldom experienced, which he took as a sign that he needed to leave well enough alone.

On Wednesday night, he had dinner with his ex-wife Beth and her husband Joe, who were in town for a few days.

"You look good, Brian," she said after they were seated at the restaurant. "All tanned and rested."

"Better than my usual look?" he asked with a self-deprecating smile.

"Which is white and pasty," Joe joked. He was a hulking Irishman with bright blue eyes and a big smile. Brian had always liked him.

"Gee, thanks," Brian said, chuckling. "Pregnancy certainly agrees with you, Beth. You're glowing."

She snorted with laughter. "I'm glowing, all right. I'm huge."

"You're adorable," Joe said, kissing his wife's hand.

She had short dark hair and big brown eyes that had once reminded Brian of Carly's. He'd been disappointed to discover the likeness was only on the surface. Beth was sweet and loving, but she wasn't Carly.

Over dinner Beth and Joe grilled him about every detail of the trial, which they had followed from their home in Chicago. While Joe was in the men's room, Brian reached for Beth's hand. "It's great to see you so happy."

"I'm beyond happy. I'm ecstatic."

It showed on her face and in her delighted smile.

"I can't wait to be a mom. But what about you, Bri? Still all work and no play?"

He shrugged. "I love the work. You know that."

"There's more to life than work, but I won't waste my breath trying to convince you otherwise. You're hopeless." She paused, studying him intently. "I worry about you."

Touched, he said, "Can I ask you something kind of weird?"

She grinned. "How can I say no to that?"

"When we were together, did you ever think of me as . . . hollow?" He hesitated. "Like something—"

"Was missing?"

He nodded.

"All the time. On the outside you were this smooth, well-put-together package, but on the inside . . ." She shrugged. "Not so much. I wondered why that was."

"I was terribly unfair to you, Beth. I'm sorry for that."

"Don't be. I had to go through what I did with you to get to where I am now. I want you to find what I have with Joe, Brian. You deserve it."

How could he tell her he'd once had it but walked away from it? "Don't worry about me," he said with a cavalier smile. "I'm happy enough."

Her expression was skeptical, but Joe returned to the table, and the conversation went in a less serious direction.

After seeing them off in a cab, Brian took his time walking home. Posters from the recent Tribeca Film Festival were still affixed to telephone poles and in store windows. Brian liked that he never knew who he might see in the eclectic neighborhood. He had once dined next to Robert De Niro in a café and passed Meryl Streep on the sidewalk.

At home he plugged his cell phone into the charger and noticed he had missed a call from his father. He checked his watch and found it was after ten, but he returned the call anyway.

"Hey," Michael said.

"Sorry it's so late. Did I wake you?"

"No, I was up. How are you? How's the vacation?"

"I'm bored out of my mind, and I've got four days to go." Michael laughed.

"I had dinner with Beth and Joe tonight. That's where I was when you called."

"How is she?"

"Six months pregnant and loving life. She said to say hi to you and Mom."

"That's nice. Good for her on the baby."

"So what's up? You've been keeping a low profile lately."

"I'm up to my eyeballs in a case."

"We sort of figured that when you blew us off in Florida last week," Brian joked.

"Believe me, I would've much rather have been there." He gave his son a quick summary of the case.

As he listened, Brian sat down on the sofa. "Jesus, Dad. You really think it's someone from Granville?"

"It's looking that way."

"And the attacks in other towns?"

"We think they were intended to draw the focus away from Granville."

"So he kidnaps and rapes three girls in other towns just to send the cops on a wild goose chase?"

"It probably wasn't the sole purpose. He also succeeded in traumatizing three pretty, popular cheerleaders, and a fourth one here in town." He told Brian his theory about the accident and the five-year pattern.

"You think it's our guy in the road," Brian said, incredulous.

"We're looking for a connection. Matt says the M.O.s don't match up, and he's right, but the common thread is all the victims were popular kids. And every one of the girls, including the carjacking victim, was a cheerleader."

"The feds will bring in a profiler. He'll tell you you're looking for a loner who was picked on or ignored by popular kids."

"If this started with the accident, we might be looking for someone you and Sam went to school with."

"I still have my yearbook. I can flip through it to see if anyone stands out."

"That would help. Thanks." Michael paused before he added, "Listen, there's one other thing I should tell you."

"What's that?"

"Carly found the last two notes—one at the accident site and another at her parents' house."

"*What?* What was she doing at the accident site?"

"She maintains it. Plants flowers, pulls the weeds."

As Brian ran a hand through his hair, he absorbed that intriguing piece of information and was swamped with helplessness and fear. "He was in her parents' yard. Mom said she walks everywhere. She's totally vulnerable."

"You talked to Mom about Carly?"

"I just asked how she was doing. Don't make it into something it's not."

"That's interesting, because she asked me about you earlier."

"She did?"

Michael chuckled. "But I won't make it into something it's not. Don't worry."

"Dad, she could be in danger. You have to do something."

"We're keeping an eye on her. She's fiercely independent, so she won't make it easy."

"You don't think it's a coincidence that the notes were put in places where she was likely to find them, do you?"

"I'm not sure, son. She doesn't live at home anymore, but everyone knows her parents are in Europe for a month. So it's possible our guy assumed she'd be taking care of the house in their absence. I'd be more concerned if the note had been left at her place."

"You have to promise me you'll keep her safe, Dad. You can't let anything happen to her."

"I'm doing everything I can to keep this whole town safe," Michael said, sounding weary. "Tomorrow we're going public with what we know. We'll also be going into the high school to talk to the students about traveling in groups and keeping an eye out for each other. If I have to, I'll institute a curfew to keep them in at night. It won't be a tough sell.

They've been freaked out since Tanya Lewis was attacked," he said, referring to the high school student from Granville who'd been raped in January.

"How is she?"

"Still recovering at home. She's had surgery twice to repair the damage that animal did."

"I just can't believe something like this could be happening in Granville."

"I know. I told Matt earlier I'm actually relieved to have the feds stepping in. We need the help."

"Well, I'll let you get some sleep. I'm here if you need to talk or anything."

"Thanks."

"It sure would be something if you could tie this guy to the accident, wouldn't it?" Brian asked softly.

"You and I have always had our suspicions there was more to it."

"People said we were grasping at straws," Brian said. "Take care of Carly, Dad. Please."

"I will. I'll keep you posted."

After they ended the call, Brian sat in the dark for a long time, his head spinning with everything his father had told him. The idea of Carly being in danger made him sick with fear. Eventually, he changed into sweats and a T-shirt and went to bed. But for hours he was awake trying to think through the facts of the case as a prosecutor, not as a concerned son, a grieving brother, or a regretful ex-boyfriend.

If the crime spree had begun with the accident, didn't it stand to reason that the perp had been targeting someone in the car? *Or someone who wasn't.* Brian sat straight up in bed. The accident had occurred on the road that led to his house and Carly's. *Had she been the intended target? Or was it me?*

"Okay, man, get it together," he muttered as he realized he

was breathing heavily and his heart was beating hard, like it would if he—or someone he loved—was in imminent danger. Unable to shake the feeling he was on to something, he got up to get his cell phone. As he waited for his father to answer, Brian paced back and forth in his small living room.

"Westbury," Michael said, his voice hoarse with sleep.

"Dad."

"Brian? What's wrong? Christ, it's four in the morning."

"I'm sorry, but I was thinking . . . What if the person he was hoping to kill in the accident wasn't in the car?"

"I don't follow," Michael said with a big yawn.

"What if he'd been counting on Carly being in that car with the others like she should've been?"

Silence.

"Dad?"

"Are you suggesting he's targeting Carly?"

"He put notes in places she was likely to find them."

"How do you know it wasn't you he was after?"

"Because he prefers girls—young girls. Cheerleaders."

"Carly's not young anymore. At least not by his standards."

"Mom said she looks exactly the same."

"She does," Michael agreed. "I hear what you're saying, son. I do. But if he was after Carly, wouldn't he have acted on it by now?"

"Maybe he is by going after girls that remind him of Carly. He could be building up to the main event."

"It's a stretch, Bri."

"Do you remember the one piece of advice you gave me when I started with the DA's office? I'm trusting my gut, Dad."

"I'll mention it at our meeting tomorrow, and I'll talk to her to make sure she's being careful."

"Thank you," Brian said, releasing a long deep breath. "I'm sorry I woke you up."

"No problem. Now, turn off that prosecutor's brain and go to sleep, you hear your old man?"

"Yes, sir," Brian said with a small smile. "I'll call you tomorrow."

CHAPTER 10

The next morning, as Michael sat at the head of the conference room table and listened to the monotone recitation of the known facts of the case, his stomach turned with disgust. He had read the reports, seen the horrific photos, and memorized the victims' chilling accounts, but to hear it all again with the added suspicion that the man they were hunting could also be responsible for the death of his own son . . . It was almost more than Michael could stand.

"Penetrated multiple times," the detective from Smithfield was saying. "Our victim is still hospitalized, recovering from the three rounds with him she remembers, and possibly more after she mercifully lost consciousness. She also suffered from exposure after spending a night naked and bound in the woods."

"The woods seem to be a possible signature, like the notes," Federal Agent Nathan Barclay commented.

The others nodded in agreement. Michael struggled to maintain his professional composure as rage threatened to consume him. Every one of these victims was someone's little girl, just as Sam had been his little boy.

"How's it possible this guy hasn't left a shred of DNA behind?" Federal Agent Jeff DiNardo asked.

"He had our girl gargle something she said smelled like Windex," the detective from Cranston said. "That took care of the DNA in her mouth."

"Ours, too," Matt Collins said.

"Each girl also reported he used two condoms at a time, except for the oral sessions."

"Jesus, what's the point?" Barclay muttered.

"What do you mean by that?" Michael asked, annoyed by the agent's cavalier tone.

"I don't know what you think of condoms, but most guys hate them because you can't feel a damned thing through one of them, let alone two," Barclay said.

"So you're suggesting he's not looking for sexual satisfaction?" Matt asked.

Barclay shrugged. "Maybe our guy has a perfectly satisfactory sex life at home and this is all about torture, plain and simple."

Michael wanted to say there was nothing plain or simple about it. And if his years of law enforcement had taught him anything, rape was never about sexual gratification.

"Let's keep our minds open to the possibility our perp might not be a loner, but a family guy with a wife and two-point-five kids at home," Barclay said.

"What else do we know about him?" DiNardo asked.

"He's big," Matt said. "The lab report on the partial footprint found at the Holbrooks—where one of the notes was discovered—indicate it was made by a work boot that was at least a size fourteen."

"And we've ruled out the home owner as bigfoot?" Barclay asked.

Matt nodded. "Steve Holbrook wears a ten-and-a-half,

and his son, who hasn't been home in more than a month, wears an eleven."

"Most shoe stores carry up to what?" Barclay asked. "Size thirteen?"

"That's right," Matt said. "I'm a fourteen. I special order most of my shoes from Gleason's. I could check with them to get a list of other local residents who special order larger sizes and see if any of them have a tread that matches the print."

"Good," Barclay said.

"Um, we also know his feet aren't the only thing that's big." Matt's face flushed with embarrassment. "An average-sized . . . man . . . doesn't do the kind of damage this guy did to these girls. They all reported he was extremely well endowed."

"Big feet, big dick," DiNardo commented.

Michael glared at him.

"Sorry," DiNardo said under his breath.

"There are a few other common elements," Matt said. "We already mentioned they were all cheerleaders, but they also walked to and from school, which is how he managed to nab them."

"We've concluded it would take a tremendous amount of time, patience, and planning to identify the cheerleaders at four schools in two different states and then to find one at each school who was vulnerable," the detective from Danielson, Connecticut, said.

"You read my mind, Detective," Barclay said. "Our guy has either a flexible schedule or a seasonable job where he has downtime in the winter."

"The attack in our town happened in late spring," the detective from Smithfield said.

"He could've planned it earlier," DiNardo said.

"We need to put out a bulletin to all high schools in

Rhode Island, Connecticut, and Massachusetts, warning them a serial rapist is targeting cheerleaders who walk to and from school," Barclay said to the administrative assistant he had brought with him.

She nodded as she typed notes on a laptop.

"You might want to add colleges, universities, community colleges, and technical schools to your distribution list," the Pawtucket police chief interjected. "Our carjacking victim—a former high school cheerleader—was a freshman at Rhode Island College."

Barclay accepted the suggestion with a gesture to his assistant. "Let's talk about tie-ins. You've mentioned the carjacking, which had the cheerleader factor as well as the absence of DNA."

"Right," the Pawtucket chief confirmed. "Except for some reason he went a step further in this case and murdered the victims."

"That was also his only known sex crime against a man," Matt added.

"Give us the details on that one," DiNardo requested.

"The guy was twenty-one, she was nineteen. They had been dating about a year. On July 6, 1995, they stopped at a convenience store on Broad Street. He left the car running and went in to buy a soda. Security cameras showed him in the store alone, so we assume while he was inside, the perp got into the back seat and pulled a weapon on the girl. The car was found ten miles away in a wooded area."

"Again with the woods," Barclay commented. To his assistant, he said, "Make a note to mention wooded areas in the warning memo."

"The victims were found in the car, arranged in a sexual position," the Pawtucket chief continued. "They were strangled, naked, bound, and bloody. Like the other victims, they'd been raped multiple times and ways, and autopsies showed their injuries were consistent with those of the recent victims. The lack of hair and fibers in the car led us to suspect the attacks took place outside the car. We compared the time from the convenience store camera with the time of death to determine he had them for five or six hours before he killed them."

He let the impact of that settle in the room before he added, "Ten frustrating years later, we haven't had a single suspect."

After fifteen years of looking for a guy in a road, Michael could sympathize with his colleague's disappointment.

"So let's recap," Barclay said, attempting to bring the two-hour meeting to a close. "We have four recent aggravated sexual assaults and a series of notes found in Granville at the graves of deceased cheerleaders, at a memorial where six cheerleaders and athletes were killed in a car accident, and another found at a former Granville cheerleader's parents' house. In addition, we have a carjacking where several elements match the current spree. Without the lack of DNA, I'd say the carjacking victim being an ex-cheerleader was a coincidence. I'm also bothered by the fact they were murdered, but I'm not ruling out a connection."

"When you add the same kind of sex and no DNA," DiNardo said with a shrug, "it sounds like the same guy to me."

"For now, we'll operate under the assumption it's connected," Barclay decided. "Anything else?" When no one answered, he said, "You've all done an excellent job thus far. I want to reiterate that we're here to help, not step on toes. So let's meet here again the day after tomorrow at nine a.m. to regroup. In the meantime, I'll be holding a press conference at noon to warn the public. I don't want to mention the possible connection to the carjacking yet. There's no sense getting the hopes of the victims' families up until we know more. Thanks very much, everyone."

The others engaged in animated conversation while they gathered up their files and belongings. As they moved toward the door, Michael said, "Wait."

"Chief Westbury?" Agent Barclay said. "What is it?"

Michael made eye contact with Matt across the room. Matt's expression urged caution. *But if there was a chance, even the slightest chance . . .* "There might be something else."

"I'm listening," Barclay said.

"In the interest of full disclosure, I should mention that the accident site where one of the notes was found . . ."

"What about it?" DiNardo asked.

"The younger of my two sons was killed in that accident."

"I'm sorry," Barclay said soberly.

"Me, too," DiNardo added.

"Thank you," Michael said. "About a month before the accident, my older son was coming home late one night and had to swerve to avoid hitting a man who was standing in the road at the exact place where the accident later happened." In a rush of words, Michael laid out his theory. When he was done, he waited breathlessly for their reaction.

"I ran a search for unsolved cases from 1990 and 2000," Matt interjected. "Nothing jumped out from 1990, but in 2000, two high school cheerleaders—one in Providence and another in Cumberland—reported attempted abductions on their way home from school. They were able to get away— one kicked him where he lives, and the other said he bolted when a car approached them."

"No description of the perp?" Barclay asked.

Matt shook his head. "All the girls who've been attacked said he grabbed them from behind and wore a face mask during the actual assaults. They did say he was big, though. So if Chief Westbury is right about the five-year pattern, our perp tried twice but failed in 2000. I also checked all the in-between years since 1995 but found nothing else that stood out as possibly connected."

Michael glanced at Matt, hoping his eyes conveyed his appreciation for his deputy's support.

Barclay stood with his hands on his hips as he contemplated Michael.

For a long moment, Michael had no idea if he was about to be dismissed as a grieving father hoping to exonerate his son.

Finally, Barclay said, "Let's hear the rest."

AT MISS MOLLY'S, everything came to a halt during the busy lunch hour as regular TV programming was interrupted to carry federal Agent Nathan Barclay's chilling announcement that a serial rapist was targeting popular young cheerleaders in Rhode Island and Connecticut. With Chief Westbury standing next to him at the podium, Agent Barclay said the investigation was focused on Granville in part because of disturbing notes found in five places around town, including the graves of the three cheerleaders killed in the 1995 car accident on Tucker Road.

As she heard that for the first time, Carly's legs gave out under her, and she sat down hard on one of the stools at the counter.

Agent Barclay called on young people to travel in groups and to be wary. He added a further warning to young women who had once been cheerleaders. "We're looking for a dangerous predator who's targeting cheerleaders and ex-cheerleaders," Barclay concluded. "However, I urge all young women between the ages of thirteen and thirty-five to be highly vigilant, especially in wooded areas, until he's apprehended."

The twenty-minute press conference ended without the agent taking any questions from the media. Patrons of Miss Molly's, stunned by the news, conversed in low murmurs rather than their usual boisterous tones.

Molly Hanson rested a hand on Carly's shoulder. "Are you all right, honey? You look like you've just seen a ghost."

Trying to shake off the unease that had settled over her, Carly nodded.

"Disturbing," was Molly's take on it. "Could be someone who sits at one of my tables every day."

The thought sent a cold shiver of fear through Carly as she glanced around the room full of familiar faces. These were people she had known all her life. The idea that she or anyone else could have reason to fear one of them was absurd.

Molly brushed a loving hand over Carly's cheek. "Do you feel up to working?"

Embarrassed that the news had rattled her so deeply, Carly nodded, got up, and reached for the coffee pot to do refills.

"Carly," her coworker Debby called from behind the counter. She waved Carly over to her. In a low tone, Debby said, "Chief Westbury called for you. He asked that you wait for him here when your shift ends. He wants to talk to you."

Carly smiled her thanks and began her rounds with the coffee, wondering if the chief wanted to talk to her about the notes she had found. What else could it be? *I guess I'll find out soon enough.*

MICHAEL WESTBURY FELT the eyes of the town on him as he walked from the station to Miss Molly's just before two. If he were a regular citizen, he supposed he, too, would be wondering why the man charged with keeping their town safe had failed so miserably.

Desmond Kane, a member of the volunteer fire department, stopped him outside the hardware store.

"What do you know, Mike?"

"Not as much as I should," Michael muttered. He glanced down at Desmond's feet and found them to be normal sized.

"You really think this guy lives here?"

Michael shrugged. "The only thing I know for sure is he has a beef with cheerleaders."

"I heard he did a real job on Tanya Lewis," Desmond said, his interest in knowing more about just what had been done to Tanya apparent on his face.

It disgusted Michael that people always wanted the details, especially in sex crimes. If they could see the pictures and read the reports, they wouldn't be so curious. The images were burned into Michael's brain, and he wouldn't wish them on his worst enemy. "Take care, Desmond," Michael said, continuing down Main Street.

Miss Molly's had emptied out for the day, and Carly was working with the other waitresses to clean up. She looked up with a smile when Michael walked in and sat in a corner booth.

Carly brought him a steaming cup of coffee and patted her stomach, raising a questioning eyebrow.

"I'm good, thanks."

With her fingers, she suggested a little something.

He smiled. "Okay. You pick."

She came back with a slice of Molly's famous chocolate cake.

He groaned. "Mary Ann's going to flip when she gets home next week and sees how fat I've gotten."

Carly crinkled up her face and shook her head in disagreement.

"Don't let me interrupt your work. I can wait until you're done."

She held up both hands to tell him she needed ten more minutes.

"Take your time. I'll enjoy this sinful cake you forced on me."

Leaving him with a smile, she went to finish refilling the creamers and sugar bowls in preparation for the next morning. By the time she joined him in the booth, the rest of the staff had left. Molly flipped the open sign on the locked door, came over to say hello to Michael, and then went to her office in the back of the building to do some paperwork.

Carly tugged out a pad and pen. "Tough day for you," she wrote.

"Tough month."

"You look tired."

"I'm not sleeping very well these days."

"You really think it's someone who lives here?"

"Unfortunately, yes." He put down his fork and wiped his mouth with a paper napkin. "Carly . . . I don't want to frighten you, but . . ." He looked around to make sure they were still alone. "It's possible, but not definite, that there's a connection to the accident."

Carly stared at him for a long moment before she wrote, "The guy in the road?"

"Yes. Brian told you what happened to him?"

She nodded. "After the accident. After he remembered it."

"I hate to dredge up your memories of that night, but you never did give us a statement about what you saw, so I need to ask . . ."

Her nod gave him permission to continue.

"Was anyone else there besides you, Brian, and the driver who stopped to help you? Did you see anyone else before the police and firefighters arrived?"

Michael watched as Carly let her mind wander back to that fateful night. She trembled, so he reached for her hand. "Take your time, honey. I know it's hard to think about."

"I can almost still smell the fire," she wrote and then shook off the memory so she could tell him what he needed to know. "But no one else was there, at least not that I can recall. I kind of lost it when I saw . . ." She looked up at him, her eyes bright with tears.

"What did you see?" Michael's stomach twisted with anxiety as he waited for details he didn't really want to know.

"I saw them burning. I started to scream and couldn't stop, like I was outside of myself watching someone else. It was surreal."

He squeezed her hand, his heart hurting for her, for both of them. "There's more I need to tell you, facts about the case we haven't made public. I know I don't need to say it, but they're things we don't want anyone to know."

Her smile was rich with the absurdity of him asking her, of all people, to keep a secret.

Because he was concerned about her safety and knew he could trust her—and would've been able to trust her even if she could speak—he shared his theory about the five-year pattern. "We think it began with the accident, which means it's most likely someone you, Brian, and the others went to school with." Pausing to let that settle, he continued. "Do you still have your yearbooks from high school?"

Seeming shocked by what he had said, she nodded.

"Can you flip through them tonight? We're looking for someone who might've had issues with you, Brian, or one of the others in the car. Someone who had a beef over what he saw as your easy success in school, in sports, in social situations, where he might not have had it so good. If you think of anyone who meets those criteria, write down his name for me. Think also about boys you and the other girls might've dated before Brian, Sam, Pete, and Toby."

He hated the overwhelmed expression on her face but pressed on anyway, knowing he had to do this. "I talked to Brian about the case last night. He made an interesting point."

Carly brightened at the mention of his son, which pleased Michael for reasons he couldn't take the time to process just then. "He suggested the person our perp was hoping to kill that night on Tucker Road might not have been in the car."

She sucked in a deep breath.

"You could be in danger, Carly," he said gently. "It's possible the notes you found were intentionally put in places you were likely to find them."

"Why me?" she wrote, her hand shaking ever so slightly.

"I don't know. That's what I need you to think about. Go back in time to before you started dating Brian. Who might've been put out by you getting a new boyfriend?"

"It was twenty years ago," she wrote.

"That's why I want you to take some time to think about it. In the meantime, let's talk about your schedule."

Her face twisted with confusion. "My schedule?"

"Your routine." He didn't want to mention yet that his officers would be keeping a close eye on her. "What days do you work here?"

Tentatively, she wrote, "Sunday through Thursday, six to two."

"Do you have certain things you do after work on various days?"

She nodded. "Mondays in the spring and summer I go to

the accident site, Tuesdays I watch my niece and nephew for a few hours so Caren can do some errands. On Wednesdays, I volunteer at the animal shelter. Walk the dogs, etc."

"Busy girl," Michael said with a smile.

Shrugging, she continued. "Thursday afternoons in the summer, I go to my niece Zoë's baseball games at Columbia Park. Fridays I chill out and do laundry and stuff at home. Saturdays I spend at whatever games my other nieces and nephews have—soccer, baseball, lacrosse."

"Sundays you go to five o'clock mass at St. Mary's, right?"

She nodded. "And then dinner at my parents' when they're in town. That's pretty much it."

Knowing what could have been, Michael was saddened by the lack of friends and a man in such a beautiful woman's life. It was a small life by some people's standards, but it would've been even smaller had her father not forced her back into the world.

"You guys are going to be stalking me, aren't you?" she wrote, the resignation showing in her eyes.

"I promised my son I'd keep you safe," Michael said with a wry smile.

Carly's eyes flew up to meet his.

"He's worried about you," Michael said, aware he was picking at something that might be better left alone.

"Maybe I should be worried about him. He wasn't in the car, either."

Michael shook his head. "This guy likes girls."

"But if your theory is true, the guy you're looking for might be jealous of Brian. Maybe he was after both of us."

"Possibly," Michael conceded. "However, because you're here and Brian isn't, I'm more worried about you." He reached into his pocket and withdrew a small can, putting it on the table in front of her.

With the lift of her chin, she asked what it was.

"Pepper spray. I want you to carry it with you everywhere you go. If you step outside your door, I want you to have it with you. Use it if you feel even the slightest bit threatened, and even if it's someone you know and think you can trust." He leaned in, his forearms resting on the table, and took her hands. "It's going to be someone you know, Carly, someone we all know. Hesitating, even for a second, could make all the difference. Trust your gut. If it's telling you you're in danger, you probably are."

Carly freed one hand from his hold and ran her fingers over the can.

Michael showed her how to use it. "Aim for the face, the eyes preferably."

She shuddered and stared at the can for a long moment.

"What are you thinking?"

Picking up the pen, she wrote, "I'm scared."

"I'll do everything I can to keep you safe. All right?"

Her face pale and pinched with anxiety, she looked him in the eye and nodded.

CHAPTER 11

May faded into June, and the tension in Granville was as thick as the humidity that settled like a wet blanket on the small town, making its annual announcement of summer's return to northwestern Rhode Island. Over picket fences, at the post office, in the shops along Main Street, at the counter at Miss Molly's, and at the car dealership on the outskirts of town, people speculated nervously about who among them was the monster.

A collective sigh of relief went through a town full of brittle nerves when Granville High School graduated the Class of 2010 without further incident. Recovered physically from her injuries, Tanya Lewis received a warm welcome from her classmates at commencement. As summer vacation began, petrified parents monitored their daughters' comings and goings. The girls, accustomed to the freedom that came with high school, chafed against the restraints.

That chafing kept Michael Westbury awake at night, waiting to hear that one of the kids in his town had reached her limit, had gone out alone, and had been attacked by a predator who was waiting for the chafe to become unbearable. With the investigation stalled, his officers, with backup from the state police and FBI, could only watch. And wait.

A court order had compelled Gleason's to turn over its list of men who special-ordered larger-sized shoes. The list had yielded four possible suspects, but each had been ruled out. One was in his sixties and didn't fit the profile. Another had been out of the country when two of the rapes occurred. The other two men had solid alibis. The few names Brian and Carly had given him from their yearbooks hadn't panned out, either. Most of them lived out of state, one had died, and another was crippled with multiple sclerosis.

Michael had officers patrolling everywhere kids gathered in the summertime—Columbia Park, the town common, the beach at the lake, the movie theater, and the bowling alley. If they saw a girl walking alone on a town road, they'd been instructed to offer her a ride home.

As the weeks passed, Michael noticed people losing the initial burst of interest that came with big news in a small town. They'd talked a blue streak about it and had finally run out of steam on the subject. He was concerned that the first wave of panic had abated, and folks had relaxed a bit. He didn't want them relaxed. He wanted them worried and afraid so they'd be vigilant.

If they were in fact dealing with an anniversary perp, he had six more months left in 2010. He was probably high on the success of the first half of the year and enjoying the goose chase he was leading law enforcement on. The task force believed he would strike again before the year was out. So while others in his town relaxed, Michael didn't.

The heat was stifling, the tension debilitating, the watching tedious. But the waiting . . . The waiting was hell.

≈

CARLY LOVED TO CLAP. Joining in a round of applause gave her the feeling, even for the briefest of moments, that she was just like the other people in the bleachers expressing their approval of her niece Zoë's strikeout. Zoë's ponytail of auburn curls—the same curls all the Holbrook women had—was pulled through the back of her ball cap, and her long legs looked even longer in white baseball pants as she prowled around the pitcher's mound.

"I keep hoping she'll start acting like a girl one of these days," Carly's sister Cate muttered as they watched Zoë strike out the side.

With a delighted wave to her family in the stands, Zoë pranced into the dugout full of boys.

"She's *all* girl, and the boys love her," Carly's mother Carol said, defending her granddaughter.

"They love her fastball," Cate said.

Carly smiled at the old debate. Zoë had insisted on joining Little League as a six-year-old and had played every year since without any regard for the fact that she was the only girl in the league. Now, at fourteen, she was a star in the summer Sandlot League.

With a huge smile on his face, Cate's husband, Tom Murphy, climbed the bleachers to where they were sitting. "Did you *see* that? Struck out the side! That's my girl."

Embarrassed by his effusiveness, Cate tugged him down next to her and told him to hush. "Everyone's looking at you," she whispered.

"So what?"

Their exchange amused Carly. Tom was a big teddy bear of a man who loved his wife and kids passionately and didn't care who knew it. Carly was struck with a familiar pang of envy over her sister's happy marriage and beautiful family.

"Dad, can we go to the concession stand?" asked ten-year-old Steve.

"Sure, let's go," Tom said.

"No more soda," Cate called after them. "And bring something for Lilly."

Tom raised a hand to let his wife know he had heard her.

Six-year-old Lilly was curled up in one of her favorite places—Carly's lap.

Carly tickled the girl and delighted in the belly laugh she was rewarded with.

"There's Auntie Caren," Lilly cried, dashing off to meet her cousins.

Looking frazzled, Caren made her way from the parking lot with four-year-old Justin and two-year-old Julia in tow.

Carly watched Lilly take Julia's hand and lead her to the bleachers. Justin and Julia gunned for Carly's lap, and she wrapped her arms around them.

Lilly ceded her coveted spot to her younger cousins and plopped down next to Carly with a long-suffering sigh.

Carly buried her nose in Julia's fragrant blond curls, wallowing in the sweet scent of baby shampoo.

"What's the score?" Caren asked.

"Six nothing, us," Cate replied. "You just missed Zoë striking out the side."

"Damn!" Caren said.

"Damn!" Julia repeated, and the adults cracked up.

"She's like a parrot lately." Caren poked her daughter's ribs playfully. "She couldn't decide what dress she wanted to wear, which is why we're late."

"Pretty dress," Julia said.

"Very pretty," Carol agreed, reaching for the child. "Tell Auntie Carly she has to share you with Grammy."

Carly tightened her hold on Julia, and the girl's peals of laughter delighted her as she handed Julia over to her grandmother.

"Look!" Justin cried. "Zoë's up!"

"Come on, Zoë!" the others hollered.

Carly clapped Justin's pudgy hands together while they watched Zoë patiently wait for her pitch. She had worked the pitcher to a full count when she finally connected, sending the ball deep into left field. Two runs scored as she rounded the bases and barreled into the second baseman, sliding in just ahead of the throw from left.

"*Mother of God,*" Cate groaned, hiding behind her hands.

With a huge smile on her face, Zoë leaped to her feet and shook a victorious fist at the dugout where her teammates were celebrating. The other team's second baseman was still flat on his back in the dirt.

Watching Zoë, so tall and lovely, so full of life, filled Carly's heart to overflowing, and for once, she was perfectly content.

CARLY WAS WALKING with her mother to Cate's house for a cookout after the game when her cell phone chimed to indicate a new text message. A week earlier, she had finally caved in to pleas from Chief Westbury and her parents and had gotten the phone, which included a GPS device. The thought that she might one day need to be located was terrifying, so she tried not to think about it.

She flipped it open to read the latest message from the chief.

"Where R U?" His use of teen message lingo never failed to amuse her.

"With my mama," she replied.

"Just checking."

"Relax," she wrote back.

"Is that Michael?" Carol asked.

Carly rolled her eyes and nodded.

"He's worried about you. We all are."

Carly hooked her arm through her mother's.

Carol stopped walking and turned to study her daughter. "You're not sleeping well, are you? You look tired."

Carly shrugged in reply.

"I haven't been sleeping too well myself. Are you sure we can't convince you to come home until this is over?"

With a smirk, Carly shook her head.

"I know, I know. We threatened to kick you out, and now we're begging you to come home. I see the irony, don't worry."

The party was in full swing by the time they arrived at Cate's house. Caren's husband Neil had come straight from work and was pushing Justin and Julia on the swings. He waved hello when Carly and her mother came in through the back gate.

Carly's dad joined them a short time later after playing golf with some friends. With a cell phone pressed to her ear, Zoë came bursting through the sliding glass door that led to the deck. She had showered and changed into a denim skirt and tank top. Carly put her arm around her niece, pressed a kiss to her wet curls, and was startled to notice the mascara and eye shadow she was wearing.

Zoë closed her phone and caught Carly looking at her eyes.

"How does it look?" Zoë asked in a conspiratorial whisper.

Carly gave her a thumbs up.

Zoë kissed her aunt's cheek and said, "Don't tell my mom." As Zoë raced off, Carly decided Cate would be thrilled to see her tomboy daughter wearing makeup.

They ate, played a cutthroat game of croquet with the

kids, and were toasting marshmallows over the outdoor fire-place when a group of Zoë's girlfriends came into the yard through the gate.

"Mom!" she called. "Can I go to the movies?"

"How're you getting there?"

"Walking?"

"No way!" Tom bellowed. "I'll drive you."

"But Dad . . ."

"Nonnegotiable, Zoë Ann. We've talked about this."

Zoë kicked at the grass. "Sucks. I'm a sophomore now, you know."

"You're not getting any help from us, baby girl," Steve Holbrook said, kissing his granddaughter's forehead. "We're on your dad's side."

"It's a conspiracy," Zoë said with a good-natured grin. She never stayed mad for long.

"Let me get my keys," Tom said. "You ladies tell your parents where you're going and that I'm driving both ways."

"Okay, Mr. Murphy," they said in a girlish chorus.

After Tom left with the girls, Caren said, "I feel sorry for them."

"We all do," Carol said. "It's a terrible way for everyone to have to live."

"Even after this guy is caught, we'll all be much more cautious than we used to be," Caren's husband Neil said. He had kicked off the boots he wore to work at the construction company he co-owned with his brothers. They had teased him earlier about his mid-shin tan line.

"Luckily the younger kids won't know what they're missing out on because they'll never have the freedom Zoë's had," Cate said. "It's been hard clipping her wings just as she was starting to spread them."

"Whatever it takes to keep her safe," Steve said.

Carly was saddened by the conversation. Until the killer

was caught, her nieces and nephews wouldn't know the simple pleasure of a walk on the beach in the moonlight or a kiss under the willow tree. The man they were all afraid of had done much more than kill and terrorize young people. He had forever altered Granville's small-town fabric.

CHAPTER 12

*C*arly was working her final shift before the Fourth of July weekend. Tony Russo, Luke McInnis, and Tommy Spellman were in their usual booth, chugging water rather than coffee.

"Freaking stifling out there," Tony said as Carly delivered their lunch and refilled their glasses.

"Are you going to the reunion, Carly?" Luke asked.

She shook her head.

"Why not?" Tommy asked. "It won't be the same without you."

She shrugged, wondering what the point would be. It wasn't like she could talk to anyone or had anything exciting to tell them, even if she could. Besides, the last thing in the world she felt like doing was hearing how successful and happy her classmates were. She was the one who should have been happily married with children she adored—Brian's children.

Until recently, very little of her time or energy had been expended on bitterness about something she had no control over. But living in fear of the man who'd taken so much from her and her friends had stirred up old feelings she thought she'd long ago put away for good.

The guys each tried a different tactic to convince her to go to the reunion, but Carly just shook her head with amusement at their campaign and moved on to other tables.

As her friends were preparing to leave, Luke walked over to her. "Are you *sure* you won't come to the reunion, Carly? You, um, you can go with me if you want to. It would be fun."

Startled, Carly looked up at him. *Is he asking me out?* She was so out of practice with such things she couldn't be sure, but it certainly seemed like he was.

"Everyone would love to see you," he added.

The only person in their class she had any interest in seeing wouldn't be there, but she couldn't very well tell Luke that.

"Thanks for asking, Luke," she wrote on the back of her order pad. "But I'm going to pass."

The disappointment on his handsome face surprised her, but he recovered quickly. "You don't know what you'll be missing," he said with a cajoling grin.

She shook her head.

"All right. Have a good Fourth."

"You, too," she wrote.

She walked home from work, aware of the subtle presence of a Granville police officer watching her and the activity on Main Street. The stores and homes along the street were decked out in festive bunting, and the stripes down the middle of the street had been painted red and blue in preparation for the parade. For reasons she didn't quite understand, the festive atmosphere depressed Carly. When she got home, she sent her mother a text message to let her know she had a headache and wouldn't be going out again that day.

The checking in was irritating for someone so fiercely

independent, but the alternative was much worse. Her parents and Chief Westbury always knew where she was. She supposed it was a small price to pay for staying safe.

After taking an Advil, she stretched out on the sofa and fixed her eyes on the jukebox that took up a whole wall in her small living room. A few years ago, she had walked past Toby's parents' house and found the jukebox by the curb with some other furniture they were getting rid of. She had plopped herself down in an orange plaid chair she remembered from the basement and waited.

Toby's dad had been startled to find her there when he got home from work. He'd aged significantly since Carly had last seen him, and she noticed right away that, like Brian's parents, Mr. Garrett wore the pain of his loss in his eyes.

"Carly? What're you doing here?"

She had rested a hand on the jukebox and looked at him with what she hoped were imploring eyes.

"You want that?"

She nodded.

"Mrs. Garrett is redoing the basement, and this old thing was taking up too much room. We don't use it much anymore. If you'd like to have it, it's yours."

She gave him a spontaneous hug that seemed to take him by surprise.

Clearing his throat, he said, "Do you have room for it in your place?"

With another nod, she clapped her hands with delight.

Amused by her glee, Mr. Garrett said, "I'll get a couple of friends to help me bring it over on Saturday, okay?"

The jukebox had lived in her apartment ever since. At first, the memories that came with it made her sad, and she wondered if she'd done the right thing by asking Mr. Garrett for it. But over time, the memories had softened, and now she was glad to have such an important souvenir from the best years of her life.

Perhaps it was because she knew Brian was thinking of her and worrying about her safety, or it could be all the talk of the class reunion. Maybe it was the holiday, which was always tinged now with melancholy, since the last time she made love with Brian had been on the Fourth of July. But whatever the reason, she wanted to give herself permission to think about him, to remember *them*, and the love they'd shared before disaster stole their every hope and dream.

Getting up from the sofa, she went over to the jukebox and turned it on. For the first time since she had owned it, she selected D8 and then returned to the sofa to let the music transport her back to that last exquisite moment a lifetime ago.

She could almost feel Brian's arms around her and smell the musty scent of Toby's basement. Tears rolled down her cheeks, but she made no move to brush them away as she listened for the soft giggles that never came from the other couples dancing to Van Morrison's "Tupelo Honey."

She ached for Brian. How long had it been since she'd felt that particular ache? Not since the first couple of years had passed, when she finally accepted he wasn't coming back, had she allowed herself to yearn for him the way she did right then. To have just a few minutes with him, an afternoon maybe . . . What she wouldn't give for an hour to do nothing more than look at him. She told herself it would be enough.

The song ended, snapping her out of her stupor. Wiping the tears from her face, she got up and got busy cleaning her spotless apartment. There was no point in sitting around feeling sorry for herself. She hadn't often allowed herself that indulgence, and there was nothing to be gained from it now. He had his life, and she had hers. Like she had told his father, it was better this way.

Mid-July in Manhattan was not for the faint of heart, Brian decided as he walked the short distance from court back to his office. Once there, he was surprised to find messages from his mother on both his office voicemail and his cell phone, which he'd forgotten to bring with him to court. Since it was unlike her to call him twice in a week, let alone twice in an hour, his stomach twisted with nerves as he waited for her to answer her cell.

"Mom? Hey, what's wrong?"

"Oh hi, honey. I'm sorry to bother you at work. I know how busy you are."

"It's fine. Don't worry about it. What's the matter?"

"I'm worried about Dad, and I needed someone to talk to."

Loosening his tie and opening the top button of his shirt, Brian sat behind his desk. "Is he sick?"

"No, it's the investigation," she said. "He's working fourteen hours a day, seven days a week, and he's not sleeping well at all. I suspect he thinks it's up to him to single-handedly protect Granville from this guy. I don't know how much more he can take."

"It's not just about protecting the town. He's out to clear Sam's name, too. This is personal to him."

"I know, but I've never seen him like this, Bri. He's completely obsessed."

"I'm not sure if it'll help, but I'll give him a call."

"It would help a lot. He listens to you. So how are you? Back to your crazy schedule?"

"Of course," he said with a chuckle.

"What does Saul have you working on now?"

"A couple of drug cases, a B&E, and two gang-related things. Nothing that'll land me on TV."

"Ugh, I hate the idea of you dealing with druggies and gang bangers."

Brian laughed. "What the heck do you know about gang bangers?"

"More than you think," she said indignantly. "I watch *Law & Order*."

"I've told you not to watch those shows. It's a lot more boring and mundane than they make it out to be."

"Have you gotten any more job offers?"

"A few."

"Maybe you ought to think about taking one of them."

"And give up my druggies and gang bangers? I'd die of boredom."

"Now you're just being fresh."

"God," he said with a laugh. "I haven't heard that word in years." It took him right back to getting in trouble with Sam in the back seat of her station wagon. "Hey, Mom? Dad's still keeping tabs on Carly, right?"

"He's got her using text messages to keep him and her parents apprised of her whereabouts."

"Great idea."

"Well, I won't take up any more of your time, honey. I appreciate you checking in with Dad."

"If you think I need to come home, Mom, I'll do it in a minute."

"I wouldn't ask that of you."

"Staying away has begun to seem foolish lately. I'll have to go home eventually. What will I do when you guys are ninety? Hire someone to take care of you?"

She snorted with laughter. "How about we cross that bridge in about thirty years?"

"Call me if you need me. Day or night, okay?"

"I will. Love you, Bri."

"You, too." Brian ended the call and sat back to think

about what she'd said. The strain was taking a toll on his dad, and despite the youthful image Brian had of him, Michael was pushing sixty. With this case taking up all his father's time, Brian realized it might be months before his parents could get away for a weekend in New York. As Brian dialed his dad's cell, he imagined himself catching the shuttle from LaGuardia to Providence. His mother would pick him up and drive him home to Granville. No biggie, right?

Yeah, right . . .

"Is this the famous prosecutor from the great city of New York calling?" Michael asked.

Brian smiled, relieved by his father's joviality. "The one and only. How's it going, Dad?"

"About the same. We're waiting and watching."

"Mom's worried about you."

"Did she call and tell you that?" Michael asked with annoyance. "She shouldn't have bothered you with it."

"Why not? You're running yourself ragged, and you're not thirty anymore."

"I'm not?"

"Don't be fresh with me," Brian joked.

Michael laughed. "You *have* been talking to your mother."

"What's the latest?"

"Not a damned thing. We spent the Fourth of July weekend watching your class reunion, but we got nothing— no lurkers, no oddities, nada. It was completely uneventful. I did see a bunch of your old friends, though, and they all asked for you. They said they'd followed the Gooding trial."

"That's cool. It sounds like you're doing everything you can."

"This town is crawling with cops and feds. You wouldn't recognize the place."

"Well, it must be doing the trick."

"I guess so," Michael said in a weary tone. "Part of me just wants to get through this year without any more trouble, because I know I'm right about the five-year pattern. But I'd hate to have to wait five more years for another opportunity to nail this bastard. Hang on a sec, son."

Brian heard muffled voices on the other end of the line.

"I've got to go," Michael said.

Brian could hear the tension in his father's voice. "What is it?"

"We just got a report from the south end of town that a dog returned home without the teenaged girl who was walking it."

"Oh no."

"I'll call you when I can," Michael said an instant before the phone went dead.

MICHAEL'S HEART pounded from a burst of adrenaline as he raced through town with lights flashing on top of his unmarked car. On the way, he tried to reach Matt Collins, who was taking a few days off on Michael's order. They'd been working nonstop for weeks, and the strain had begun to take a toll on both of them.

"Goddamn it," Michael uttered when he realized Matt's cell phone was turned off—another thing he'd ordered his deputy to do. "Matt, it's Mike. Call me the minute you get this message."

Maybe the dog just got away from the kid. Maybe it's nothing. Even as he thought it, though, he didn't believe it. The affluent subdivision was in chaos when he arrived just behind the FBI and several of his patrol officers. The neighbors had poured out of their houses to watch the unfolding scene.

Agent Barclay stood in the driveway of the missing girl's

home, attempting to get a statement from her hysterical mother.

"*He has her, doesn't he?*" She clawed at Barclay's shirt. "You have to do something! Before he hurts her, *do something!*"

"Ma'am, we're doing everything we can," Barclay said in a calm, professional tone that Michael admired. Nathan grasped the woman's hand. "But we need your help. Can you get us a recent picture of Alicia?"

She glanced at her teenaged son, and he ran for the house.

"Does she have a cell phone?" Michael asked.

The woman wiped the tears from her cheeks and nodded. "She has it with her everywhere she goes, even to walk Chester."

Hearing his name, a yellow lab bounded over to her, still dragging a leash behind him.

She brushed him aside with the absent wave of her hand. "But when I tried to call her, the phone was turned off." Breaking down again, she said, "That phone is *never* off."

"The dog isn't protective of her?" Barclay asked.

"He's still a puppy." She sniffed. "He loves everyone."

Michael had to bite his tongue to keep from asking how she could've let her fifteen-year-old daughter wander around *alone—with a rapist on the loose*—with a dog that could be bought off with a pat on the head or a treat. Just as he had feared, the initial shock had worn off, and people had gotten complacent. His worst nightmare had come true.

A fancy sports car came to a screeching stop at the curb. Dressed in a shirt and tie, Alicia's father bolted from the car and ran up the driveway to his wife. "Did you find her?" he asked frantically.

"No," she moaned. Her legs suddenly gave out from under her, and she sank to the grass.

Her husband sat next to her and put his arm around her.

"Is it possible she's at a friend's house and forgot to check in with you?" Barclay asked.

"Alicia always tells us where she is," her father said. "Always. And she'd never let Chester run around unattended. She's raised him since he was two months old. She adores him."

"How about her activities?" Michael stopped short of asking the one specific question he and Barclay were both dying to ask.

"Um, she plays soccer in a summer league."

"And during the school year?"

"She's a junior varsity cheerleader."

Michael's blood ran cold as he exchanged glances with Nathan Barclay.

CHAPTER 13

*Z*oë Murphy was inconsolable. Alicia Perry had been a good friend of hers since preschool, and even though Alicia was a year older than Zoë, the two had remained close over the years. As the disappearance stretched into a second day, Zoë's family rallied around her, doing what they could to keep the girl's spirits up.

Carly found her on a swing in the backyard of Cate and Tom's house. As Carly took the swing next to Zoë's, she noticed her niece's cheeks were wet with tears. Carly reached for her hand.

Zoë wrapped her fingers around Carly's. "Thanks for coming by."

As they sat in silence for several minutes, holding hands and swinging slowly, Carly was filled with longing for everything and everyone she'd lost in the accident. Being with Zoë, in good times and bad, made her yearn for the things that were missing in her life, especially the husband and children she should've had by now.

"My mom and I were talking earlier," Zoë said. "She told me what happened to you when you were a senior. I'm so sorry, Auntie Carly. I never knew those crosses on Tucker Road were for your friends. I can't imagine what that must've been like for you."

With a squeeze, Carly released Zoë's hand to pull a pad and pen from the back pocket of her jeans. "Alicia is going to be fine." She underlined the word fine several times.

"He's hurting her," Zoë said, breaking down again.

"She's strong," Carly wrote.

Zoë nodded.

"You have to be strong, too."

"I'm trying."

Carly got up and reached for the girl.

Sobbing, Zoë fell into her aunt's embrace and held on tight.

BY THE THIRD DAY, Alicia's disappearance had brought the town to its knees in a way that reminded long-time residents of the week that followed the Tucker Road wreck. Other than a candlelight vigil for Alicia on the second night, people kept their kids inside and limited their outings to essential trips only. The local churches held daily services, and counselors were available for students at the high school.

Miss Molly's was as quiet as Carly had ever seen it. The few customers they did have were members of the local and national media that had lined the town common with their satellite trucks. The story had been carried by most of the national news channels, and one show had devoted an entire hour to Alicia and the case, including an interview with Chief Westbury.

"If you want to take off early, feel free," Molly offered.

Embarrassed to be caught staring out the window when she was supposed to be working, Carly shrugged. There was nothing she particularly felt like doing. Worrying about what that poor girl was going through had left Carly feeling drained and listless.

"Suit yourself, honey," Molly said, patting Carly's shoulder.

"Hey, Carly," Debby said. "Chief Westbury called. He wants you to meet him by the willow at the lake when your shift ends. He said he's got something he wants to show you."

Carly's cheeks grew hot at the idea of meeting the chief in the place where she used to make love with his son. *What could he possibly want to show me there?* Her stomach knotted with anxiety. The willow was the one place from her old life she had never returned to. The memories were just too painful. But if the chief needed her for something, she would go.

Since there wasn't much cleaning up to do at Miss Molly's, she left at the stroke of two and set out for the lake. With the police on a desperate search to find Alicia, Carly noticed with uneasiness the absence of officers on Main Street that afternoon. She reached into her pocket and wrapped her fingers around the ever-present can of pepper spray.

Twenty minutes later, she arrived at the appointed spot but found no sign of the chief. Several hundred yards down the beach, a few scattered families were enjoying a warm day at the lake, despite the crisis unfolding in town. Carly supposed the kids couldn't be held captive inside forever.

Where is he? Tugging the slim cell phone from her back pocket, she sent him a text message. "Where R U? I'm at the lake waiting 4 U."

While she awaited his reply, she wandered over to the willow and was assailed by a flood of memories and feelings. What would it hurt to step inside just for a minute? Fingering the delicate shower of leaves, she summoned the nerve to part the curtain. She closed her eyes, took a deep breath for courage, and walked through the branches. When she opened her eyes, she found Alicia Perry's lifeless, naked body in the very spot where she and Brian used to make love.

Carly opened her mouth and screamed.

MICHAEL WORE a path in the conference room rug as he heard an update from the patrol officers and detectives who were finishing their shift. "Nothing new," they reported for the third straight day. "There's no sign of her anywhere."

"It's like she vanished, Chief," one of the younger patrolmen said, his eyes wide with dismay.

"She did," Michael snapped, annoyed by the stupid statement. "Anyone who can stay for second shift is requested to do so." His department's overtime expenses were threatening to bankrupt the town, but that was the least of his worries at the moment. "That's all."

He stormed into his office and slammed the door, feeling impotent and exhausted at the same time. Except for quick runs home to shower and change clothes, he had worked around the clock since Alicia's disappearance but was no closer to finding her today than he'd been three days ago. For at least the tenth time, he stood in front of the TV to watch the video they had taken at the candlelight vigil. Every face was familiar to him, but they'd captured nothing out of the ordinary on the film, no sign of a monster in their midst.

The frustration settled in his chest as he collapsed into the chair behind his desk. He popped two more antacid tablets and rested his head against the soft leather. Matt had called to check in from out of town, and was cutting his vacation short to get back tomorrow.

In his absence, Michael had found himself relying more

and more on Nathan Barclay, who'd turned out to be a pretty good guy—for a fed. If Michael were being honest, he'd have to admit that Barclay had been tremendously helpful and supportive. That the feds were equally stumped by the case also made Michael feel less like a loser.

A week before Alicia's abduction, Barclay's request for additional agents had been denied. Since the abduction, four more agents had been assigned to the case. He prayed it wasn't too late for Alicia and hoped the extra manpower would result in an arrest this time.

With his eyes closed, Michael released a deep breath. They had nothing. Not a scrap of evidence, not a clue to follow, and nothing they could do but wait. Bloodhounds had followed Alicia's scent for a quarter mile to where it had abruptly disappeared. So they knew she had been trans-ported in a car. A complete sweep of her neighborhood hadn't yielded a single witness, nor had multiple aerial searches by helicopter told them anything new.

When Michael imagined the torture that girl was suffering through, his stomach began to ache as badly as his chest did. Too much time had gone by. They should've found her by now. He never kept them this long, so Michael was further tormented by the image of Alicia injured, naked, and alone in the woods hoping someone would find her.

"*Damn*," he whispered with a hand on his chest. "This frigging heartburn is killing me."

His cell phone chimed with a text message. "What the hell?" He read Carly's message a second time. "Why's she waiting for me at the lake?" A heartbeat passed before panic set in. Leaping to his feet, he bolted for the door, stopping short when a sharp pain ripped through his chest. Bent in half in the doorway, he tried to breathe his way through it.

"Chief," the dispatcher called to him. "They found her. They found Alicia."

"Carly!" Michael cried, gripping his chest.

"Chief!" The dispatcher tossed his headset aside and ran to Michael. "What's wrong?"

Michael collapsed. "Find Carly Holbrook," he gasped. "At the lake."

BRIAN WAS HAMMERING out a plea agreement in the conference room when Sally, one of the administrative assistants, came in with a message from his mother. He took one look at the pink slip of paper and said, "I'm sorry, we'll have to do this another time."

"Where're you going?" the defense attorney sputtered.

In the hallway, Sally handed Brian his cell phone and held his suit coat for him. "Run home and pack a bag. I'll get you a flight out of LaGuardia."

Thirty minutes later, his cab inched along FDR Drive in the late afternoon traffic, leaving Brian with far too much time for recriminations. He should've gone home when his mother first told him she was worried about his dad. He should've put aside his own selfish concerns and done what was best for his parents. After all, he *was* their only child. And now, if his father died . . . Collapsed at work, collapsed at work . . . What did that mean? Was it is his heart? A stroke? What did collapsed *mean*?

After Sally called with his flight information, Brian dialed his mother's cell phone again. Mary Ann still didn't answer, which only added to Brian's anxiety. *Why isn't she answering her phone?* He tried unsuccessfully to reach her numerous times before he boarded the five thirty shuttle to Providence.

When the plane touched down at T.F. Green Airport just after seven, Brian was back on Rhode Island soil for the first time in almost exactly fifteen years. He turned on his cell the moment the plane landed. A message from his mother told him his father was in stable condition and had been admitted to Rhode Island Hospital for tests. He immediately called her back.

"He's in room seven twenty-two," she said, sounding weepy. "He'll be so glad to see you. Thanks for coming, Bri. I know how difficult it is for you to come home. I'll see you soon."

Brian realized coming home wasn't difficult at all under these circumstances. He jogged through an airport that was much bigger than he remembered and emerged into the humid evening to find a cab.

"Rhode Island Hospital," he told the driver. "And hurry. Please."

The drive from Warwick to Providence along Interstate 95 was surreal in that nothing had changed. The Thurbers Avenue curves were as treacherous as Brian remembered, and the big blue termite, known locally as Nibbles Woodaway, still sat atop the New England Pest Control building. With the State House dome looming in the distance, the cabbie took the hospital exit.

Brian tossed two twenties to the driver and bolted from the car. On the seventh floor, he asked for his father at the nurse's station and was directed to a room at the end of a long corridor. After taking a moment to prepare himself for whatever he might find inside, Brian pushed the door open.

Mary Ann turned and let out a happy yelp as she launched herself into her son's arms.

"Tell me you did *not* call the boy home over this," Michael groaned to his wife.

Overwhelmed by the sound of his father talking—and bitching—Brian released his mother and bent to kiss his father's forehead. "Shut up, Dad." Michael was pale and his hair had gone completely gray in the few months since Brian had last seen him, but otherwise he looked fine. Brian could have collapsed himself from the sheer relief.

"You shouldn't have come," Michael grumbled even as he reached for his son's hand. "It's nothing. Just a bad case of heartburn."

Brian turned to his mother. "What's the real story?"

"Thankfully, it wasn't a heart attack," she said. "They want to rule out any arterial blockages, so he's having some tests tomorrow. They think it could've been an acute anxiety attack."

"Stupid waste of time. I need to get back to work." Michael pushed himself up, chafing against the monitors attached to his chest.

"You're not going anywhere, Dad. Not now, anyway."

"They found her," Michael said with a grim set to his face. "They found Alicia Perry, and no one will tell me anything other than that. I'm the freaking chief of police! This is *my* case! I need to know what's going on!"

Mary Ann went around to the other side of the bed and eased her husband back down to the pile of pillows. "You need to relax, Michael. All that stress is what landed you here in the first place."

"If you expect me to relax, you have to find out, *please*, if they located Carly and if everything's all right with her."

"Carly?" Brian said. "What does she have to do with it?"

"I got a text message from her, right before this happened," Michael said with a gesture to the monitors. "That she was waiting for me at the lake. I never asked her to meet me there, so I need to know they've got her and she's safe."

"Mom?" Brian asked, his own chest tightening with tension. "Do you know if she's okay?"

Mary Ann appeared to be weighing whether she should

tell them what she knew. She rested a hand on Michael's shoulder as she said, "Honey, Alicia's dead."

"*No, no, no.*"

"Dad, take it easy."

Mary Ann took a deep shuddering breath. "Carly found her under the willow at the lake."

"Under the willow?" Brian gasped. "Are you sure that's where she was?"

Mary Ann nodded. "Dave DeSilva picked me up at home and drove me here to meet Dad," she said, referring to a Granville patrolman. "He filled me in on what was happening. Carly's safe. There were people on the beach who heard her screaming and went to help her. One of them called the police."

"She screamed?" Michael asked, incredulous.

Mary Ann nodded. "That's what Dave said."

"Why would he put Alicia there, of all places?" Michael wondered.

"I might know why." Brian swallowed hard as the implications swirled through his mind.

His parents looked at him with interest.

"That's where Carly and I used to go when we, um, wanted to be alone." Brian couldn't believe how embarrassed he was, even at thirty-three, to be confessing such a thing to his parents. "That's where we were the night of the accident."

Michael ruminated over that information for a moment and then glanced at his son. "Did anyone else know that was your spot?"

"I never told anyone, and I doubt she did, either."

"Then whoever this guy is, he somehow knew about it, and that's why he sent Carly there to find Alicia's body." Michael was all but bursting to get out of that bed. "Any doubt I had that this is somehow connected to Carly and the accident just disappeared. Call the station," he directed Mary Ann. "Tell Nathan Barclay I need to see him. Tonight."

"Michael, surely it can wait until tomorrow—"

"Tonight, Mary Ann," he said in a tone that left no room for argument.

AGENT BARCLAY DROVE Brian and his mother home to Granville close to midnight. Slumped against the back seat, Brian was drained and mortified after the grilling he'd withstood about how often he and Carly had gone to the willow, exactly what they'd done there, and whether he was sure no one else knew about it. They were the secrets of his youth, secrets he'd never expected to share with his parents, of all people, and secrets he'd never imagined would factor into a murder investigation.

"You're sure Carly is safe?" he asked Barclay. He'd learned earlier that she was spending the night with her parents.

"We have people keeping an eye on the house. Don't worry."

Right, don't worry. "She really screamed when she found the body?"

"That's right. Apparently, she was also able to tell the people who came to her rescue that there was a body under the tree."

"Amazing," Brian said. "Those are the first words she's spoken in more than fifteen years."

"So I'm told," Barclay said.

"Does this mean she can talk again?" Mary Ann asked.

"We don't know yet if it was temporary or not," Barclay said. "She was a mess, so we decided not to push her for a statement tonight."

"Poor Carly," Brian said. "Like she hasn't already been through enough."

Mary Ann turned around in the front seat and reached for Brian's hand. "I'm sorry, honey. This is not quite the homecoming I'd imagined for you."

Brian shrugged and worked up a wry grin for her. "I left in the midst of high drama, so why not come home to it, too?"

They crossed the town line into Granville, and Brian was grateful that from this direction they wouldn't have to take Tucker Road. This day had been enough of a bitch without having to face that, too. In the dark, he couldn't see much of anything, which was fine. There'd be time enough for that tomorrow.

A few minutes later, Barclay pulled into the driveway at the house, which had been painted white in his absence. He helped his mother from the car and thanked Barclay for the ride.

"Let me know how your dad makes out," Barclay said.

"I will."

He drove off, and Brian stood in the driveway with his mother, remembering the night he'd waited there with Officer Beckett to tell his parents that Sam had been killed in the accident. The memory sent a shudder rippling through him. "I like the white," he said, forcing himself to say something as they climbed the front stairs.

"I do, too. We did it about four years ago, I guess. The brown was so depressing. I was sick of it."

Walking into that house was like taking a step back in time. The furniture was new but arranged the way he remembered it. The smell was the same—a spicy mix of potpourri and candles—and the old school pictures of him and Sam still hung on the wall.

"I'm sorry I didn't have time to clean out your room or

get anything ready for you," Mary Ann said. Her shoulders stooped with exhaustion as she led Brian past the closed door to Sam's room.

Resting his hands on her shoulders, he turned her to face him and pulled her tight against him as she finally broke down.

"I'm sorry," she said between sobs. "I was just so scared earlier when they said Dad had collapsed, and it's so good to have you here, even though I know it's hard for you."

"Shh. Don't be sorry. For anything. I'm right where I need to be tonight."

Brian Westbury had finally come home.

PART III
AUGUST 2010

A time to mourn and a time to dance . . . a time to embrace and a time to refrain from embracing; a time to lose and a time to seek.

Ecclesiastes 3:5-6

CHAPTER 14

*S*ince Carly had taken the bed from her room to the apartment when she moved out of her parents' house, she was sleeping in Cate's old room, which was now outfitted for grandchildren. A crib occupied one corner along with a narrow twin bed with Disney characters on the sheets where Carly was pretending to sleep.

As if she could sleep.

Every time she closed her eyes she saw Alicia Perry's battered body. She had been on her back with her legs splayed open to ensure that the person who found her would be certain to see what she'd been through. That Alicia's killer had arranged for her to be the one to find the girl was a thought Carly had yet to fully process. The ramifications were so overwhelming.

And that she had screamed, actually *screamed*, when she found the body was another thing she couldn't quite believe. She'd just opened her mouth and done what anyone else would've done in that situation. Apparently, she had screamed loud enough to attract the attention of people way off in the distance, people who'd come running to see what was wrong.

In the melee of police and chaos that followed the grim discovery, Carly hadn't tested her voice again to see if the scream and the words she'd said to those who had come to her rescue were a one-time thing or a miracle in the midst of disaster. On the order of the FBI agent in charge of the investigation, a female Granville Police officer had driven her to her parents' home and explained the situation to her overwrought parents.

Through the wall, she could hear them in their bedroom talking about her the way they had after the accident.

Her mother was crying. "She's in danger, Steve. I just know it. Why would he pretend to be Michael Westbury and lure Carly to the place where he'd left that poor girl? Why Carly?"

"I don't know, honey, but Michael's been saying all of this is connected to the accident. I have to admit I wondered if he was so desperate to clear Sam's name that he was creating a link to the accident. But now it certainly seems possible."

"And he's in the hospital, with maybe a heart attack," Carol said. "It's all so unbelievable."

Hearing that, Carly got up and went to their room, her own heart beating so hard it echoed in her ears. She had wondered why he hadn't come to the lake earlier, but no one had mentioned his name.

"Honey?" Carol sat up when she saw Carly standing in the doorway. "What is it?"

Carly looked at her parents and said, "What's wrong with Chief Westbury?" Her voice was hoarse from lack of use, but she wasn't about to complain.

"*Oh!*" Carol cried, flying out of bed. "*Oh my God!* Steve! Did you hear that?"

"I sure did," he said, his own voice catching with emotion. "Do you think maybe you could say it again?"

"Did he have a heart attack?" Carly asked.

Carol broke down as she wrapped her arms around Carly. "Listen to you! Your voice is deeper and more mature, but it's you, all right. Oh, it's definitely you!"

Steve joined them in a group hug, and the three of them stood there like that for a long time.

Finally, Carly drew back from them. "I want to know what's wrong with him."

"They don't know, honey." Carol cradled Carly's face with her hands. "He collapsed at the office, and they took him to Rhode Island Hospital. That's all we know."

"Can we call Mrs. Westbury?"

"It's kind of late," Carol said.

"I don't care! I need to know he's all right."

"I'll go call," Steve offered, his eyes glued to Carly as if he was afraid he might be dreaming.

Carol led Carly to the bed and urged her to get in.

With her head resting on her mother's shoulder, Carly reveled in the comfort.

"When did you realize you could talk again?" Carol asked, combing her fingers through Carly's long curls.

"When I saw Alicia under the willow and I screamed. I can't stop thinking about her. There was blood everywhere . . . between her legs, on her chest . . ."

"My poor baby. What an awful thing to see."

"Mom?"

"Hmm?"

"I used to make love with Brian under that willow."

Carol's hand froze, and she sat up.

"I know that's probably something you don't want to know, even now, but—"

"He put her there on purpose! He's telling you he knows you two used to go there!"

"I think so, too."

"Oh, *God*, Carly. God."

"I'm scared," Carly whispered.

Carol tightened her arms around her daughter. "Nothing's going to happen to you. We won't let it."

Steve came back.

"What did she say?" Carly asked. "Is he all right?"

"It wasn't a heart attack, but they're keeping him overnight for some tests."

Carly and her mother exchanged relieved glances.

"There's one more thing you should probably know," Steve said hesitantly.

"What?" Carly asked.

"Brian's home."

～

A NAMELESS, faceless man who wanted to hurt her haunted Carly's dreams. She ran until her chest ached and her legs threatened to buckle beneath her. He chased her through town to the lake, where he pushed her inside the willow tree. She fought him, and the branches slashed at her face. Then all at once she was a little girl. Brian was there, and he was in danger. She wanted to warn him but couldn't speak.

A car was on fire. Inside was her family, the family she'd had with Brian. *Her children were in that car*. Frantic, Carly rushed toward them, but someone held her back with strong arms that didn't feel friendly. The bad man returned, and this time he had Zoë. Again Carly was under the willow, but instead of Alicia, it was Zoë she found lifeless and beaten.

Carly awoke with a muffled scream, and the sound coming from her own mouth startled her. Her body was bathed in sweat, her heart pounding. She was still in her parents' bed where she had slept with her mother. Forcing herself to take deep breaths, she managed to eventually slow her heart rate. As she lay there recovering from the vivid nightmare, an image of Alicia Perry under the willow flashed through her mind. Alicia's killer had made sure to leave Carly with an image that would haunt her forever.

She hurt for Alicia's family and friends, including Zoë. They were waking up today without the hope they'd clung to since Alicia's disappearance. She knew that feeling. She knew it all too well.

And then she suddenly remembered.

Brian is home.

Was he really just seven hundred and eighty-six steps from her at that very moment? The idea filled her with the kind of comfort and contentment—and anticipation— she hadn't experienced since the day he left. She wondered if she would see him. *You can't be disappointed if you don't. He's here to take care of his father. But would he really come to town and not see me? Especially after what happened yesterday? I guess I'll find out. Maybe I'll even see him today.* Her heart literally skipped a beat at that thought. *Stop it, Carly.*

"Are you awake?" her mother whispered from the door.

Carly began to nod and then remembered she didn't have to. "Yes."

"It didn't go away overnight," Carol said with a smile as she came into the room and perched on the bed. "I was afraid it would."

Carly was unaccustomed to the sound of her own voice and the odd rumble in her throat. "I sound weird."

"You sound like a grown-up. Your voice is rusty from lack of use, but we'll take it."

"I feel bad that Dad got bounced out of his own bed."

159

"It was for a good cause. He didn't care." She took Carly's hand. "How are you feeling?"

"Sort of guilty."

"Why guilty?"

"Because all I can think about is that Brian's home. Isn't that awful when there're so many bigger things going on right now?"

"If I were you, that's my first thought today, too."

"It wasn't my *first* thought," Carly said. "But it was my second, third, fourth, and fifth thoughts."

Carol chuckled and then sobered. "I don't want you to get your hopes up."

"I was just giving myself the same lecture. Don't worry. I know. I might not even see him."

"I'm sure he's upset about what happened to you yesterday."

Carly shrugged. "Maybe."

Carol held out her arms, and Carly sat up to hug her mother. "I can't *tell* you how good it is to be sitting here talking to you. If you want to know *my* first thought this morning, that was definitely it."

Carly absorbed the comfort of her mother's embrace for a long moment. "Have you talked to Cate? How's Zoë?"

Carol shook her head with dismay. "Terrible. She was up all night."

"I want to see her." Carly got out of bed. "If anyone understands what she's going through, it's me."

"I went over to your place earlier to pick up some clothes and a few other things I thought you might need," Carol said. "It's all in the kids' room."

"Thank you. I know I should be too old to want my mother taking care of me, but it sure feels good right now."

"I'm glad you feel that way, because Dad and I want you to stay here with us until they catch this guy."

"Before yesterday I would've argued with you, but not anymore."

"Good. Then it's settled. Why don't you take a shower and get dressed while I make you some breakfast?"

"I need to call Molly." Carly stopped herself. "I can't believe I *can* call Molly—like anyone else would."

Carol hugged her daughter. "It's a miracle—a true-blue miracle. And don't worry about Molly. She called earlier and said not to come to work until you feel up to it."

"That's nice of her. She's been so good to me." Carly hesitated before she asked, "Do you think maybe I've been able to talk for a while and didn't know it? I haven't tried very often, in fact, not since I tried to call 911 when I found the notes when you were in Europe. So it's possible I could, isn't it?"

"You would've known," Carol assured her.

"Yeah, I guess you're right," Carly said, but she wasn't entirely convinced.

AFTER BREAKFAST, Carly and her mother walked the short distance to Cate's house where Tom greeted them with hugs. "Let's hear it," he said, framing Carly's face with his big hands.

"Hello, Tom," Carly said with a small smile.

"Wow," he said, amazed. "You sound just like Caren."

Carly screwed up her face. "I do *not*!"

"Ah, yeah, you do."

"Do I, Mom?"

Carol chuckled at their banter and held up her hands. "I'm not getting into this one."

"I'll forgive you," Carly said to Tom, "because there's something I've been wanting to tell you for a long, long time."

"And what's that?"

"You're a good guy, Tom Murphy, and my sister is lucky to have you. We all are." Carly went up on tiptoes to kiss his cheek, which had gone red with embarrassment.

"Thank you," he mumbled.

"How's Zoë doing?" Carly asked.

"Awful." He shook his head. "What the hell do you tell a fourteen-year-old about something like this?"

"The truth," Carly said without hesitation. "You tell her the truth, because if you don't, she'll hear it from someone whose parents told *them* the truth."

"That's what Cate said, too."

"Can I see her?"

"She's in her room. You just missed Cate. She took Steve and Lilly over to Caren's for the day so we can focus on Zoë."

"If she asks me what I saw, what do you want me to tell her?" Carly asked.

Tom studied her for a moment before he said, "As much of the truth as you think she can handle, I guess."

With a nod, Carly climbed the stairs to Zoë's room. She was in bed with the curtains drawn. Carly knocked softly on the door. "Can I come in?"

"*Oh*," Zoë gasped, sitting up in bed.

Carly was grateful to her miracle for giving her niece a moment's reprieve from her grief.

"My mom said you'd gotten your voice back, but to hear it . . ."

Carly slid under the covers next to her. "Your dad says I sound like Auntie Caren. What do you think?"

"Maybe a little."

Carly poked her in the ribs. "Do not."

Zoë's smile was small and pained.

"Can I tell you something I've wished I could tell you at least a million times over the last fourteen years?"

Zoë nodded.

"I love you so much. From the first instant I ever saw you, you've had my heart."

Zoë broke down and slumped into Carly's outstretched arms.

"Why did this have to happen?" Zoë whispered as she shook with brokenhearted sobs. "*Why?*"

"I don't know. I wish I could tell you. I asked myself that same question over and over again after my friends died. Sometimes I still wonder."

"My dad said you were the one who found her."

"Yes."

"Was it bad?"

Carly nodded and was grateful that Zoë didn't ask for more.

"I want him to die for doing this to her," Zoë said fiercely. "Does that make me a bad person?"

"No, honey. That's a natural response to something like this. You want the person who did it to pay. Chief Westbury, the police, and the FBI are doing everything they can to find him. And when they do, they'll make sure he pays." Carly wasn't sure who she was trying to convince, herself or Zoë. "He'll pay."

"Am I ever going to feel good again, Auntie Carly?" she asked in a small, shattered voice.

Carly took a deep breath. "It might take a while, but one day you'll wake up and be surprised when you actually notice the sun is out, the fireflies are back, and the jasmine's in bloom." Her heart ached as she was flooded with memories of a long-ago summer when she had been the heartbroken young girl. In a whisper, she added, "One day you *will* feel better, but that won't mean you've forgotten Alicia. It only means life goes on. Even when you think it can't possibly, somehow it just does."

"Is that how it was for you?"

"That's exactly how it was for me."

"And you lost *six* friends. I can't imagine that. One is bad enough."

"Grief doesn't come in sizes, honey."

"Do you still miss them?"

"Every day, but I tell myself that by missing them, I'm keeping them alive, even if it's only in my heart and mind. Does that make sense?"

Zoë nodded.

Carly held Zoë close to her for a long time until she realized the girl had drifted into a restless sleep. She eased Zoë's head onto a pillow and watched her sleep. Her face was puffy and red from crying, which infuriated Carly. That the same man was probably responsible for both their tragedies . . . They had to find him—and soon. Enough was enough.

CARLY WAS on edge all day. A steady stream of people dropped by her parents' house to check on her. Molly and Debby came after the coffee shop closed for the day. They were still there when Matt Collins and Agent Nathan Barclay arrived to take a statement from Carly about what she had seen at the lake.

They also grilled Debby about the call she had taken from the man pretending to be Chief Westbury.

"He sounded just like him," Debby insisted. "It never occurred to me that it wasn't him. I'm so sorry, Carly." Debby's soft brown eyes filled with tears. "If anything had happened to you . . ."

"I'm fine," Carly assured her friend.

They stared at her every time she opened her mouth. She

supposed it would take some time before they got used to hearing her talk and stopped staring.

Molly and Debby left a short time later. While Carly recounted her story to Matt and Agent Barclay, the doorbell rang again. This time it was a neighbor bringing over brownies. Carly hated that she was waiting for Brian and that every time the caller wasn't him, she had to absorb a fresh wave of disappointment. *So much for not getting my hopes up.*

"How's Chief Westbury?" she asked Matt.

"He's doing great. He passed all the heart tests, so they sent him home with orders to take it easy for a few days."

"That's a huge relief."

"From what Mary Ann told me, he's been desperately worried about you, though," Matt added. "I'm sure you'll hear from him."

Agent Barclay handed Carly his card. "Give me a call if you think of anything else."

"I will."

Carly's mother showed them out and then came back to the living room. "What do you feel like having for dinner? Anything you want."

"I miss your meatloaf," Carly confessed.

"Then meatloaf it is. Do you think maybe you could try to take a nap before dinner? You look beat."

"I am." She stretched out on the sofa.

Carol spread a light blanket over her.

Carly smiled at her. "You're spoiling me rotten, Mother."

"And enjoying every minute of it. Go to sleep."

While Carly dozed on the sofa, the phone rang a couple of times, and her father came home. Before she knew it, her mother was shaking her awake. "Honey? Dinner's ready."

Carly sat up and tried to emerge from the deep sleep she had fallen into.

"Do you feel any better?"

"Yeah," she said with a big yawn.

"Chief Westbury called while you were sleeping. He really wants to see you. I told him we'd take a walk over after dinner."

Startled, Carly looked up at her mother.

"That is, if you feel up to it."

"Of course I do," Carly responded in what she hoped was a light, breezy tone. "Why wouldn't I?"

Carol snorted with laughter as she folded the blanket and returned it to the back of the sofa. "Whatever you say."

CHAPTER 15

*C*arly took a shower after dinner. She told herself it was because she'd woken up hot and sweaty after her nap, but she knew better. Brushing her long curls until they were shiny and soft, she studied her reflection in the mirror. *I wonder what he'll see when he looks at me. What will I see when I look at him? Will he have changed so much I won't recognize my Brian in the man he is now? Will he think I've changed, too? Maybe* he *won't recognize* me.

Never one to wear much makeup, she settled on just a light coating of mascara along with lip gloss and went into the kids' room to put on a skirt, sleeveless top, and leather sandals. She checked herself one last time in a full-length mirror behind the door to Caren's old room before she went downstairs.

"You look lovely," Carol said.

"Not like I went to too much trouble, though, right?"

"As lovely as always."

"My heart is pounding, and my palms are sweaty," Carly confessed.

Carol reached for Carly's hands. "I'd be worried if your palms weren't sweaty right now."

"Whose palms are sweaty?" Steve asked as he joined them by the front door.

Carly tugged back her hands. "No one's. Let's go."

Carol brought a basket containing the extra meatloaf she had made for the Westburys as well as some of the brownies from the neighbor. They stepped into the soft summer evening to make the short walk.

Seven hundred and eighty-six steps . . . Had it ever taken so long to walk seven hundred and eighty-six steps? By the time they stood in front of the Westbury's house, Carly had to remind herself to breathe—in, out, in, out.

Carol must have sensed Carly's anxiety, because she slipped an arm around her daughter's shoulders.

Mary Ann answered the door with a delighted smile and hugs for all of them.

Carol handed her the basket of food. "So you won't have to cook one night."

"It smells wonderful, Carol! Thank you so much. Can I get you all something to drink? How about a beer, Steve?"

"I won't say no to that."

"That sounds good to me, too," Carol said.

"Nothing for me, thanks, Mrs. Westbury," Carly said.

"Carly," Mary Ann said, reaching out to caress Carly's cheek. "It's so good to hear your voice, but you're old enough to call me Mary Ann."

"Isn't it amazing to hear her talking again?" Carol asked, her eyes filling with tears that she brushed at with impatience. "I said I wasn't going to cry about it anymore, and then here I go again."

Steve put a comforting arm around his wife.

"Come on up." Mary Ann led them up the short flight of stairs to the living room where Michael rested in a recliner.

He dropped the footrest and got up. "I can't tell you how happy I am to see you, young lady."

Wondering where the heck Brian was, Carly crossed the room to the chief and wrapped her arms around him. "You scared me," she whispered.

"Right back atcha, honey," he said, his voice heavy with emotion. "You shaved about ten years off my life yesterday afternoon."

Carly hugged him for a long moment before she pulled back to study his face. He looked pale, but otherwise there was no sign of his recent ordeal. "Everything's all right? With your heart?"

"Hale and hearty," he said with a smile.

Every nerve in Carly's body was suddenly on full alert, and she knew without turning around that Brian was hugging her mother and shaking hands with her father.

"That's a relief," she forced herself to say to the chief. "You need to take better care of yourself."

"Not you, *too*," Michael groaned. "I thought you and I were friends."

"We are." Carly poked him lightly. "That's why I want to keep you around for a while."

"I can't get over you chattering away like you never stopped."

"I'm still getting used to it myself."

"My son is waiting patiently to say hello to you," he whispered loud enough for the whole room to hear him.

"Your son's here?" she whispered back. "I hadn't heard that."

Everyone laughed, which made it easier for her to finally turn around. And then there he was—her Brian, only older and, if possible, even more handsome than she could've imagined. Neither the pictures in the paper nor the TV cameras had done him justice. Feeling as if all the air had been sucked from her lungs, she stood perfectly still as he closed the distance between them.

"My mother said you hadn't changed at all," he said. "I didn't believe that was possible, but it seems she was right."

Carly had forgotten how tall he was. Looking up to find his hazel eyes fixed on her, she had no idea what she was supposed to do. Overcome by a thousand emotions, she wanted to hug him, kiss him, hold him, never let him go . . .

He solved the problem for both of them by hugging her.

Surprised, Carly was slow to respond. But then her hands were on his back, and she relaxed against him, willing herself not to cry. *Not with an audience. Later, maybe, but not now.*

Carly heard sniffling and realized one or both of their mothers hadn't been so strong.

"Well," Mary Ann said brightly. "How about those drinks?"

The others followed her into the kitchen to give Brian and Carly a moment alone.

Brian released her, but she couldn't take her eyes off him. He seemed to be having the same problem.

"It's good to see you," she said, putting it mildly.

"You, too." He looped one of her curls around his finger. The familiar gesture took her breath away.

"And to hear you talking again . . ."

Swallowing hard, she had to remind herself she was expected to say something. *What would he think if I kissed him instead?* "It's been a strange, crazy day."

"I know what you mean. I woke up this morning in my old room and had no idea where I was."

"I woke up in my mother's bed because I was too afraid to sleep alone."

"When I heard what happened to you yesterday . . ." With what seemed to be great reluctance, he let his hand drop from her hair. It landed on her shoulder. "Are you all right?"

Touched by his concern and distracted by the feel of his warm hand on her shoulder, she said, "I have good moments and bad moments." Her cheeks heated with embarrassment. "You heard where he put her."

Nodding, he said, "We probably should talk about that, but right now do you think maybe I could . . ."

"What?" she stammered, undone by the intensity of his gaze.

"I really want to hug you again."

She stepped into his strong arms, but this time she made no attempt to stop the tears.

BRIAN HELD her for much longer than he should have. He had told himself to play it cool, but the moment he saw her, all his good intentions disappeared. Judging by her tears, this moment was as overwhelming for her as it was for him.

"Carly," he whispered. "Don't cry."

"I'm sorry." She pulled back from him and wiped her face. "I can't seem to help it. I've imagined what it would be like to see you again, but nothing could've prepared me."

Cradling her face in his hands, he touched his lips to her forehead. "I've thought about you, too. More often than I should probably admit to. I walked in here when you were hugging my dad, and it was an odd feeling to realize you're closer to him these days than you are to me."

"That wasn't my choice," she reminded him with a small smile.

"Touché," he said, grinning. "I need to let you go now so we can visit with our parents, but what I really want is to take you by the hand and get the hell out of here."

"And go where?" The dashing and almost dangerous edge to him was new—and exciting.

He clutched her hands. "Anywhere."

"I wondered if I would see you while you were home," she confessed.

"Did you really think I'd be here and not see you?" he asked, incredulous.

"I didn't know."

"Yes, you did."

She held his gaze. "It might've been better if we hadn't."

"Safer, maybe, but not better. Not better."

In that moment, a zing of awareness passed between them—everything they had once felt for each other was still there. Perhaps even stronger than before.

"Brian . . ."

"Let's go spend some time with the parents. I'll walk you home later."

"Just like old times?" she asked with a smile.

He returned her smile. "Only better."

"I'D FORGOTTEN how quiet it is here," Brian commented as they left his parents' house two hours later.

"Anywhere must be quiet compared to New York City. How do you stand it?"

He shrugged. "I hardly notice it anymore. At first it was completely overwhelming—so many people, so much noise and chaos. But you do get used to it."

Their hands bumped together, and he took advantage of the opportunity to lace his fingers through hers. The touch of his hand electrified her. To be walking through a quiet summer night holding hands with Brian Westbury, like fifteen years hadn't passed since the last time she held his hand . . . What was left of her common sense compelled her to let go while she still could, but somehow she couldn't bring herself to do it. Just a few weeks ago, she'd thought an hour with him would be enough. How foolish that seemed now.

"I was surprised to hear you were in New York." She wanted to know everything about his life, every detail since she'd last seen him. "I never pictured you for the city."

"It was the job that appealed to me more than the location. The D.A., Saul Stein, is a good guy to work for."

"I followed the Gooding trial," she confessed. "I was *so* proud of you, Brian."

"That means a lot. Thank you."

"Why didn't you go to Harvard for law school?"

"Do you know everything about me?" he asked with a chuckle.

Embarrassed, she looked down at the sidewalk.

He stopped walking and turned to her. "It's flattering to know you didn't forget about me."

"*Forget about you?*" She released a choppy laugh. "It's safe to say I did *not* forget about you."

With his hands on her face, he asked, "Has there been anyone else?"

She shook her head.

"Carly," he whispered as he leaned in to kiss her.

His lips were soft and undemanding, and for a moment, she allowed herself to simply feel the sensations that spiraled through her. His kiss was familiar and yet new at the same time. Then reality came crashing down to remind her he was home for only a few days, and she couldn't let him do this to her. She wouldn't survive it a second time. With a hand on his chest, she gently pushed him away. "Don't."

"I'm sorry. I couldn't resist. I've missed you so much. I don't think I had any idea *how* much until I saw you tonight."

"Please don't do this," she pleaded. "We can't pick up where we left off like nothing ever happened. In a few days, you'll be back in New York, and I'll be left here again. I can't go through that again. It was bad enough the first time."

"Do you want to know why I didn't go to Harvard?"

She nodded, grateful the conversation was headed in a less intense direction.

"Because I was such a mess after leaving you here that my freshman year was a bit of a disaster. I would've lost my scholarship, but my mother—in her infinite wisdom—had mentioned to my academic counselor that I'd lost my brother and asked her to keep an eye on me. So the counselor went to bat for me. I got my act together the second year, but my grade point average never recovered. I was very, very lucky to get into Northwestern Law."

Overcome, she rested her head on his chest.

Putting his arms around her, he spoke softly and close to her ear. "By the time I got to Ann Arbor, it was too late to get out of the lease on the apartment. I had to live alone in the place we were supposed to share. There were days when I was so paralyzed by grief and sadness I couldn't even get out of bed, let alone go to class."

"Brian," she whispered.

"I was so sure I'd done the right thing, but leaving was easy compared to living without you."

Carly broke free of his embrace and ran toward her parents' house.

He chased after her. "Carly! Wait!"

She tugged her arm free of his grasp and kept running.

At her parents' front gate, he caught up to her and pulled her into his arms.

"I can't start this all up again and then watch you leave," she said, breathless from running and the emotions he had reawakened in her.

"If we start this up again, I'll never let you go. I wouldn't make the same mistake twice." He captured her mouth in a hot, passionate kiss that was full of longing.

This time she reached for him, her arms tight around his neck as her tongue tangled with his in a fierce burst of desire that made her head spin. She hadn't felt anything like it since the last time he held her.

With a gasp, he tore his lips free of hers and kissed her face, her jaw, and then her neck.

Carly's knees were weak, and only the tight hold he had on her kept her from sliding into a puddle on the sidewalk.

"I looked for you everywhere I went," he whispered. "I married one woman because she reminded me of you and another because she was nothing like you. But I discovered there's only one you, Carly. I'm not going anywhere until this guy is caught and you're safe. And when the time comes for me to leave, either you'll go with me, or I won't go at all."

His lips brushed over her ear, making her tremble.

"Tonight, when you're in bed, I want you to think about that, all right?"

Somehow she managed a small nod.

He kissed her again, long and deep, and when he pulled back from her, he looked down at her with his heart in his eyes. "I'll see you tomorrow." Opening the gate, he nudged her inside and waited until she was in the house.

She rested her forehead on the screen door.

With a wave, he turned and walked away.

CHAPTER 16

*B*rian knocked on the front door at the Holbrooks' house at noon the next day.

Carol came to the door.

"Hi, Mrs. Holbrook."

"Hi, Brian. Come on in, and my name is Carol."

Stepping into that house was like returning to his second home. "Is Carly around?" he asked, just like he used to.

"She's at work."

Surprised, he said, "She is? How'd she get there?"

"Steve walked her into town first thing this morning. She was determined to get back to normal and not to let this guy drive her back into seclusion in her parents' house."

Brian smiled. "Good for her."

"How's your dad doing today?"

"Chomping at the bit to get back to work. The doctor said he can go back on Monday, but I'm afraid he's going to drive my mother nuts before then."

Carol chuckled as she hugged him. "It's just so good to see you."

"You, too. It's good to be home."

"Is it? You're feeling all right about . . . everything?"

"To be honest, I'm wondering why I stayed away for so long. It seems kind of ridiculous now."

"You did what you needed to do to survive a terrible thing. Life's too short for regrets."

"And yet, after just a few hours with Carly last night, I seem to be riddled with them." He followed her into the kitchen and accepted the cola she poured for him.

"You two," she said, shaking her head. "From the time you were what? Thirteen? You just had something so special."

"Yes, and when I left here, I was under the misguided impression it would turn up again if I spent enough time looking for it."

"And it didn't?"

"Never even came close."

"I love all my children," Carol said. "But Carly . . . she's special. I know I don't have to tell you she's a gentle soul. Her nieces and nephews adore her. I guess kids don't need words to know a person's heart." She looked up at him. "If you get her hopes up, Brian, and then go back to your life, I don't know if she'll be able to bounce back again. It took such a long time before."

He reached across the counter for her hand. "I'll tell you the same thing I told her last night—if we're able to get back even a shred of what we had before, I won't walk away from it again. I promise you that."

"I'm going to hold you to it."

"Be my guest." He took a long drink of the icy cola. "How's she getting home after work?"

"I was going to meet her when her shift ends at two."

"Do you mind if I do it?"

"Be my guest," she said with a smile.

BRIAN LEFT the Holbrook's house and headed for Tucker Road, figuring he may as well get that over with if he was going to be sticking around a while. As he approached the accident site, his stomach clenched with anxiety. It didn't take much, even after all this time, to recall the horror of that night . . . the sights, the sounds, the smells.

Thanks to the obvious effort Carly had expended, the site looked almost festive. The splash of color from the bank of wildflowers that framed the six crosses was eerily beautiful. Brian crouched down to pick a drooping cosmos and let it dangle between his fingers as he studied the names on the crosses. So many memories were attached to every one of those names, memories that had come to life again now that he was home.

Reaching out to run his hand over Sam's cross, he felt the familiar cloud of sadness begin to settle over him, so he stood and shook it off. He didn't want to be sad today, the first day in longer than he could remember that he had woken up thinking about something—or *someone*—other than work. He hadn't seen her in fifteen years, and just then another fifteen minutes seemed too long.

If he were wise, he would hightail it back to New York while he still could. But he was tired of being wise, and he was tired of feeling like half of him was missing. So he set off toward town, toward the only person in the world who could fill his empty places.

The town was pretty much as he remembered it, except there were more stores and more traffic. The town common was packed with media, and the police patrolling Main Street were an omnipresent reminder that a madman was on the loose. As he walked along the street, he saw a few people he recognized, but they didn't notice him.

Miss Molly's was exactly the same. When he walked in, his eyes immediately sought out and found Carly, who was sharing a laugh with three guys in a corner booth. As if she'd been waiting for him, Carly turned, their eyes met, and his heart fluttered.

Brian wondered if everyone in the coffee shop felt the current that passed between them as he walked over and kissed her cheek. "Hello."

Flustered, she murmured, "Hi."

"Brian Westbury!" one of the guys in the booth said.

He took his eyes off Carly long enough to say hello to Tommy, Luke, and Tony, all of whom he had known since elementary school.

"Want to join us?" Luke asked, pulling his feet back from the other side of the booth to make room for Brian.

"Sure."

"Can I get you something?" Carly asked.

Her cheeks flushed with color, which Brian found adorable. He liked knowing he had thrown her off just by walking in the door. "What's good?" he asked the other guys.

"Molly's burgers are still the best," Tony said.

"Sold," Brian said. "Medium, please."

Without looking at him, Carly scurried away to place the order.

Brian chuckled softly to himself as he watched her go.

"So how long are you home?" Tommy asked.

CARLY HUNG BACK as a parade of locals stopped by the booth to say hello to Brian. Eventually, the other guys left to go back to work.

Molly stepped away from the grill to bring Carly the burger she had ordered for Brian. "Go sit with your young man while he eats."

"He's not my young man," Carly protested, despite the

fact that she had floated through her day thinking only of him and what he had said to her the night before. "And my shift's not over."

"It is now." Molly nudged her. "Grab yourself a drink and go."

Carly did as she was told and slid into the booth across from Brian.

Raising an eyebrow in amusement, he asked, "Sitting down on the job?"

"Boss's orders. Are you enjoying your moment in the sun?"

He gestured her closer to him.

She leaned across the table.

"Is it me, or did everyone get old and fat?"

Carly laughed.

"Except for your parents and mine, that is."

"We come from good genes."

"You surely do." He shook ketchup onto his fries. "I can't get over how you look exactly the same as you did at eighteen. That's really not fair to other women."

"If you look close, I've got crow's feet starting."

"I'll have to look close," he said, lowering his voice. "Later."

Her cheeks turned bright red.

He laughed at her reaction and pushed his plate to the middle of the table so she could share his fries. "You still chew on your straw."

She looked down, surprised to discover he was right. "I guess I do."

"I'm assigned to your security detail this afternoon."

The thought of spending the afternoon with him filled her with excitement and anticipation. She was still afraid she might be dreaming. Was Brian really sitting here talking to her like he always had, like nothing had ever come between them? And how long did they have before he had to leave again?

"What are you thinking right now?"

"That I can't believe you're really here."

"And?"

"How do you know there's more?"

"I can still see everything you're feeling in your eyes. Just like always."

"Brian . . ."

He finished the burger and pushed the plate aside. Reaching for her hands, he said, "Tell me."

"I was wondering how long you're going to be here."

"I talked to my boss this morning and took a one-month leave of absence."

She gasped. "How can you just do that?"

"How can I go back to work when you're in danger and my father's working himself into an early grave?"

"A whole month." She settled back against the booth. "Can you afford that?"

He laughed. "Yes, I can afford it. Since I just recently took my first vacation in six years, I still have eight weeks on the books. Even if I didn't have vacation time, all I do is work, so I have plenty of money sitting in the bank."

Still trying to absorb that she had a whole month to spend with him, she asked, "Why do you work so much?"

"Because I don't have anything better to do." He squeezed her hand. "Or I didn't, until now. Can we get out of here?"

She looked around and was surprised to see the shop had cleared out. "Sure."

He paid the check and slipped a ten-dollar bill into her apron pocket.

"What's that for?"

"It's for the lovely waitress who brought me the best burger I've had in years."

"That's more than the check!" she protested, trying to give it back to him.

"Don't be silly."

They left the shop and walked slowly along Main Street.

"Do you want to get changed?" he asked.

"I'd love to. What do you feel like doing?"

He shrugged. "What do you normally do on Thursday afternoons?"

"I go to my niece Zoë's baseball game, but it's cancelled today."

"Your niece plays baseball?"

"She's an incredible pitcher," Carly said as she led him up the stairs to her apartment over Carson's.

"This I need to see."

"Hopefully, she'll be up for playing by next week. Alicia Perry was her good friend. She's taking it really hard."

Brian shook his head. "Poor kid. You and I can relate, can't we?"

"All too well, unfortunately."

Carly unlocked the door and went in ahead of him.

"Oh, wow," he said. "What a great place. It's so . . . you." He wandered into the living room and came to a stop when he saw the jukebox. When he turned back to her, the surprise showed on his face.

She pulled her hair free of the ponytail she had worn to work and shook it loose. "Toby's parents were getting rid of it, so I asked Mr. Garrett if I could have it."

Brian ran his hands reverently over the vintage jukebox. "I can still remember that last day. Every moment of it is etched permanently in my mind."

"Mine, too. I've had the jukebox for about three years and was just recently able to bring myself to play 'Tupelo Honey' for the first time. I cried my eyes out."

"I heard that song once, a few years back when I was with

some of my coworkers having a drink after work. We were in a pub near the office, and I was actually having a pretty good time."

The way he said it told her that didn't happen very often, which made her sad for him.

"And then the song came on over the sound system. It was so loud in there I shouldn't have been able to hear it, but it was like all the other noise faded away. It was the first time I'd heard it since that night, and I felt like someone had punched me or something."

Carly walked over to him and rested her hands on his chest.

He put his hands over hers but was a million miles away from her, locked in a memory. "I'd heard of a song transporting people back to some moment in time, but it'd never happened to me before. I got up from the table and went outside because I couldn't bear to listen to it. I remember sliding down this brick wall in the alley next to the bar and just bawling my head off."

Slipping her arms around him, she held him close to her for a long, quiet moment. "Do you think, maybe, if we listened to it now, together, we could create a new memory that would make the old one less painful for both of us?"

He glanced down at her. "That might work."

She went to plug in the jukebox and select the song. When she returned to him, she was suddenly filled with shyness.

Reaching for her, he brought her into the shelter of his arms and kept her there as the first notes of the song filled the room. They didn't dance so much as sway.

"I wanted so badly to get you out of there," he recalled. "All I thought about back then was getting you alone. I just wish I had known those were the last minutes I'd ever have with my brother, with all of them."

"Do you ever wish we'd gone with them?"

He pulled back from her so he could see her eyes. "There've been times when I thought it might've been easier. But then I think about my parents losing both of us, and I know I wasn't in that car for a reason, and neither were you."

"Sometimes I'm not quite sure what that reason is. My life has been very small. I haven't left this town in more than fifteen years. I have my job, my family, my nieces and nephews . . . but not much else."

"That's about three times as much as I have. Even your apartment is a real home. Mine has a sofa, a TV, a bed, and twenty suits hanging in the closet." He sang along softly to the song, like he had so long ago.

"I've pictured you living a glamorous life in New York City."

He snorted with laughter. "If you only knew how boring and empty it is."

"You must have friends, people you do things with."

"Not really. I never went to the trouble to make new friends. It didn't seem worth the risk."

Her eyes burned with tears. "Our lives are a lot more alike than I ever would've imagined."

"When I was in Florida, my mother was going on and on about how courageous I'd been to go off and have my life despite what happened. She said I didn't let it ruin my life. But in so many ways it *did* ruin my life and yours. When I think about what we should have, compared to what we *do* have . . ."

Carly looked up at him.

He brushed his lips softly over hers. "How's this for a new memory?"

"It's working for me," she said, breathless. Burying his face in her soft tangle of curls, he said, "Me, too." The song ended, and three more came and went before he lifted his head from her shoulder. "It was kind of funny today. People in town didn't seem to recognize me until I was with you at Miss Molly's."

"You look a lot different—even more handsome than before, if that's possible. In fact, you remind me of your dad when I first knew him."

"You think so?"

"Totally."

"Would you've known me if you saw me somewhere and hadn't seen me on TV?"

"I would've known you anywhere."

He combed his fingers into her hair and tilted her face to receive his kiss. "I still love you, Carly. I realized the instant I saw you last night that I've always loved you, and I always will."

Her eyes grew wide with wonder. "You never stopped? Even when you were mar—"

He quieted her with his fingers on her lips. "I never stopped." Reaching for his back pocket, he said, "I want to show you something."

Carly watched as he opened his wallet and withdrew a piece of paper from one of the leather compartments. When she realized what it was, she gasped. "You still have that?"

"I've carried it with me since I left. Whenever I thought I couldn't go another minute without you, I'd take it out and read it again. The reminder that you love me made it possible to keep going."

Tears rolled down her cheeks. "If you missed me so much, why didn't you just come back?"

"Because I said I wouldn't. My foolish pride and a whole lot of stubbornness kept me away."

"That stubbornness got you through college and law school," she reminded him. "Don't forget that."

"Did I stay away too long?" He put his wallet back in his

pocket and then brushed his thumbs over the tears on her cheeks.

"No," she whispered. "I meant what I said in that note. You're the only one I've ever loved, the only one I will ever love."

He hugged her tight against him. "That's all I need to know. We'll figure this out, Carly, and this time, nothing will stop us from having it all. Nothing." He lifted her to him and kissed her.

Carly clutched his shoulders and moaned when she felt his hands slide up the back of her legs to hook them around his waist.

Her skirt impeded him, so he pushed it up and out of the way.

She tightened her arms and legs around him.

A groan rumbled through him, straight into her.

The sensation of falling had Carly opening her eyes just as she landed on the sofa.

Brian settled on top of her and gazed down at her.

She tucked her hands under his shirt, desperate for the feel of his warm skin.

"I want you," he said softly as he slid his lips over hers. "But I'm afraid we're moving too fast." He sucked in a sharp, deep breath when she pushed her hands into the back of his shorts.

Smiling, she said, "Am I moving too fast for you?"

He answered with a passionate kiss, and desire surged through her. She wrapped her legs around him, lifting her hips to press against him.

"Carly," he said hoarsely. "Are you sure?"

She nodded and brought him back for another kiss.

His fingers brushed against her chest as he unbuttoned her yellow uniform dress. He moved slowly, his lips following his fingers on a path straight down the front of her. His hazel eyes went hot with lust when he caught the first glimpse of her lacy bra. "Do you always wear such sexy underwear to work?" he asked as he unhooked the bra and pushed it out of the way.

"I wore the good stuff today—just in case."

He chuckled. "In case of what?"

"In case I got very, very lucky." With her fingers buried in his hair, she directed him to where she wanted him most and gasped as he drew her nipple deep into his mouth. "*Oh*," she said, turning her head away as if to escape from the over-whelming sensations. She opened her eyes and shrieked when she caught a glimpse of someone watching them through the door.

Pushing at Brian, she urged him up. "He was there!" she cried. "He was watching us!"

Brian bolted from the sofa and raced for the door.

With shaking hands, Carly quickly buttoned her dress.

Brian returned a minute later, his expression grim. "He's gone. Call the police."

CHAPTER 17

*B*rian kept his arm tight around Carly as she told Matt Collins and Nathan Barclay what she had seen.

"And you're sure you didn't catch *any* part of his face?" Matt asked again.

"She already said she didn't," Brian snapped and then immediately regretted his tone. Matt was only doing his job. "I'm sorry."

"Don't be," Matt said. "I know this is frustrating as hell for you. It is for us, too."

The man who had been so good to Brian the night of his brother's death had remained remarkably youthful looking in the years since Brian had last seen him. He kept his blond hair short, and only a few lines in the corners of his blue eyes indicated that he was approaching his mid-forties.

"He had a hat on that shaded his face," Carly said. "But he was tall. I'm sorry I can't tell you more."

"We already have people canvassing the downtown area," Barclay said.

"I'm sure he's long gone by now," Brian said. "Do me a

favor and don't tell my dad about this. He's supposed to be taking it easy, and this'll get him all fired up."

"I'm afraid it's probably too late for that," Matt said with a smile. "You know he's got his ear pressed to the scanner."

"Great," Brian mumbled. "I'll call him."

They left a few minutes later, promising to keep Carly and Brian posted on the investigation.

Brian saw them out and then returned to sit with Carly on the sofa. He took her hand and was alarmed by how cold it was. Rubbing both her hands between his, he asked, "What are you thinking?"

"That he just keeps taking things from us," she said in a small voice. "Your brother, all our friends, the willow, each other." She turned to him, and the sadness in her eyes tugged at his heart. "We were going to make love, and I wanted to. So badly."

"We will," he assured her. "And when we do, that creep won't be watching us. I'll guarantee you that."

"He has before," she said with a shudder. "Under the willow, he was watching us."

"That makes me sick." He had never imagined himself capable of killing someone, but to have just one minute with this guy . . . Just one minute. That's all it would take to get revenge on behalf of Sam, Carly, and the others. He would be lying if he said he didn't want some for himself, too.

"You're all tense, Bri."

"I just wish I could somehow get you out of this town and away from all of this."

"I'd like that, too."

"But with the whole car thing, I don't know how we could do it."

"I've been thinking I might be ready to try that."

Surprised, he looked over at her. "Really?"

189

She bit her bottom lip and nodded. "I'm so tired of being afraid. If you were with me, I think I might be able to do it."

He thought it over for a minute. "My dad bought my mom a convertible a couple of years ago. You've probably seen it."

"She's adorable roaring around town in that little red car."

Brian laughed as he imagined what the police chief would have to say about his wife "roaring" around town. "I'm sure she'd loan it to us. Having the top down might make it easier for you the first time."

"What if I can't do it? Will you be disappointed in me?"

"Of course not." He kissed her cheek. "If it's too much for you, I could call the psychologist who prepped the Gooding children to testify. He specializes in trauma, and I wondered at the time if he might be able to help you."

"You thought of me like that?"

"I thought of you *all* the time. That day in court, when the jury found Gooding guilty? You were the first person I wanted to tell."

She hugged him for a long, quiet moment. "There's something I want to show you." Carly went into her bedroom and returned with what looked like a photo album.

"What've you got there?"

She handed it to him. "I thought of you, too."

Brian opened the book and was stunned to find clippings from the local newspaper about his graduations from Michigan and Northwestern and his appointment as an assistant district attorney in Manhattan. He winced when he found mention of both his marriages. "I wondered if somehow you knew," he said in a hushed tone.

"Keep going."

The rest of the book contained articles about all the major cases he had prosecuted, with the Gooding trial dominating the last few pages. "How did you get this stuff?" he asked, incredulous.

"I subscribed to *The New York Times*," she confessed, looking almost embarrassed. "I wanted to know what you were doing."

"I have no idea what to say. That you cared enough to do something like this . . . I'm amazed and humbled, Carly."

She leaned in to kiss him. "Carly Holbrook loves Brian Westbury," she whispered.

Overwhelmed by the familiar words, he put the book on the coffee table and wrapped his arms around her. "And he loves her right back."

"Get me out of here, Brian. Please."

"You're off for the next two days, right?"

She nodded.

"Call your parents and pack a bag. I know just where we should go."

CARLY APPROACHED the cherry red convertible with trepidation. Behind her, Brian and his parents watched.

"Do you think you can do it, hon?" Brian asked.

"I want to, but I'm afraid I'll lose my nerve the minute we drive away."

Brian rested his hands on her shoulders and kissed the top of her head. "If you do, we'll come right back. I promise."

Carly turned around. "Thank you for loaning us your baby, Mary Ann."

She smiled as she hugged Carly. "It's my pleasure."

Michael kissed Carly's cheek. "I'm proud of you for even trying this. You're not letting him win."

Something about that statement seemed to fill Carly with

courage. She reached for Brian's hand. "Let's go before I chicken out."

He held the door for her and crouched to secure her seat belt. With his hands resting on her legs, he kissed her. "Okay?"

She nodded.

"I'll see you in a couple of days," he said to his parents as he walked around to the driver's side. "Call my cell if you need to reach me."

"Have a good time," Mary Ann said.

Brian started the car and let it roll slowly out of the driveway. He glanced over at Carly. Her face was set in an unreadable expression, and her hands were clenched together in her lap. On the way out of town, he took a roundabout route to avoid Tucker Road.

"Doing all right?"

She nodded.

"Your knuckles are white." He reached over to work his hand in between hers. "I'd forgotten how much I like to drive. I don't get much chance, living in the city."

Her head whipped around to face him. "How long has it been?"

He laughed. "It would probably be better if I didn't tell you."

"*Brian!*"

Laughing, he said, "Relax, honey. I drove my mom all over the place when I was in Florida."

Carly closed her eyes and turned her face into the warm summer breeze. "You were right about the convertible. I don't feel closed in."

"How *do* you feel?"

"Free," she said softly. "I feel free."

~

As THEY MADE their way south, Brian was amazed he remembered so much about getting around his home state. He had purposely avoided the interstate and had kept a watchful eye in the mirror to make sure they weren't being followed. By the time they crossed the town line into East Greenwich, he was confident they had made a clean escape.

"You still haven't told me where we're going."

"It's somewhere we went a few times, once with Toby and Michelle. You probably don't remember," he teased, knowing that, like him, she had forgotten nothing about the years they'd spent together.

She mulled it over for a minute. "Oh! I know! Newport, right?"

"Damn. You guessed."

Clapping her hands with delight, she leaned over to kiss his cheek. "That's perfect."

He was surprised when her delight faded as fast as it had come. "What's wrong? Will it remind you too much of Toby and Michelle?"

"No."

"Then what?"

"Right now, right in this very moment, I feel better than I have since before the accident. I'd almost forgotten it was possible to feel this way."

"That's good, isn't it?" he asked, pleased to hear her say that.

"It's just that I feel guilty, too."

"Why?"

"With everything that's going on, it seems selfish for me to feel so good. Zoë's devastated over Alicia, this guy is torturing and killing young girls, maybe because of some grudge he has against me. All those devastated families and kids. All because of me."

Brian pulled off the road and reached for her. "Baby,

listen to me. You have nothing to feel guilty about. This guy's a psycho, and his actions are no reflection on you." Struggling to think of some way to make her feel better he said, "Remember when John Hinckley shot President Reagan and then said he'd done it for Jody Foster?"

She nodded.

"Did anyone blame Jody Foster?"

"No, but I'm sure she felt bad about it."

"But it wasn't her fault, just like it isn't yours. We're going to find out this guy's had a very unhappy life, and he was envious of us. You can't take on the guilt, honey. You haven't done anything wrong."

"I just keep racking my brain, trying to remember if I was mean to someone without intending to be or who I might've disappointed by going out with you, but I come up empty every time."

"It'll probably be someone you never knew had a thing for you. Hell, it could be anyone. You were the prettiest girl in school, and I couldn't believe how lucky I was when I asked you out and you said yes."

"You've never told me that before." She caressed his face. "I always thought I was the lucky one."

He took her hand and pressed his lips to her palm. "We were both lucky, and other people knew it, too. The fact we had something special was obvious to everyone who knew us. That's not our fault, Carly. So no more guilt?"

"I'll try."

"What? There's something else isn't there?"

"It's just . . ."

"What, honey?"

"I have so many questions about what happened to me, about why I lost my voice, and how I got it back the way I did. I don't understand why I couldn't talk a month ago when

I tried to call 911, but when I found Alicia, it was just there again. Why do you suppose that is?"

"I wish I could tell you."

"I guess I'll never really understand it."

"You know, I'm sure my doctor friend in New York would talk it through with you. I could call him next week and arrange something, if you're interested."

"You really think he would?"

"We worked very closely on the Gooding trial and spent a lot of nights eating cold Chinese together. He'd do it for me if I asked him to."

"Thank you."

"Now can I have just one little smile?"

"I can do better than a smile."

His voice was rough with desire when he said, "Yeah?"

"Uh huh."

He touched his lips to hers for a light kiss, and was startled when she reached up to keep him from pulling away.

Her mouth opened under his in invitation.

He had forgotten how potent her kisses could be, so sweet and yet so hot he melted into her. Their tongues mated in a dance as familiar to him as anything in his life. When he couldn't stand another minute without having more of her, he finally drew back.

From the stunned look on her face, he could tell she felt all the same things.

He kissed the hand that had wrapped around his and then her lips again. "I have a sudden burning need to get to the hotel."

"Since I seem to have the same need why are we just sitting here?"

He laughed and shifted the car into gear. When he would have floored it, he had to remind himself to drive slowly so he wouldn't scare her.

The sun was setting over Narragansett Bay by the time they crossed the Newport Bridge and took the exit for the City by the Sea.

"It's as pretty as I remember," Carly said as they drove down narrow cobblestone streets with Colonial-era houses and gas-powered streetlights. "I can't believe I've been less than an hour from here all these years."

"Now that you've conquered your fear of cars, the whole world is open to you again. You can go anywhere and do anything you want."

"When you put it that way, it's sort of overwhelming."

"Do you think you might want to go to college?"

She shrugged and rested her head against the leather seat.

"Seriously, if you could do anything you wanted, what would it be?"

Turning so she could see him, she said, "I don't know."

"Come on," he urged. "There has to be *something*."

"If I tell you, it'll freak you out."

"No, it won't."

She laughed. "Trust me, it will."

"Okay, now I have to know." When she still didn't answer, he tried pleading. "*Carly, tell me.*"

Hesitating for another moment, she finally said, "I want to have a baby." She said it so softly he almost didn't hear her.

Almost.

He took his eyes off the road to glance over at her.

"I told you it would freak you out."

"Do I look freaked out?" he asked indignantly.

"Yes!" She snorted with laughter. "You look like you just got hit by a bus."

"I do *not*!"

"Yes, you do."

They were still playfully arguing when he pulled up in front of a downtown hotel and handed the keys to a valet.

Brian carried their two small bags, and within minutes, they were riding the elevator to the third floor. Their room looked out over Newport Harbor, which was packed with boats.

"Is this all right?" he asked, taking a quick look at the sunset.

"It's beautiful. I can't believe you arranged it so quickly."

"My mother might've helped me," he confessed.

She smiled. "Why do I feel so shy now that we're finally here?"

"We don't have to do anything. I'm happy to be in the same room with you."

"You always did know just what to say to me." She put her arms around him. "Didn't you?"

He kissed her cheek and then her lips before he hugged her tight against him. "Do you want to take a walk or get some dinner? We can do anything you want."

"Anything?"

"You name it."

She surprised him when she reached for the hem of his polo shirt and tugged it up and over his head. "Anything at all?" she asked, looking up at him with a coy smile as she turned her attention to his chest. Her tongue flicked his nipple, drawing a gasp from him.

He took as much of that as he could handle before he buried his hands in her hair and captured her mouth in a kiss that went from zero to ninety in about two seconds flat. "Jesus, Carly," he whispered as he unbuttoned her blouse and pushed it off her shoulders. "No one has ever been able to fire me up the way you do."

Her face clouded briefly, and Brian wanted to shoot himself for reminding her, especially right then, that there had been others. He framed her face with his hands and looked into her eyes. "You're the only one I've ever loved, the only one who's ever really mattered to me. Do you believe me?"

She nodded and reached for him, wanting more. Her kiss told him she wanted everything.

Pulling frantically at clothes, they were suddenly unable to wait another minute for what they'd lived fifteen years without. As her bra fell to the floor, Brian tightened his arms around her and trembled at the feel of her soft breasts pressed to his chest.

She closed her hand around his erection, and he gritted his teeth against the burning need that spiraled through him.

"Carly," he whispered as he caressed her face and leaned in to kiss her.

"I had forgotten."

"What, honey?"

"How you feel." She stroked him gently as her other hand cruised over his chest. "How it feels to be with you like this. I thought I remembered, but I didn't."

"There's no substitute for the real thing," he said as he urged her onto the king-sized bed. "What we wouldn't have given for a room like this back in the day, huh?"

"We had that one night in Ann Arbor." She wrapped her arms around him. "I've relived it a million times."

He nuzzled her breasts. "You don't have to relive it anymore, because we have every night for the rest of our lives to make new memories." His hand traveled down to find her ready for him. "I don't ever want to go to bed again without you next to me." He teased her with his finger as he tugged her nipple into his mouth.

She gasped and squirmed under him. "I'm so afraid this is a dream, and I'm going to wake up to find you're still in New York, that you never came home."

Raising his head so he could see her eyes, he kissed her softly. "For the first time since I was last with you, I'm right where I belong, Carly, and I'll never leave you again. I promise."

"Did you bring, you know, protection?"

"Yes, but we don't need it."

"I'm not on the pill anymore. There wasn't any point."

"I know." He kissed her breasts and worked at keeping his ravenous desire in check, afraid he would scare her if she had any idea how badly he wanted her.

She tipped his face up. "But we can't just—"

"Why not?"

Her withering look made him laugh.

"You want a baby. Isn't that what you told me?"

"Yes, but—"

"Since I wouldn't want you going to anyone else to get what you want, you'll have to settle for me." As his tongue caressed hers, he entered her slowly, taking care to remember how long it had been for her. Rocking his hips against her, he looked down at her with a smug smile and whispered against her lips, "I told you I wasn't freaked out."

CHAPTER 18

"*D*o you think it worked?" he asked an hour later.

She laughed and snuggled closer to him. "If it didn't, it won't be for a lack of trying."

He laughed softly and kissed her. "Are you hungry?"

"Getting there."

"Do you want to go out?"

She shook her head. "I never want to leave this bed again for the rest of my life."

"Then room service it is."

When he would've gotten up, she stopped him. "Don't go just yet."

"I was coming right back." He turned on his side and brought her closer to him. Tracing a finger over her cheek, he asked, "Why so pensive all of a sudden?"

"What were they like?"

His eyebrows knitted with confusion. "Who?"

"The other women you were with. The women you married."

He groaned and turned his face into the pillow. "We are *not* going to talk about that now."

"Why not?"

"Because. This is a time to be looking ahead not back, and this night is about you and me. No one else."

"Do you think I won't understand that you were lonely, Brian? I will, because I was, too."

"Why didn't you ever go out with anyone else? There must've been no shortage of men who were interested."

"It's kind of hard to date when you can't talk."

"What if you could've talked? Would you have dated then?"

She shrugged. "It's hard to say, but I doubt it. The only man I wanted was the one I couldn't have."

He closed his eyes and exhaled a long deep breath. "I was so sure I was doing the right thing when I said I was leaving for good. You know the main reason I did that was to try to force you to come with me, don't you?"

"Of course I do."

"I was desperate, Carly. And once that ultimatum was out of my mouth, it was kind of hard to take it back. I wished so many times I hadn't made such an all-or-nothing stand. Now that I'm back with you again, I realize what a big mistake I made and how much I denied us both. Even a little bit with you would've been better than nothing."

She brushed his hair off his forehead and kissed him. "You were eighteen years old and traumatized. Don't beat yourself up for doing what you thought was right at the time."

He was quiet for a long moment as he studied her face. "It took me three years to even think about being with someone else," he finally said as he combed his fingers through her curls. "I didn't bother dating or getting to know anyone, because that would've taken too much effort, and it didn't really matter. I was lonely and bitter about losing you and everyone who mattered to me, so I was looking for a purely physical thing. I picked up a girl in an off-campus bar, and we went back to her place."

Carly caressed his chest as she listened to him.

"I can only imagine what you must be thinking. It sounds awful, even to me," he said as he looked up at the ceiling. "So we started, you know, fooling around." He glanced over at Carly. "You're sure you want to hear this?"

She nodded.

"One thing led to another, and we ended up in her bed. I kept wishing I'd had more to drink so I wouldn't have been so aware of what I was doing or that everything about it—and her—felt wrong. And then I kind of lost my . . . enthusiasm, so to speak." He brought Carly's hand to his lips. "Even though we weren't together anymore, I felt like I was cheating on you."

Her eyes filled with tears. "Bri," she whispered.

"I made a bunch of excuses about drinking too much and got out of there as fast as I could. I hit a pretty low point for a while after that. It was as close as I ever came to just saying fuck it and going home. I wondered if I was destined to be alone for the rest of my life, if that's what I had doomed us both to. Then I met Beth. She lived in the apartment across the hall from me during our senior year. She had short dark hair and brown eyes that reminded me of yours. She's really the only good friend I've made since I left home, but even she doesn't know the whole story."

"You were married to her, and you never told her?"

"I've never told anyone."

Carly shook her head with dismay. "I thought it was harder to be the one who got left behind at home, but at least I had my family around me. You were so alone in the world."

"Beth made me feel less alone, which is the one and only reason I married her. Of course, that wasn't very fair to her, and it didn't take me long to realize I'd made another huge mistake."

"But you stayed with her for a while."

He nodded. "She came home a few weeks before I graduated from law school and told me she'd met someone else and wanted a divorce. I could hardly blame her. She married Joe, and they're very happy. I like him a lot. In fact, I just had dinner with them recently when they were in New York. I was lucky she forgave me for being a crappy husband and kept me as a friend."

"What about Jane?"

Brian smiled. "Ah, yes. And then there was Jane. My mother couldn't stand her."

Carly's eyes widened. "Really? I can't imagine your mother not liking her own daughter-in-law."

"Jane wasn't much of a daughter-in-law or a wife. As my mother said in Florida, 'There wasn't an ounce of warmth in that woman.'"

"Then why'd you marry her?"

He winced. "She was a bit of a looker—tall, blonde, blue-eyed. You get the picture."

Carly made a face. "Spare me any further details, please."

He quickly added, "She was also an ADA, and she worked as much as I do, so it was more a marriage of convenience than anything. Then she started talking about having a family and buying a house in the burbs. I was like, whoa, that's not what I signed on for. I certainly didn't want that stuff with her. She was so self-absorbed that she would've been a horrible mother. Things got kind of ugly toward the end with her."

"How long were you with her?"

"About three years, married for just over a year."

"And since then?"

"I've been married to my work."

Carly released a long deep breath and rested her head on his shoulder. "Thanks for telling me."

With his finger on her chin he tilted her face up so he could see her. "I want you to understand . . . Both times, I knew in the very moment I was saying 'I do' that I was making a mistake, because everything inside me was crying out for you."

"Brian."

"I mean it."

"I know you do."

"Can I ask *you* something?"

"Of course."

"It's kind of a big deal."

"Okay."

"Which do you think would be worse? Being my third wife or never being my wife at all?"

Carly laughed until she cried. "Never being your wife at all," she was finally able to say through her tears. "That would definitely be worse."

"Good to know. Can I get up for a second?"

She lifted her arm and leg to let him up and then wiped the tears from her face.

He went over to rummage around in his bag and came back to flop down next to her. Perched on his pinkie was a diamond ring.

"*What?*" she cried. "*Where did you get that?*"

"It was my grandmother's." The utter shock on her face was exactly what he'd hoped for. "You should've seen how my mother bawled when I asked her to get it out of the safe for me today." Wiping the tears from Carly's face, he touched his lips to hers. "Remember the first time we got engaged, and I told you I'd get you a ring as soon as I could? You said I shouldn't spend the money because we'd need it for things like food?"

Dealing with a new flood of tears, Carly nodded.

"Well, I knew this ring was coming to me when I was ready to get married, and I'd planned to give it to you the next day. Then everything happened, and I never got around to it. I regretted that, Carly. After all, we *were* engaged. I spent a lot of time after I left wondering if I'd given you the ring and made it official, if we might've somehow found a way to stay together."

"Why didn't you give it to Beth?" she asked softly.

He shook his head. "The only person I ever could've given it to is you." Reaching for her left hand, he said, "Will you marry me, Carly? Will you make my life complete by spending the rest of your life where you should've been all along? With me?"

"Do you even have to ask?" she whispered.

He slid the ring onto her finger. "I love you, and I'm sorry it took me so long to come home to you."

"All that matters now is you did and nothing has changed between us." She raised her hand to take a better look at the ring. "It's absolutely beautiful. Thank you."

"I want to get married as soon as we can."

Surprised, Carly glanced up at him.

"What kind of wedding do you want?" he asked.

"Something small. Is that all right with you?"

He snorted with laughter. "I couldn't care less how we do it, as long as we do it—and very, very soon. I've lived long enough without you. Are you going to be okay with not getting married in church? They'll frown on a two-time divorcee."

"Father Joe might make an exception for us."

"I don't want you to get your hopes up, honey."

"Maybe we can do something in my parents' backyard and ask Father Joe if he would marry us. If we're not in church, it might not be an issue."

He tightened his hold on her. "I can't believe we're in bed together talking about getting married. I used to spend tremendous amounts of time imagining us just like this. I hope you won't mind if I keep you in bed for most of the first year we're married."

She laughed. "Just the first year?"

"I'll have to go back to work at some point so I can take care of you."

"I don't know if I can live in New York, Brian."

"You don't have to."

"But your job—"

"We can live in the burbs, and I'll commute, or I'll quit and do something else." He shrugged. "Whatever you want."

"You love that job. I'd never ask you to quit."

"You didn't, so don't sweat it. I've had a bunch of offers since the Gooding trial. We can do anything we want. I'm ready to find something with more regular hours, so I can spend most of my time with you. And the baby." He ran a hand over her flat belly. "What will we name him? Or her?"

"You don't already know?"

"Should I?"

She nodded.

"Hmmm. I'm stumped."

"We'll name him—or her—Sam."

"Carly," he whispered as he pressed his lips to hers. "My parents would love that. Thank you." He noticed the new tears in her eyes. "Hey! What's this?"

"I'm just . . ."

"What?"

"Happy."

Pulling her to him, he held her as tight as he could. "Good. That's the only thing that matters to me."

"And scared. We're so close to having everything we've

ever wanted. I'm afraid he'll find a way to take you away from me again."

"I won't let him touch us, Carly. I promise you that." He poured all his love for her into a kiss that left them both breathless. "Guess what I discovered out there in the world?"

Amused by his expression, she said, "What's that?"

He kissed her neck until she trembled with desire. "There're *tons* of ways to make love. We've only scratched the surface." He kissed his way down to her belly and dipped his tongue into her belly button.

She clutched handfuls of his hair. "*Brian!*"

Laughing softly, he said, "I'd forgotten about your hang-ups. We'll have to get you over that—and fast. I've got *lots* of stuff to show you."

"Oh, *God*," she groaned.

ON THEIR WAY back to Granville late on Saturday, they called Brian's parents and Carly's sisters, requesting everyone meet them at Carly's parents' house.

"Did you ask her?" Mary Ann said breathlessly.

"I'm not saying a word," Brian replied with a wink for Carly.

"*That's not nice!*" Mary Ann complained.

"See you at seven thirty," Brian said, smiling as he ended the call.

"She knows," Carly said.

"She *thinks* she knows."

"She gave you the ring," Carly reminded him.

"I told her not to get her hopes up and not to tell my dad about the ring, just in case."

"In case of what?"

"In case you said no."

Startled, Carly spun around in her seat to stare at him. "Did you *really* think that was a possibility?"

He shrugged. "I wasn't sure how you felt about me being married before. And I was afraid I might be hitting you with too much too soon." Pausing, he added, "If I am, you know, going too fast for you, it's okay to say so."

She held his hand between hers. "You're not, Bri," she said. "I want everything right now, too. I feel like my life has been on hold for fifteen years, and now that it's finally moving forward again, I don't want to waste a minute of it."

He squeezed her hand. "In that case, how about Labor Day weekend?"

"That's in three weeks!"

"That *long?*"

"We can't get a wedding together in *three weeks!*"

"Sure we can. I've got nothing but time right now since I'm not working. Tell me what to do, and I'll do it."

"I know you're quite experienced with planning weddings—"

"*Watch it,*" he said in a teasing growl.

She giggled. "But you're still a guy, and no woman in her right mind would trust her *one* and *only* wedding to a *guy.*"

"You'll pay for that later."

"I'll look forward to it," she said with a saucy smile.

"What do you say to quitting that job of yours so you won't have to trust the wedding planning to a dreaded *guy?*"

She shook her head. "Not until we're married and figure out where we're going to live and everything."

"Why?"

"Because it's the right thing to do. Molly has been so good to me."

"The right thing would be for you to take the next three weeks to enjoy every minute of planning your *one* and *only* wedding without any pesky distractions like a job. I'll move in with you and pay for everything, so you can focus on the wedding." He kissed her hand. "Let me do this for you, honey. Please?"

"I'll think about it."

"What's there to think about?"

"I've been taking care of myself for a long time, Brian. Just let me have some time to get used to the idea that I'm not going it alone anymore."

"You're *not* alone anymore."

"I know, and you're very sweet to want to come in on your white horse and take care of me. But even if I do say yes to this plan of yours, I'd have to give Molly some notice."

"Fine. Tell her tomorrow you're leaving at the end of the week."

"*Brian.*"

As they crossed the line into Granville, Carly felt her tension return. Somewhere in this town she called home was a man who wanted to harm her for a transgression she could neither remember nor repair. Her worries about who he was and when he might strike again took something away from her happiness, and that made her mad. Hadn't he already taken enough from her? When would the debt be repaid?

"Hey." Brian rolled their joined hands around on her leg. "What's going on over there?"

"He's out there somewhere, waiting for us to come back. It's like I can feel him watching me."

"Why don't we go to New York until the wedding? There's no need for you to live like this when I've got a place sitting empty in New York. Let's get you out of here until they find him."

"What's to say he won't follow us there?"

"He'd be out of his element in the city."

Carly thought about that as Brian rolled the car to a stop at a four-way intersection. "You can take Tucker Road," she said. "There's no sense going all the way around."

"Are you sure?"

She nodded, and he took a right.

"So what do you think about New York?"

Turning her head so she could see him, she said, "Would you think I'm a silly, sentimental girl if I said I want to be with my mother, my sisters, and my nieces before the wedding?"

"Of course not."

"Then we can stay here at least until the wedding?"

"Only if you'll consent to spending twenty-four hours a day with me."

"I don't know if I could stand that," she joked.

He poked her ribs, and she was still laughing as they took the last curve before the accident site. Her laughter faded to a shriek when Brian slammed on the brakes to avoid hitting a person standing in the road. The car fishtailed wildly for what felt like an endless second before stopping just a few feet from where Sam and their friends had died.

In the time it took for Brian to regain control of the car, the man dashed into the thicket of trees that lined the road. Brian sprinted from the car and disappeared into the woods after him.

"*Brian!*" Carly screamed. "*Come back!*"

Fumbling around in her purse, she found her cell phone. With shaking hands, she dialed 911.

CHAPTER 19

*C*arol pressed a cup of hot tea into Carly's cold hands. "I added a shot of whiskey to warm you up."

"Thanks, Mom." She took a tentative sip of the hot brew and felt the whiskey burn its way through the numbness. "Where's Brian?"

"In a huddle on the back deck with his father, Matt Collins, and the FBI agent, Nathan someone."

"Barclay," Carly said as she took another sip of tea. "Nathan Barclay. Is Brian still bleeding?"

She nodded. "His mother's after him to have it looked at, but he's keeping the towel on it and brushing off her attempts to hover."

"We were coming to tell you we're engaged." Carly's eyes filled, and she blinked back the tears. She refused to give in to the overwhelming desire to weep. "We just wanted to tell you."

Carol took hold of Carly's left hand. "Your ring is beautiful, honey. You must be thrilled."

"I'm so far beyond thrilled, I don't even know what the word is," Carly admitted. "He wants to do it in three weeks.

Do you think we can get it together that fast? Nothing fancy, just something small."

"Of course we can." Carol eased her daughter's head onto her shoulder and stroked a loving hand over Carly's hair.

"Did Cate and Caren leave?"

Carol nodded. "They took the kids home to bed."

"Where was Zoë?"

"A group of her friends got together to spend the night at someone's house. They figured they'd do better together than they were doing alone."

"Cate took her there, right?" Carly raised her head to look at her mother. "You're sure she's safe?"

"Of course, honey. Don't worry."

Carly put down the teacup and stood. "I need to see Brian." With an odd feeling of detachment, she walked through her parents' house, aware of worried glances from her father and Brian's mother, who were talking quietly at the kitchen table.

She slid open the screen door and stepped onto the deck.

"There's *no way*," Brian was saying. His back was to her, but she could see him dabbing at his face with a paper towel. A branch had caught him just under the eye, cutting open his cheek. One glimpse at his bloody, furious, frustrated face emerging from the woods after an interminable wait had caused Carly to faint in the road next to his mother's convertible. A day that had begun with such promise had ended with fear and pain. "You are *not* using her as bait. I don't want to hear another word about that, Dad. Think of something else."

"I'll do it," Carly said, startling them.

Dropping his hand from his face, Brian spun around.

She winced at the angry cut beneath his eye, which had swollen shut. That he had come so close to losing his eye . . . A quarter of an inch higher and he would be in the hospital.

He reached out to her. "Are you all right, honey?"

"You want to use me to lure him out of hiding," she said to Michael as she took Brian's hand. "I'll do it."

"The hell you will!" Brian said. *"No fucking way!"*

"It's me he's after," Carly argued. "Let me do this before he hurts someone else."

Brian's angry outburst had caused the wound to reopen. "It's not an option," he said, wiping the fresh blood from his face.

Carly took the paper towel and gently tended to him. "This seems to have begun with me, so doesn't it seem fitting it should end with me, too?"

"No, it does *not* seem fitting. It seems stupid and risky. Call me crazy for not wanting to dangle my fiancée in front of a psychopath."

"Your *fiancée?*" Michael asked, the delight all but radiating from him.

"That's what we were coming to tell you," Brian mumbled.

Michael put his arms around them both and simply held them.

Nathan Barclay cleared his throat. "Well, it seems you all have other fish to fry tonight. We can discuss this in the morning." To Brian, he added, "Get that looked at. You might need stitches."

After congratulating Brian and Carly, Matt left, too.

"I found a couple of butterfly bandages," Carol said.

"Let's see if we can get one on without getting too close to your eye." Mary Ann took Brian by the hand to lead him inside. "Come in here under the light."

Carly watched Brian work at standing still while his mother fussed with the bandage.

"There," Mary Ann said. "That ought to do it. If it's still bleeding in an hour, I'm taking you in."

"I don't have to do what you tell me anymore," he reminded her in a teasing tone.

"Where'd you get that misguided idea?"

The others laughed, and the tension that had filled the air suddenly lifted.

"What we need is some champagne," Steve Holbrook declared. He rummaged around in a kitchen cabinet, returning a moment later with a bottle he held up with a smile. "The good stuff left over from my retirement party. I've been saving it for a special occasion, and I can't think of one more special than this."

He popped the cork and poured it into the glasses Carol had gotten out. When everyone had one, Steve raised his glass. "To Brian and Carly, may your future be bright and full of all the happiness you so richly deserve. Congratulations."

"Hear, hear," Michael said, touching his glass to Mary Ann's.

After they polished off the first bottle, Steve went looking for another.

As she listened to their mothers discuss what needed to be done to throw together a wedding in three weeks, Carly began to believe for the first time that it might actually be possible. Caught up in their excitement, she almost didn't notice when Michael stepped out on the deck.

HE RESTED his hands on the rail and hung his head, rolling it back and forth in an effort to relieve some of the tension that had gathered at the base of his neck. Better there, he had discovered, than in his chest.

"Dad?"

Turning, Michael could have swooned once again with relief at the sight of his boy, even with the nasty cut on his face. He was safe, he was alive, and that was all that mattered to Michael. When he considered what could have happened earlier, in the very same place as before . . . It didn't bear thinking about.

"How's the cut, son?"

"Hurts like a bastard."

"Maybe you should get to the E.R. You'll have a scar if it doesn't heal right."

"A scar would add to my rakish good looks."

Michael smiled. "What kind of B.S. has that lady of yours been filling your head with?"

"The very best kind," Brian said. "The kind I somehow managed to live without for far too long."

"I'm happy for you, Bri. You can't know just *how* happy."

"Then what're you doing out here by yourself when there's a wedding to be planned?"

"I'll leave that to the ladies."

Brian snickered. "I'm told I have no place in the process."

"You know what I did for my wedding?" Michael asked, resting back against the rail.

"What's that?"

"Got married."

Brian laughed. "Sounds like the wisest course of action." A moment of quiet passed between them before Brian said, "Why didn't you collapse or do something equally dramatic to force me home sooner?"

"Because it wouldn't have been time."

"You could've saved me—hell, all of us—a lot of aggravation if you'd come up with something, *anything*, to get me back with her again."

"You wouldn't have wanted to hear it, especially from your old man, even if he's all-knowing and filled with wisdom."

Amused, Brian said, "You'll be my best man again, won't you?"

The burst of pleasure in the midst of mayhem surprised Michael. "Of course," he said, touched to be asked and at the same time oddly saddened, as he'd been twice before, to know there was no one else his son could ask. "We should have it down to a science by now."

Brian hooted with laughter. "You *had* to say that, didn't you?"

Michael shrugged. "In this case, the third time will definitely be the charm."

"Yes, it will. Do something for me?"

"Anything."

"Let go of this idea of using Carly as bait. It's not going to happen. I can't believe you'd even consider it."

"She'd be surrounded by cops and FBI. She'd be safe."

"You can't guarantee that."

"Don't you want to *nail* this guy, Bri?" Michael pleaded. "For Sam, for the others?"

Brian shook his head. "Don't play that card with me, Dad," he fumed. "Don't make this a 'who do you love more' thing, because the answer is Carly. She'll *always* be the answer. I want to clear Sam's name as badly as you do, but he's not here anymore and she is. I plan to keep it that way, so think of a plan B."

"What if this guy gets to her before we get to him?"

"He'd have to kill me to get her."

"You underestimate him at your peril and Carly's. For whatever reason, you seem to have what he wants. Do you honestly think he'd hesitate to kill you?"

Brian looked down at the deck, a tick of tension pulsing in his injured cheek.

"You'd better be thinking of your mother, and you'd better be thinking of me," Michael said softly. "We've already buried one son. Don't you dare get yourself killed by thinking you can outsmart and outmaneuver a madman, Brian Westbury. Do you hear me?" His voice broke. "Don't you dare."

Brian took a step to close the space between them and put his arms around his father. "I won't."

~

Michael drove Brian and Carly to her apartment in downtown Granville. After ensuring the officers positioned at the bottom of her stairs and across the street at the town common understood they were guarding his son and future daughter-in-law, Michael left them for the night.

When they were alone, Brian rested his hands on Carly's shoulders. "How're you doing, hon?"

She shrugged him off. "Don't."

Surprised, Brian followed her into her yellow and white bedroom. "What's wrong?"

"Don't treat me like I'm fragile and might break under the strain." She took off her sandals and flung them into the closet. "I can handle that kind of mollycoddling from my mother and yours but not from you, too. That's not what I need from you right now."

He moved fast, so fast she had no time to anticipate his intentions before he was devouring her mouth in a hot, breathtaking kiss. Wincing, he turned his head so he could delve deeper.

"Wait," she gasped. "Your cut. You'll split it open again."

"Don't mollycoddle me." Unbuttoning her blouse, he worked quickly to get rid of her clothes. When she was naked, he stepped back to look his fill.

Carly trembled under the heat of his gaze.

He kissed the palm of her hand but never once looked

away from her. "You make me want like I've never wanted before, Carly."

"Then take." She reclined on the bed and reached out to him. "Don't go slow. Just take."

He tugged the shirt over his head and dropped his shorts. He covered her, held her, took what she offered, and lost himself in her.

Her nails scored his back, fueling the flame that blazed through him. Filling his hand with a breast that was fuller now than it had been when she was younger, he laved at her nipple and sent her into a soaring climax.

Sweat stung the cut under his eye, but it didn't slow the frantic beating of his heart or the rapid-fire pace of their coupling.

She must have sensed he was hurting, because she forced him onto his back, straddled him, and took him in. Arching her back, she cried out when she was surprised by a second orgasm.

"*Carly*," he moaned, burying his hands in her waterfall of curls and bringing her down to him to give her a moment to recover from the rush. "I love you so much. So very, very much."

She kissed him, a sweet, innocent brushing of her lips against his that undid him. "I love you, too," she whispered. "More than you'll ever know."

He held her tight against him and came with a choked cry of release.

THE HAPPINESS, the bone-deep satisfaction of having everything she'd ever wanted, had Carly floating through her routine over the next week. Every time she turned around, Brian was there. She woke up to him every morning, went to bed with him every night, shared every meal, every thought, every dream with him. Nothing, not even the threat of the man who would do them harm, could detract from her joy.

Brian had finally succeeded in convincing her to quit her job at Molly's. On Thursday morning, the day of her last shift, he walked with her to the coffee shop and then lingered for a while to have breakfast and read the paper.

Carly's regulars were delighted about her engagement but sorry to hear she was leaving the shop. She would miss seeing them and would miss the women she worked with, too. Miss Molly's had given her more than just a job for all the years when she'd had nothing else.

The people there—both her coworkers and the customers —had been like a second family to her. That one of them might be the man terrorizing the town was a thought she wouldn't allow in today, not on a day that signaled the end of one phase of her life and the start of a new, exciting phase with Brian.

He stood and dropped a twenty on the table. With a cute nod of his head, he called her over to him. *Will my heart still skip a crazy beat when he does that five years from now? Definitely.*

"Can I get you anything else, sir?" She reached up to caress his cheek, which was still bruised. The swelling around his eye had gone down, and the cut had scabbed over. They hoped it would heal in time for the wedding.

He hooked an arm around her waist, pulled her to him, and surprised her with a passionate kiss.

Miss Molly's patrons hooted and hollered.

Carly's face burned with embarrassment. "Stop," she whispered.

"I will, but I don't want to." He kissed her again, a light touch of his lips that was somehow more than the first one, which had said, "I want you." This one said, "I love you."

"What're you doing today?" she asked, flustered by him. She was still getting used to the feelings he had resurrected in her, feelings she had never expected to experience again.

"I'm going over to bother my mother for a while, and I need to check in with my office to make sure they're not hosing up my cases. I'll be back by two." He took a measuring look around at the people sitting in booths and at stools at the counter. "Don't talk to strangers. Don't talk to anyone, for that matter, and don't step foot outside that door until I get back. You hear me?"

"Yes, dear."

He smiled at her easy obedience. "We're still on for your niece's game, right?"

Carly nodded, her stomach fluttering with nerves.

"Good. She's the only new member of the Holbrook family I haven't met yet. Looking forward to it." He kissed her one last time. "I love you."

"Love you, too. Have fun with your mom, and be careful."

"I will."

Carly watched him go out the front door, hating the trip of fear that came with letting him out of her sight. Only the knowledge that the police were keeping a close eye on both of them made it possible for her to start bussing the table he had vacated.

"It does my heart good to see that some things never change," Molly said.

Carly turned to her.

Molly shook her head and smiled. "You and that Westbury boy, just as cute as you were when you were kids."

The description of Brian as "that Westbury boy" amused Carly. "You'll come to the wedding, won't you, Molly?"

Resting her hand on Carly's shoulder, Molly said, "You bet your life I will. I'll miss you like crazy around here. We all will, but I'm so delighted for you, Carly. So very, very delighted."

Carly's eyes burned with tears as she hugged Molly. "Thank you so much for everything, for giving me a place in the world when I had nowhere else to be."

"There'll always be a place for you here."

As the coffee shop bustled around them, Carly held the older woman for a long moment. When they finally released each other, both brushed tears from their cheeks. With a sheepish smile for her friend, Carly went back to work.

CHAPTER 20

A police officer trailed behind them at a respectful distance as Carly and Brian walked hand-in-hand through town on their way to Columbia Park to watch Zoë's game.

"You're sure you don't mind if I have all the kids in the wedding?" Carly asked him.

"Whatever you want, hon. I told you that."

"Julia's only two. She's apt to freeze up."

"She's so cute." Brian chuckled. "She'll be fine."

"Lilly's over the moon about going dress shopping this weekend. Craig's boys, on the other hand, begged me to leave them out of the whole thing. Mark actually called my mother and said, 'Please ask Auntie Carly if I can just come and watch.'"

Brian laughed. "How old is he?"

"Almost fifteen. Allison was expecting him that last summer, remember?"

"Yeah." He brought her hand to his lips. "That seems like a lifetime ago, doesn't it?"

"That's because it was. Anyway, his brother Peter, who's thirteen, apparently feels the same way. So that leaves me with Zoë, Lilly, Julia, Justin, and Steve. You're sure about this?"

"Absolutely. So then Zoë would be your maid of honor?"

"I think that would be better than trying to choose between my sisters or having them both. I don't want the wedding party to outnumber the guests."

"True," he said, amused by her excitement. "Speaking of guests, I was wondering . . ."

"About?"

"What would you think of inviting the Garretts, Randalls, Townsends, and the other parents? I was thinking they might like to see us get married, after everything."

"That's a wonderful idea, Bri."

"Would you mind terribly if I also invited Beth and her husband?"

"She's your friend. You should invite her."

"Wow. You didn't even have to think about that."

Carly shrugged. "She's no threat to me."

He dropped her hand and slung an arm around her shoulders to pull her close to him. "I adore you, Carly Holbrook."

"Which is why I couldn't care less if your ex-wife comes to our wedding."

"She's getting along in her pregnancy, so she may not be able to fly by then."

"Invite her anyway."

"I will. Thanks for understanding."

"You know what I've got to get busy practicing?"

"What's that?"

"Saying Carly Westbury loves Brian Westbury. It doesn't roll off the tongue quite as smoothly."

He laughed. "As long as it rolls off regularly, I don't care if it's smooth or not. Carly Westbury," he said. "That's got quite a ring to it."

"Sure does. I used to write it all over the inside covers of my notebooks in high school. I never imagined it would take this long for it to happen."

"We couldn't have imagined a lot of things."

"Even Hollywood couldn't have come up with our story," she said with a smile.

"No kidding."

They arrived at the field as the two teams were warming up. None of Carly's family was there yet, so she lingered with Brian at the chain-link fence that lined the field.

"There she is." Carly pointed to the tall girl standing in the infield.

"The ponytail was kind of a giveaway," Brian said.

"Cate keeps hoping she'll outgrow her baseball phase, but so far there's no sign of it."

"I can't see her face with the hat on."

"She'll come over to say hello before they start."

Zoë was engaged in a series of stretches and didn't notice them watching her. She swung her arms around in windmill style and then walked onto the mound to throw to her catcher.

"Damn," Brian muttered when Zoë unleashed a fastball that snapped into the catcher's mitt. "That's outrageous." He looked down to find Carly watching him anxiously. "What?"

"Nothing." She turned back to Zoë, who had an equally impressive curve ball and sinker.

"She's really good."

"I know. At her last game, she slammed into the other team's second baseman and knocked the wind out of him. I thought Cate was going to expire on the spot."

He laughed. "That's awesome. I love it."

"Hey, guys."

They turned to find that Matt Collins had replaced the other officer.

"Hi, Matt." Brian extended his hand. "What're you doing here?"

Matt shook Brian's hand. "Shift change. We're short-handed with everyone working overtime, so it's all hands on deck. How're the wedding plans coming?"

"Getting there," Carly said.

"That's your niece, right?" Matt said, referring to Zoë.

Carly nodded. "Oh, here come Tom and the kids."

"I'll let you visit with your family," Matt said. "I'll be right over there if you need me."

"Thanks," Brian said.

Carly's niece Lilly ran the short distance from the parking lot. "Auntie Carly, Auntie Carly, check out my new shoes!"

Carly reached down to scoop up the girl. "Oh, they're so pretty."

"They're jellies," Lilly said solemnly.

"I see that. Do you remember my friend Brian, who you met at Grammy's the other night?"

"Uh huh. You're going to marry my Auntie Carly, aren't you?"

"Would that be okay with you?" Brian asked, his face set into a serious expression that tugged at Carly's heart.

"My mommy says you're a nice guy, so I guess it's all right. But you aren't going to take her back to New York with you, are you?"

"Nope." He played with a lock of Lilly's hair. "I got a job today with the Rhode Island attorney general, so we'll be staying right here, or at least somewhere nearby."

Carly almost dropped Lilly as she stared at Brian. "Really?"

He nodded.

Before she had a chance to absorb the news or jump all

over him for keeping secrets, her brother-in-law Tom strolled up to them with Steve in tow.

"How's it going?" he asked Carly.

She kissed his cheek and mussed Steve's hair. "Pretty good. You remember Brian, right?" They had met briefly the other night at her mother's house.

"Sure." Tom extended his hand to Brian as he sought out Zoë on the field.

Brian shook his hand. "Good to see you again."

"You, too. We're going to grab some seats." Tom nodded toward the bleachers. "Are you coming?"

"In a minute," Carly said.

The moment Tom had walked away with the kids, she pounced. "When were you going to tell me?"

Brian flashed a big satisfied smile. "I was getting around to it."

"Oh, I should be so mad at you." She punched his shoulder playfully. "But I really just want to kiss you right now."

"Please feel free."

"Later," she said with a meaningful look that made his blood boil. "Tell me everything. How did it happen?"

"I called the attorney general and told him I was looking to relocate to Rhode Island. He said he'd followed the Gooding trial and asked if I'd be interested in heading up the criminal division. The whole thing took, I think, four minutes."

"Are you sure, Bri? You love your job in New York."

"You'd hate it there, hon. Your family is here, and I'd like to be closer to my parents, too. This is where we belong."

Carly hurled herself into his arms and kissed him. "Thank you, thank you, *thank you*." She sank into the kiss, oblivious to where they were or who was watching.

"Gross."

Carly tore her lips free of Brian's and laughed at the look of total disgust on her niece's face. "Um, Brian, this is Zoë."

He turned, and his heart stopped. She was the very image of Carly, right down to the auburn curls, and the light dusting of freckles across the bridge of her nose. Only her hazel eyes were different.

"Nice to meet you," she said.

He released Carly to reach over the fence for Zoë's hand. "You, too. I'm sorry to stare, but you look so much like Carly. It's crazy."

Zoë wrinkled up her nose at her aunt. "How many times have we heard *that*?"

"A few," Carly said with a small smile. "Have a good game, honey. I've told Brian what a great pitcher you are, so strike out the side for me, okay?"

"You got it." She put her hat back on and trotted over to the dugout to join her teammates.

"She's lovely," he said in a hushed tone, his eyes glued to Zoë across the field.

"Yes."

It seemed too impossible to fathom, too outrageous to believe, but suddenly he had to know. His heart in his throat, he looked down at Carly. "Is she ours?"

She looked up at him with tears in her eyes. "Yes."

The roar in his ears all but deafened him as he stood perfectly still and tried to contain the urge to scream, to run, to strike out at someone. At her. At Carly.

"Bri—"

"Don't say a word," he managed to say. "Just don't say a word." Carly's shattered expression failed to move him. He couldn't think of anything but the girl on the field, the girl with his windup, his fastball, his hazel eyes. His daughter. A sudden overwhelming urge to be sick had him turning away from the fence.

Carly followed him.

"Does she know?"

"No."

"Who does?"

He walked so fast that Carly had to trot to keep up with him. "Only my parents and my siblings. And Dr. Walsh, who delivered her."

Suddenly he stopped. "How could you do this? How could you keep something like this from me? From my parents? *Do you have any idea what this would've meant to them after losing Sam?*"

"If you'll let me explain—"

He held up his hand to stop her. "Save it." He snorted harshly. "No wonder why your brother-in-law, the man who's raising *my daughter*, can barely bring himself look at me. He must be *thrilled* that I'm back in town."

"Brian, please," she begged, tears streaming down her face. "Let me tell you—"

"*There's nothing you can say, Carly!* Go back with Tom and the kids. I need to get out of here before I say something I'll regret."

She grabbed his arm. "Please, Bri. You don't understand."

"You're right." He shook her off. "I don't. I can't do this right now, and I can't leave you here alone. I'm asking you to go."

"Will you come home later? Will you talk to me? You have to let me explain. We can't let this ruin everything!"

"Too late." Knowing Matt would see Carly safely home, Brian turned and walked away.

Carly stood sobbing in the field and watched him until he was out of sight. Wiping her face, she turned to find Cate waiting for her.

For an endless moment, the sisters stared at each other before Cate closed the distance between them. "He knows."

"He took one look at her, Cate." Carly wiped the dampness from her face. "I know I promised you and Tom I'd never tell anyone, but when he asked me straight out, I couldn't lie to him. I just couldn't."

"I always knew this day might come." With tears running down her face, too, Cate put her arms around her sister and held her. "When you explain everything to him, he'll come around. He loves you too much not to. He just needs some time to absorb it."

"I don't know. He's furious, and I don't blame him."

Cate took her by the shoulders. "Listen to me, Carly. You did what you thought was best for him, for Zoë, for all of you. Remember the way things were back then? You couldn't talk, you couldn't leave the house, he was halfway across the country in college. You were both traumatized by an unspeakable tragedy, and neither of you were in any condition to raise a child. You did the right thing—the *only* thing you could do. You can't question everything just because he reacted badly."

"He'll want to know her."

"And he will. She'll be his niece."

"What if that's not enough for him?"

"It'll have to be. He's not capable of destroying the life of a child he doesn't even know just so he can have the satisfaction of hearing her call him Dad. She has a dad, one she loves very much. He'll see that."

"I can't lose him again, Cate," Carly whispered. "It'd be the end of me."

"You're not going to lose him. Let's get through Zoë's

game, and then we'll go find him. Tom and I will go with you. We'll find him, and we'll explain it to him."

Wondering if there was any explanation Brian would accept, Carly let her sister lead her to the bleachers where Tom waited for them with a stricken expression on his face. "Cate?"

She clutched her husband's hand and kissed his cheek. "Everything's fine. What's the score?"

PART IV
AUGUST-SEPTEMBER 2010

A time to love and a time to hate; a time for war and a time for peace.

Ecclesiastes 3:8

CHAPTER 21

*B*rian walked for hours. His mind raced with questions, disbelief, anger, and sadness. The sadness was unbearable. All this time there had been a child, his child, his child with Carly. *No wonder why she wants a baby so badly. She wants one she can keep. She's had to watch her sister raise the one she did have.*

When he thought about the years he'd spent so completely alone only to find out he'd had a child! *All that time!* He had asked Carly if she'd known what having a grandchild would have meant to his parents. What about what it would've meant to *him* to have a daughter? Had she considered that?

He walked the length of the beach at the lake and ended up at the willow. Studying the tree that had been their haven, he wondered if Zoë had been conceived there on the night of the accident. Or had it happened in Carly's bedroom on the Fourth of July? He had no idea, but suddenly he wanted to know. He *needed* to know.

Turning toward town, Brian had worked up quite a head of steam by the time he made it to downtown. He was cognizant enough to realize that charging into Carly's apartment in his current state of mind wasn't wise, so he crossed Main Street, cut across the town common, and went up the hill to the cemetery.

The late afternoon sun was warm on his back as he stood at his brother's grave. He sat down and rested against the large stone. "Hey, Sammy." Brian closed his eyes and took a deep breath. "I'm sorry it's been a while. I was away for a long time."

Brian pulled absently at the grass around the base of the stone. "I found out today I have a daughter. Can you believe that? She's fourteen and gorgeous. She looks so much like Carly. It's unbelievable. And you should see her pitch! She's got a smoking fastball, just like I used to have. Remember?

"You just wouldn't believe all the shit that's happened since that last night. It's like my whole life is divided squarely in half—before the wreck and after. And let me tell you, after has pretty much sucked. Until recently, that is. Things have been pretty good lately. Being back with Carly has been, just, well . . . amazing." His eyes filled. "We're supposed to finally get married in two weeks." He closed his eyes and tipped his face into the sunshine. "I just can't believe she kept this from me, Sammy. I feel so cheated. Zoë, my daughter's name is Zoë, is almost grown, and I don't even know her."

After sitting there a long while, Brian slowly rose to his feet, brushed off his shorts, and ran a hand over the stone that marked his brother's grave. "I miss you, buddy. That's one thing that hasn't changed. I'll be back soon." He turned to leave and was surprised to see Luke McInnis on his way up the hill.

"Hey, Brian. How's it going?"

Brian shook the hand Luke offered. "Pretty good. What brings you here?"

"My grandfather is buried right over there." Luke nodded

to the row just past Sam. He fixed his eyes on Sam's grave and shook his head. "I don't suppose you ever really get over something like that, do you?"

"No." Brian was reluctant to discuss his late brother with someone he barely knew and hadn't seen since high school. "Well, I've got to get going. See ya around."

"You're probably headed to Carly's. I just saw her."

Brian turned, studied him, wondered. "Where?"

"She was with her sister and brother-in-law. I think they were headed up to her place."

"I'm meeting them there."

"Well, don't let me keep you. Good to have you back in town, Brian. I hope you and Carly will be sticking around for a while."

"Take care, Luke." Brian walked down the hill and crossed the street to the town common. He glanced back over his shoulder and saw Luke still watching him. Reaching into his pocket, he withdrew his cell phone and punched number one on his speed dial. "Dad? Hey, how's it going?"

"Another frustrating day without an ounce of progress. That's how it's going."

"You aren't getting stressed out again, are you?"

"Trying not to."

"So listen, I just had an odd conversation with Luke McInnis. He didn't do anything wrong, per se, but he showed up at the cemetery as I was leaving and said he'd just seen Carly. Something about the whole thing creeped me out."

"Why aren't you with Carly?"

"We had a, ah . . . a fight."

"You didn't leave her alone somewhere, did you?" Michael asked with a frantic edge to his voice.

"Please, Dad. Give me some credit, will you? She's with her sister's family."

"I'm sorry. Of course you wouldn't leave her. This whole

thing is turning me into a paranoid freak. I'll have someone take a look at Luke. I don't really know him very well. What do you remember about him?"

"Not much. He was always just kind of there. I didn't know him well, either."

"Ask Carly what she remembers."

"I will. Eventually."

"So what in the world do you two have to fight about?"

"You wouldn't believe me if I told you," Brian mumbled.

"You'll be with her tonight, right?"

Brian stood at the bottom of the stairs that led to the apartment where they'd spent so many blissful hours since they'd been back together. He looked up, knowing she was there with her sister and brother-in-law, waiting to tell him how he'd come to have a child he hadn't known about for fourteen years. "Yeah," he said. "I'll be with her."

"Let me know what she says about Luke."

"Tomorrow."

"Are you all right, son? You sound odd. And you've been to the cemetery?"

"I hadn't been to see Sam since I got home. No biggie, Dad." He had no idea what he would tell his parents about Zoë. He needed to hear what Carly had to say before he decided anything. "You'd better get home, or Mom will come and drag you out of there in front of all your people."

"I'm going. I'll talk to you in the morning."

As he trudged up the stairs, Brian closed the phone and returned it to his pocket. By the time he reached the small deck where Carly's flowers filled the air with sweet fragrance, his throat had constricted and his heart was pounding.

He rested his hand on the doorknob for a long moment, working up the courage to take the next step. What would he hear? How would he feel about it? What would it mean for his future with Carly? Would there even *be* a future with her? Questions he thought had been answered were now back in play, and the stakes had never been higher for them.

Carly opened the door.

Despite his huge desire to be pissed with her, he was affected by her ravaged face. He hated that he wanted to take her in his arms and do whatever he could to make sure she never looked that way again, but he couldn't seem to move.

"I'm glad to see you." She reached for his hand. "Come in."

He let her lead him inside.

Tom and Cate, who didn't look much better than Carly, jumped up from the sofa when they saw him.

"Brian," Cate said, taking a step toward him.

"I was wondering," Brian said in the low, controlled tone he had practiced on his way into town, "if the three of you could maybe tell me how this happened." He turned to Carly. "When did we, you know, make a baby?"

"Fourth of July." Carly linked and unlinked her fingers as she all but vibrated with tension.

They were getting into personal terrain here, and Brian hated doing it with an audience, but that didn't stop him. "And didn't you tell me then you were still on the pill?"

Carly looked down at the floor and then back at him, the sadness in her eyes so deep and so overwhelming that had he not needed the answers so badly, he would've stopped right there. It was just too much. "I hadn't left the house in almost two months by then," she said softly. "I couldn't very well send my mother to Planned Parenthood to get my pills for me."

"You could've sent me."

"I never thought of it. I wasn't expecting to have the . . . opportunity to make love with you again."

"So you lied." Where there should have been anger, there

was only hurt and confusion. "Why would you do that, Carly?"

As if she couldn't wait another moment to touch him, she went to him and rested her hands on his chest. "I knew by the Fourth of July that I wasn't going to be able to go with you to Michigan. I was so afraid we wouldn't get another chance to be . . . together . . . like that before you left. I knew I was taking a risk, but I needed you so badly, Brian. I needed us to be *us* again, even if just for a short time. We'd spent two endless weeks apart—other than the week of the accident, the worst two weeks of my life up to that point—because you were frustrated with me for not talking. Can you remember what it was like then? How awful everything was? And how badly we needed each other that night?"

"Yes," he said hoarsely. Tom and Cate faded away, and there was only Carly. He looked down at her. "Did you know you were pregnant when I left for school?"

"I suspected."

"*Why didn't you tell me, Carly?*" he cried. "Why did you let me leave and not tell me we might've made a baby? Did you think I wouldn't care?"

"I knew you would. And I knew you'd give up your scholarship, your chance to go to Michigan, and your dream of going to law school. When you told me you were leaving and not coming back, I realized that was what you needed to do to survive what'd happened to us. I couldn't saddle you with a child at the expense of everything else you wanted and needed."

"And it *never* occurred to you I might want to make that decision for myself?" he asked, his voice growing louder.

"It never occurred to me to give you the chance. You'd made your choice to go, and at the time, I could see how it was the best thing for you to make a clean break the way you did. It was what you needed, Brian. Being stuck with a wife who couldn't talk or leave her parents' house and a baby who needed everything wasn't the life I'd imagined for you. You were destined for better things. It also never occurred to me to wonder if you would've done the right thing by me—and Zoë—had you known."

"I would have."

"I know that. I've always known that. But you might not have made it through college or become the great attorney you are today. I couldn't ask you to sacrifice your whole life, and because I was in no condition to raise a child, that's where Cate and Tom came into it."

"We got married shortly after you left," Cate said. "We eloped, actually. Tom was going to graduate school in California, and I wanted to go with him. We came home a year later and told our extended family and friends we'd had a baby. Because Carly hadn't left the house since the accident, no one but us even knew she was pregnant. So no one outside of our family ever questioned whether the baby was ours."

"What your parents must've thought of me," Brian said, shaking his head. "To leave you alone and pregnant."

"They never blamed you, Bri," Carly said. "They knew I hadn't told you."

"And you just stepped in willingly to raise a child that wasn't yours?" Brian asked Tom, trying hard not to resent the man for something that wasn't his fault. "How do you do that?"

"It was simple, really," Tom said with a shrug. "I love Cate, and she asked me to. And then when I saw Zoë for the first time, any doubts I had just faded away. I've loved her from the first instant I ever saw her." Tom's voice broke. "She's my little girl. I can't imagine how you must feel right now, but I love her, and I've tried to be a good father to her."

Wiping at her own tears, Cate put her arm around her husband.

Suddenly exhausted, Brian sat down on the sofa. "When was she born?"

"April 5, 1996," Carly said softly.

Brian looked up at her with a gasp. "On Sam's birthday?"

Tears rolled down Carly's cheeks as she nodded. "It was like a sign from above that he was watching over me. I can't even explain how that felt."

Brian let his head fall into his hands as he, too, was felled by tears. "Oh, God, Carly," he said, his voice muffled by his hands. "What that would've done for my parents. For me. To know that."

Carly sat down next to him and put her arm around him, drawing his head to her chest. "I'm so sorry, Bri. I tried to do what was best for all of us, what was best for you and our baby. And I'm sorry I lied to you about being on the pill, but I'm not sorry we got Zoë from it. She's the best thing that's ever happened to me. You and Zoë are the best of me, Brian."

"You got to watch her grow up. You got to be part of her life."

"Yes, and I'm so sorry you didn't. I'd give anything to have been able to share her with you. I've always thought of Zoë as one more thing we lost that night on Tucker Road."

He raised his head and wiped his face. "I want her to know where she came from—"

"No," Tom said. "I won't let you turn her life upside down."

"She's my *daughter*. I have a right to know her, and she has a right to the truth."

Cate moved to sit on the coffee table and took Brian's hands. "You're not a selfish person, Brian, so I'm asking you to think long and hard about what you'd be doing to Zoë by telling her this. Everything we did, everything we *all* did, was done out of love—not only for Zoë but for you, too."

Brian knew his skepticism showed on his face and made no effort to hide it.

"When you told Carly you were leaving and not coming back, she respected you enough and loved you enough to let you go, even though losing you broke her heart," Cate said. "I can see how you feel wronged by what we did, and I understand that, but please don't take it out on Zoë. Don't give her reason to question everything she knows to be true. I don't think she'd recover from that blow on top of the one she's just suffered."

"If there's one thing I've learned as a prosecutor, it's that the truth comes out eventually, and when it's controlled, it does a hell of a lot less damage than when it happens by accident, like it did today."

"There's no reason for her to ever know," Carly said. "She's a happy, well-adjusted kid who would never, ever suspect Cate and Tom aren't her biological parents. I'm begging you, we all are, to put what's best for her ahead of what's best for you."

"If I hadn't guessed, would you have ever told me?"

"No."

"And you could've married me with that kind of secret between us?"

"Without hesitation. I love you more than life itself, and I have since I was thirteen."

"When we were in Newport and talked about having a baby, why didn't you tell me then?"

"Because the one thing Tom and Cate asked of me when they did this incredible thing for me was that I never tell anyone, including you, that she was mine. It was their only stipulation. But when you asked me straight out today, I couldn't lie to you."

Trying desperately to absorb it all, Brian took a deep breath. When he looked up, the three of them were watching him, all of them rigid with anxiety. "I understand what you're saying about not telling Zoë. I hear you on that, Cate. I don't want to upset her life any more than you do. But I have a stipulation of my own."

"What's that?" Tom asked.

"I want my parents to know she's mine. I want them to know she was born on Sam's birthday, the first birthday after he died."

"They'll want to be involved in her life," Tom said, the fear written all over his face.

"They'll do—or not do—whatever I ask them to. You have my word on that."

Cate and Tom exchanged glances.

"I guess we could live with that," Cate said.

"There's one other thing," Brian said. "I want to spend some time with her. I want to get to know her. Carly and I could take her away for a few days under the pretense that we understand what she's going through since we lost our friends, too."

"I don't know about that," Cate said, glancing at Carly.

"You're close to her, right?" Brian asked Carly.

"Yes."

"So why would she think it odd to be spending a few days with you and your fiancé?"

"She wouldn't, I guess."

"Then what's the problem?"

"It's up to Tom and Cate," Carly said. "They're her parents."

"Can we sleep on it?" Cate asked. "We need to talk about it."

"Of course," Brian said.

Cate hugged her sister and then surprised Brian by hugging him, too.

"We'll talk to you in the morning," Cate said as she and Tom moved toward the door.

"Cate?" Brian said.

They turned back.

Brian went over to them. "I don't like that this was kept from me, but that has nothing to do with you two, and it doesn't mean I don't appreciate the enormity of what you guys did for Carly and Zoë and for me, too, I guess. So, um, thank you."

Tom shook his hand. "It's been our pleasure," he said in a hushed tone. "Entirely our pleasure."

Brian saw them out the door, and when he turned back to face Carly, he had absolutely no idea what to say to her.

$\mathcal{B}$rian wandered over to the antique armoire that held Carly's television. On the shelf above the TV was a cluster of framed family photos. He picked up one of Zoë and studied it.

"How old was she here?"

"I think maybe eleven."

"Do you have other photos? From when she was little?"

Carly went into her bedroom and came back with a thick photo album, which she handed to him.

His expression tight and unreadable, he sat on the sofa and flipped the book open to find Zoë as an infant, squalling with outrage during her first bath.

"She lifted her head off my chest on the fourth day and looked me right in the eye, as if to say, 'Bring it on, world.' She's been going full tilt ever since."

Brian ran a finger over a picture of Zoë, bright-eyed and alert. "I want to know everything—how you felt when you were pregnant, what the delivery was like, whether you breastfed her, how old she was when she went to live with

Cate and Tom, what schools she's gone to, who her teachers were. Everything."

Overwhelmed by his intensity, Carly rested against the back of the sofa. "I was sick as a dog for the first three months of the pregnancy. That was actually the first sign I was pregnant. I was so sick."

Brian winced. "I can't imagine anything worse."

"Oh, I can," Carly said with a chuckle. "Labor was no picnic, let me tell you."

For the first time since Cate and Tom had left, he looked right at her. "It was bad?"

"Horrible. Twenty-four hours of hard labor. The doctor wanted to take me to the hospital for a C-section, but the idea of them taking me from the house petrified me. So I summoned the energy from God knows where, and she was born a short time later, at seven in the morning, screaming her head off." She smiled at the memory. "In the fifteen years we were apart, I never wanted you more than I did in that moment. I wanted so badly to share her with you. I was overjoyed and heartbroken at the same time. I've never experienced anything quite like it."

As she watched him study every photo, Carly's stomach tightened with anxiety. He was sitting right next to her, but there were miles between them. The distance frightened her. *What will I do if he can't forgive me?*

"How much did she weigh?"

"Eight pounds, nine ounces, twenty inches long."

"What's her middle name?"

"Ann."

"Shit, I don't even know what her last name is."

"Murphy. Zoë Ann Murphy."

"You always said you'd name your daughter Jordan."

Surprised he remembered, Carly said, "I found I couldn't use that name under these circumstances."

"Did you name her Zoë? Or did Cate and Tom?"

"I did."

"I like that name. It's unique." Brian flipped to photos of Zoë as a toddler, her face covered in spaghetti sauce, surrounded by bubbles in the tub, and dancing in high heels and a pink tutu. "God, she was just so adorable," he whispered.

Carly nodded in agreement. "She came out with the bright, sunny disposition she still has, although she's been giving Cate fits the last year or so with her teenager attitude."

"How long did you have her? After she was born?"

"Almost two months, and yes, I breastfed her. I loved that."

"I wondered why you seemed, you know, bigger there."

"I got to keep them," Carly said with a laugh.

"But there're no other signs you had a baby."

"Probably because I was so young. I bounced back fast." She fiddled with the fringe on the blanket that hung over the back of the sofa. "Faster than I did from giving her up."

"It was hard."

A statement, not a question, Carly thought. *He knows me well enough to imagine what it was like.* "Yes," she whispered, traveling back in time to the very darkest days of her life.

"Carly?"

Pulling herself out of the past, she glanced at him. "It's difficult to talk about, even after all this time."

"You don't have to. Not now if you're not up to it."

"Do you hate me for this?" Her eyes filled, but she made no move to wipe away her tears. "Because I wouldn't blame you if you did."

"I don't hate you. I hate that I never knew I had a daughter. I hate that I was with your mother the other day, and the whole time she and I were talking, she knew I have a daughter, but I didn't. I hate that, Carly."

"I'm sorry," she whispered. "I'm so very sorry. I was so certain I'd done the right thing, but *you* were right earlier when you said I should've let you decide for yourself."

He reached for her hand. "You probably *did* do the right thing," he conceded. "We were both such a mess after the accident."

"That night, on the Fourth of July, when I lied to you about being on the pill?"

He nodded.

"That's the only time I've ever lied to you about anything. I swear."

"I know, and I also know you could've lied to me today, but you didn't. You didn't even hesitate."

"I saw you watching her, when she was pitching, and part of me wanted you to figure it out. I wanted you to know she'd gotten her fastball from you." Her voice caught. "I hated keeping her from you, and I *did* think of your parents when she was born. I did, Brian. That broke my heart, too."

"You understand why I want them to know, don't you?"

"Of course I do."

"I can't get over her being born on Sam's birthday," he said, still incredulous. "It's just unbelievable."

"That was such a gift in the midst of it all. I can't begin to tell you what it meant to me at a time when everything else was so uncertain and painful. To think that maybe Sam was keeping an eye on me . . ." After a long moment of silence, she said, "Are we going to be able to get past this, Bri?"

He hesitated, only slightly, but he hesitated nonetheless. Hurt radiated through Carly.

"I need some time to get my head around it."

"Our wedding is in two weeks." She hated the stammer in her voice, which conveyed just how afraid she was that she might've lost him for good at some point during that long day. "We can postpone it."

247

"We don't have to decide anything tonight."

That he even had to think about it . . . Carly stood. "I'm, um, going to take a shower," she mumbled, needing to get out of there before she lost it completely in front of him. In the bathroom, she shed her clothes and tossed them into the wicker hamper. Standing under the pulsing water, Carly was racked by sobs. When her legs would no longer support her, she sank to the floor of the tub and stayed there until the water turned cold. She trembled violently as she fought her way into her robe and tied it tight around her waist.

Her reflection in the mirror was nothing short of frightening, so she didn't linger. She brushed her long curls and secured them in a ponytail. When she emerged from the bathroom, she found Brian absorbed in the photo album, so she left him to it. Lying facedown on her bed, she hugged a pillow tight against her chest and was surprised to discover there could be more tears.

After a while, Brian came in and stretched out so he faced her.

She wiped frantically at her face, not wanting him to see the devastation.

He stopped her and finished the job himself. "That night? The Fourth of July? I never forgot it," he said as he brushed the dampness from her cheek. "The way you took my hand and led me inside. You floored me with that, Carly. My heart was beating so hard I was afraid it would burst right through my chest."

Carly hiccupped and fought a losing battle to stop the tears.

"If I'd known you weren't on the pill anymore, I probably would've risked it, too. That's how badly I wanted you. I'd missed you so much since the accident. I guess what I'm saying is I don't blame you for taking that risk at a time in our lives when we had nothing else. I relived that night, and the last time at the willow—the night of the accident—probably a million times when we were apart. Those memories sustained me. So even knowing what I know now, I don't regret what we did that night, Carly. I couldn't.'"

"But you regret I didn't tell you about Zoë. You're angry."

"I want to be angry, and I was earlier. I won't deny that. I want to be outraged over everything I missed with her. But more than anything else, I'm sad. To think of you going through what you did, having to make such big decisions, having to give up your baby after everything you'd already lost." He shook his head with regret.

"The pregnancy, waiting for her, knowing your child was growing inside of me . . . She was the only reason I survived that first year without you. And after she was born, I briefly entertained the illusion I could keep her. But I couldn't sing to her, I couldn't comfort her when she cried, I couldn't even tell her how much I loved her. I couldn't take her for a walk or for a ride in the car when she was colicky."

Brian's eyes were bright with tears as he listened to her.

"It was Cate's idea, actually, that she and Tom might be able to help. It seemed so good on paper—Zoë would have a normal home and upbringing with two parents who would love her, and I'd get to keep her in my life. But in reality . . ."

Brian held her hand tight against his chest.

"I had trouble weaning her, and after she was gone, I produced milk for days. It just kept coming, as if someone hadn't gotten the memo that there was no longer a baby to feed. I was hugely, darkly depressed. I won't deny I thought about how easy it would be to just end it all. I hate to even admit that, but it's true."

"Carly," he said, tears spilling down his cheeks as he brought her into his arms.

"After a couple of weeks, my dad finally laid down the law and gave me an ultimatum—either I got a job or went to school or he would kick me out of the house. I'm still not sure if he actually would've done it, but I suspect he would have. I spent that whole night working up the nerve to leave the house. I got dressed for work at three o'clock in the morning and then sat on the edge of my bed until it was time to go. At five thirty, I got up, went downstairs, and walked out the door like I'd been doing it every day. I think I was able to do it because I had nothing left to be afraid of. Leaving the house was no big deal after losing you and Zoë."

"You were so brave."

"No, I was shattered, but over time, amazingly enough, I began to feel better. The job helped, and getting this place of my own did, too. In many ways, Zoë helped the most, though. As she got older, we just had this thing. I don't know. I can't explain it. It didn't matter to her that I couldn't talk. She loved me anyway, and in a lot of ways that saved me, you know?"

As he nodded, Carly noticed his face was still damp with tears.

"You really think it's wise not to tell her the truth?" he asked.

"I really do."

"So many people know, though. What if it comes out years from now and she hates us all for keeping it from her?"

"It won't come out. The only people who know are my parents, Cate and Tom, Craig and Allison, Caren, and Dr. Walsh, who's retired now. Caren's husband Neil doesn't even know and neither do Tom's parents. We all understood at the very beginning how important it was that no one know."

"The lawyer in me wonders how you do something like this and not create a paper trail."

"We put Cate and Tom's names on the birth certificate."

"So they never actually adopted her?"

"No."

Brian groaned. "Shall I enlighten you as to the potential legal ramifications of that?"

"Please don't. The important thing is no one who knows would ever in a million years tell her, Brian. Never. I know you're just finding this out, and I understand how horribly shocking it must be for you—"

His eyes flashed, but with emotion, not anger. "*Do you? Do you really?*"

"No, I guess I don't. But what I was going to say is she's such a great kid. You'll see that once you get to know her."

"I saw that in thirty seconds today."

"Then you'll not want to do anything to change who she is, will you?"

"I hate that fearful look you keep giving me, like I'm some unreasonable ogre who's going to turn your whole life upside down."

"You already have," she said with the first smile she had mustered in hours. "But in all the best ways."

He combed his fingers through her still-damp curls. "I let you think, for a second earlier, that I'm having doubts about marrying you, Carly. That was wrong of me. I'm upset and all churned up inside over finding out about Zoë, but I'm not having doubts about us. Not after hearing the whole story. So I don't want you awake all night worrying about that, okay?"

She tried to swallow the huge lump that suddenly settled in her throat. "Okay."

He pressed his lips to her forehead. "Brian Westbury loves Carly Holbrook, forever and always."

She dissolved into deep, racking sobs.

Brian held her tight against him until the sobs became hiccups. After a long while, she slept.

CHAPTER 23

*E*arly awoke often during the night, and each time her first thought was to see if he was still there. He slept on top of the comforter, still dressed in shorts and a polo shirt. Her robe had twisted around her, so she gently removed his hand from her hip, got up to shed the robe, and slid under the covers. She laced her fingers through his and watched him for a long time before exhaustion overtook her and she fell back to sleep.

The next time she opened her eyes, it was morning, and Brian's back was to her as he stared out the bedroom window. His hair was wet from the shower, and he had changed into a T-shirt and faded jeans that hugged him in all the right places. He held a steaming mug of coffee as he watched the action on Main Street.

"What are you thinking about?" she asked, her voice hoarse from sleep.

"That we need to buy a house and cars."

"I don't have a license anymore."

"You can renew it."

"I don't know about that. It's one thing to ride in a car. It's another thing altogether to drive one."

He turned away from the window and came over to sit on the bed. Handing her the coffee, he said, "You'll have to try it and see how it feels."

"One of these days, maybe." She took a sip from the mug and gave it back to him. "Did you sleep?"

"Off and on. How about you?"

"The same. I dreamed about the accident. That hasn't happened in a long time."

He seemed startled. "You dream about it?"

"Not as much as I used to but occasionally."

"I do, too."

"Really?"

He nodded.

"I never knew that. My dream has changed a lot over the years, but some parts are the same. There's always someone in the car I can't get to. Sometimes it's Sam and the others. And then it'll be you and Zoë and other kids I know belong to us. The smell is the one thing that doesn't change. It's the same god-awful smell as that night."

He winced. "In my dream, I see it happening over and over. Like yours, the dream comes and goes. It always knocks me for a loop for a couple of days afterward."

"Me, too. I feel sort of like I did in the days just after it happened."

He shook his head with regret. "I can't tell you how badly I wish I could go back in time to make it so you didn't have to see what you did. So neither of us had to. If you hadn't seen that, you never would've stopped talking or locked yourself away in your parents' house. The loss would've been unbearable, but we would've been able to go ahead with our plans, despite it."

"I hate that I wasn't there for you the way I should've

been after you lost Sam. When you came to my house after his funeral, I wanted to tell you how sorry I was to have missed it. I should've been right by your side through the whole thing, and I'm sorry I wasn't."

He brought her hand to his lips. "We need to be looking forward not backward."

"Yes." Her heart ached when she thought of the question she needed to ask him. It had been on her mind all night during the wakeful periods.

"What's wrong? Something just upset you."

She smiled despite the overwhelming sadness. "I should be freaked out by the way you read me so easily. I'd forgotten about that."

"What's going on inside that head of yours?"

She studied his handsome face for a long moment, wanting to memorize every detail. "Do you think it's possible that too much has happened to us? That we're deluding ourselves by thinking we can ride off into the sunset toward happily ever after? Maybe we just weren't meant to be, Bri."

His eyes flashed with emotion. "Do you really believe that?"

"I don't know what I believe anymore."

"Do you believe I love you?"

"Yes," she said softly. "I do. I believe that."

"And since I have no doubt that you love me, too, can you think of anyone who deserves happily ever after more than we do?"

She thought about that for a moment. "I can't say I do."

"Good." He leaned over to kiss her. "Then no more talk about not meant to be or any other such foolishness, okay?"

"All right," she said, but she still wasn't sure. He was saying all the right things, but the conviction he'd once had was gone. She hoped it would be back in time for their wedding.

"I'm going to go talk to my parents about Zoë."

"I want to come with you."

"You don't have to."

"Yes, Brian. Yes, I do." She got out of bed and reached for her robe. "Give me twenty minutes."

AFTER A QUICK BREAKFAST at Miss Molly's, they walked through town to Tucker Road with a police officer following them. They stopped for a few minutes at the accident site where Carly pulled weeds and pinched off some dead blooms from the bank of wildflowers.

"I don't even know what he does for a living," Brian said absently as he watched her fuss with the flowers.

Still in a crouch, Carly turned and looked up at him. His hands were in his pockets, his eyes fixed on the white cross bearing Sam's name. "Who?"

"Tom."

"He's a vice president at a pharmaceutical company. He oversees their New England sales force."

"Sounds like a good job."

"It is. He does well. And it's flexible, so he can go to all the kids' games and stuff. That's important to him."

"So then Cate doesn't work?"

"She keeps threatening to go back now that Lilly's in first grade, but she's up to her eyeballs in all the kids' activities. I don't know where she'd find the time for a job."

"They sound like good parents."

"They are."

His eyes shifted from the cross to her. "That's what I'd want for our kids—a full-time mom and a dad who doesn't miss much. Would you want that, too?"

"Yes."

"You wouldn't want to work?"

"Not if we could afford for me to stay home."

"We could." He rattled off the salary the attorney general had offered.

Her eyes widened. "For real?"

He nodded. "Do you think you might be pregnant? Can you tell yet?"

"Not yet. But I can take a test in a week or two."

"I hope you are. I want you to have a baby you can keep."

Carly stood and put her arms around him. "I want that for both of us."

He held her close for a few minutes before he kissed her and said, "Let's get this over with."

CARLY WENT up the short flight of stairs that led to the Westbury's living room. Brian hung back for a moment to talk to his father, who had come home from the station when Brian called and asked him to.

"Did you talk to her about Luke?" Michael asked.

"Shit, I never thought of it."

Michael stared at his son, astounded. "What the hell could be so important you'd forget about that?"

"Come on up, and I'll tell you."

They went up the stairs to the living room.

"Is everything all right?" Michael asked.

"Sit down, Dad."

"You're making me nervous, Brian," Mary Ann said. "What's going on?"

Brian and Carly exchanged glances.

With a deep breath for courage, he said, "I found out yesterday that Carly was pregnant when I left for college."

"*What?*" Mary Ann gasped.

Brian told them the whole story, an abbreviated version that hit on all the important details. He held back the part about Zoë's being born on Sam's birthday, fearing that might be one detail too many at first.

When he finished, his mother's face was frozen with shock. "You mean to tell me all these years I've had a *grand-daughter* living less than two miles from me?"

"Mary Ann—"

She held up a hand to stop Carly. "Please. Don't."

"I know this is terribly shocking, Mom. It was for me, too. But after hearing Carly's side of it, I can see how she did what she thought was best for me and for Zoë."

"Zoë Murphy is my granddaughter," Michael said, more to himself than anyone else.

"Yes," Brian said. "And after talking to Carly, Cate, and Tom, they've convinced me that telling Zoë the truth now would not be in her best interest."

"What about *your* best interest?" Mary Ann's eyes were hot with anger. "What about *ours*?"

"It was important to me that you and Dad know the truth, but I assured them you wouldn't do anything to upset her life. It's too late for us with her, Mom. There'll be other grandchildren. We hope soon."

"When Brian and I get married, the two of you will become part of my family—if you want to, that is," Carly said. "There'll be holidays, birthdays, graduations. You'll have the opportunity to get to know Zoë."

Mary Ann glanced at Carly with hard eyes. "And that's supposed to be enough?"

"Don't you remember how awful everything was then, Mom?" Brian asked with a pleading edge to his voice.

"Do you think I need to be reminded of that?" Mary Ann snapped. "I live with it every minute of my life."

"Then maybe you can try to understand the situation

Carly was in after I told her I was leaving and not coming back. She couldn't talk. She couldn't leave the house. What was she supposed to do?"

"*I would've raised her!*" Tears spilled down Mary Ann's face. "I would've done it without a second thought!"

Brian looked over at Carly and saw that she too was crying.

"I'm sorry," Carly whispered. "I didn't know what to do. I didn't want to upset Brian's life and his plans. I wanted him to get past what'd happened. I was thinking of him."

"You were thinking of yourself," Mary Ann said.

Carly shook her head to say no.

"Mary Ann . . ." Michael got up to sit next to her. When he tried to slip an arm around her she shook him off.

"You know Carly, Mom. Can you even begin to imagine what it cost her to give up her baby after she'd lost me and every friend she had in the world? Can you try to image that?"

Carly sent him a look that told him she appreciated him defending her.

Mary Ann swiped impatiently at her tears. "How can you stand having a daughter who'll never know you're her father? How can you *stand* that, Brian?"

"I can do it because it's what Carly asked me to do. She knows Zoë, and she convinced me this is what's best for her. She'll be my niece. That'll have to suffice."

"And we're expected to just fall in line and keep quiet about it?"

"I didn't have to tell you," Brian reminded her. "I assured Carly, Cate, and Tom that you and Dad would do whatever I asked you to. And what I'm asking you to do is what's best for a girl who came into this world under less than ideal circumstances and who's flourishing despite it."

"How did you find out about her?" Michael asked.

"I took one look at Zoë, and I knew." He added in a whisper, "I just knew."

"So you weren't going to tell him?" Mary Ann asked, her tone accusatory.

"No, I wasn't," Carly said.

Exhaling a snort of disbelief, Mary Ann sat back against the sofa to study her son. "How can you go forward with this marriage, knowing she would keep such a thing from you?"

"How can you ask me that after what we've been through? She did what she thought was best for me. She gave up her baby so I could get through college and law school. If that doesn't tell me how much she loves me, *what the hell ever could?*"

"Brian," Carly said, reaching for him.

He squeezed her hand, stood, and ran a hand through his hair as he fought to calm down. "I'm sorry, Mom. I just can't bear the idea of you holding this against Carly like she set out to maliciously deny you your granddaughter."

"He's right, Mary Ann," Michael said. "Those were dark days for all of us. It wouldn't be fair to judge Carly on decisions she made at that time in her life."

"Thank you," Carly said to Michael.

"I'm sorry I can't forgive and forget so easily," Mary Ann said. "I understand it must've been a terrible time for you, Carly. As a mother, I get that. But how you could just leave us out of the whole thing . . . I'm sorry. That part I can't forgive."

"I hope in time you'll be able to forgive me," Carly said. "I've always loved you very much, and I've been so looking forward to being your daughter-in-law."

"Now don't you do that." Mary Ann wiped furiously at tears. "That's not fair."

Carly moved to squat down in front of Mary Ann. "I thought of you. I did. How could I not think of you? And I knew what it would've meant to you to have Zoë in your life, especially at that time. But I put what I thought was best for Brian ahead of what was best for you. I hope you can forgive me for that."

Mary Ann didn't resist when Carly hugged her. "Again, that's not fair." She sniffled.

"There's something else," Carly said.

"Carly." Brian's tone was full of warning. "This might not be the time."

"For what?" Mary Ann asked.

Carly clutched the other woman's hands when she said, "Zoë was born on Sam's birthday."

Brian's parents gasped.

Mary Ann whimpered. "Oh, Michael, did you hear that?"

As he dealt with a torrent of tears, Michael said, "I did. Yes, I did."

"That sure is something, isn't it?" Brian asked, sharing an intense moment of wonder with his parents.

"It surely is," Michael agreed.

"He was with me," Carly said. "I felt him all around me that day."

Mary Ann suddenly stood. "I'm sorry. I just need . . . I'm sorry." She left the room.

Michael got up to go after her. "She'll need some time, but she'll get past this." He bent to press a kiss to Carly's forehead. "She loves you, too. So don't you worry." On his way out of the room, he said to Brian, "Talk to her about Luke."

Startled, Carly looked at Brian. "Luke? Luke McInnis? What about him?"

Brian urged her to her feet and put his arms around her. "Later, honey. We'll talk about that later. Are you all right?"

Carly shrugged. "I feel beat up."

"I know. I do, too."

"Thank you."

His eyebrows knitted with confusion. "For what?"

"The way you defended me. Earlier I was wondering if you'd ever be able to truly forgive me for this, but it seems like maybe you already have."

"I'm still getting used to the whole thing, but I *do* forgive you, Carly. I just hope my mother can, too."

"Will you be able to live with it if she can't?"

"If you can, I can."

"I should've told you." She shook her head with regret. "My mother wanted me to. She warned me that someday you might find out, and I'd have to face the music."

"You did the right thing. I would've come home and married you. We probably would've made a terrible mess of things between us and with Zoë. It was better this way. Maybe not for the rest of us, but definitely for her."

"I'm glad to hear you say that. I knew you would've come home. I knew that for sure, Brian. But I also remembered what you said before you left about getting married and having to live in my parents' house because I couldn't leave there. As I thought about whether or not I should tell you, I just kept wondering how I could condemn you to that."

"It overwhelms me to know you put me first, even after I walked away from you."

"You didn't do it because you'd stopped loving me," she reminded him.

"I never stopped loving you." He tipped up her chin so he could see her face. "You believe me, don't you?"

"Yes, I do."

He kissed her forehead. "What you said, about my parents being part of your family and getting to know Zoë? That was good. I think it'll help my mom to cope with this."

"I hope so."

He took a deep breath to clear his mind and refocus. "Do you think *your* mother would give us a ride to one of the car dealers on the south side?" he asked.

"I'm sure she would. You want to do that now? Today?"

"I'm getting tired of walking everywhere, and I was thinking I'd like to take my fiancée and my . . . niece out to Cape Cod for a couple of days. What do you say?"

For the first time since the day before, Carly smiled, a genuine smile that made it all the way to her expressive eyes. "Your fiancée and your niece would love that."

CHAPTER 24

$\mathcal{F}$or the second time in his life, Brian Westbury had fallen flat-on-his-face in love.

Zoë hadn't taken a breath in over an hour, chatting with excitement about Carly and Brian's new midnight blue SUV, about the slumber party she had been to with her friends, and about the unexpected trip with her aunt and newfound uncle.

"I can call you Uncle Brian, right?"

As he looked at Zoë in the rearview mirror and fought through a storm of emotions, Carly reached for his hand. "I'd like that." He was still getting used to how much she resembled Carly and had to remember not to stare.

"That was fun yesterday, wasn't it, Auntie Carly? Wait 'til you see the dress she bought for the wedding—"

"Ah!" Carly cried, putting up a hand to stop her. "Don't tell him anything about it."

"Duh. I know *that*. What do you think I am? A kid? Jeez. Can I plug my iPod into the stereo?"

Brian reached back for it. "Sure."

"Be prepared," Carly said, amused. "She has eclectic taste in music."

"That's all right." *Whatever she wants,* Brian wanted to add but didn't. He cringed when rap music filled the small space.

Carly chuckled. "Told you."

Brian turned it down. "Did you find a dress, too, Zoë?"

"Uh huh." She made a face that he caught in the mirror. "It's this frilly purple thing."

"Lilac," Carly corrected her. "And it's lovely on you. We found smaller versions for Lilly and Julia."

"I'm the maid of honor. Did Auntie Carly tell you?"

"I've heard that rumor." Brian tried not to dwell on how surreal it would be to have their daughter serve as a witness to their wedding. *She's not your daughter. She's your niece. Keep telling yourself that. Maybe one day you'll believe it.*

"Does that mean I have to dance with your father?" Zoë snorted. "Me and the chief of police. How funny is that? My friends are going to *freak.*"

Brian glanced over to find Carly looking stricken. Clearly she hadn't considered that pairing. "I'm sure he'll love having such a pretty girl to dance with," Brian said.

"How cool is it to be riding in a car again, Auntie Carly?"

Zoë shifted gears so fast Brian struggled to keep up—and to hear her over the horrible music.

"I'm getting used to it," Carly said. "I like being able to get out of Granville once in a while."

"I can't imagine not leaving that boring-ass town for fifteen years."

"Zoë. " Carly frowned at her niece's language.

"Someday that boring town might look pretty darned good to you," Brian said, speaking with some authority on the subject.

Zoë shrugged. "I doubt it. I can't wait to get out of there."

"And go where?" Brian asked.

"I don't know. Anywhere." Shifting gears yet again, she said, "So you're a lawyer?"

"That's right."

"I wouldn't mind being a lawyer."

Brian had to remind himself to take the next breath. "Is that so?"

"Uh huh. My mom says I'd be a good one, cuz all I do is argue."

Brian and Carly laughed, and he could honestly say he had never been happier in his life than he was in that moment. It had been a long time coming.

MICHAEL WAITED UNTIL MATT COLLINS, Nate Barclay, and the other FBI agent, Jeff DiNardo, had taken seats in the conference room. He had spent so much time with Nate and Jeff in the last month that he'd *almost* forgotten they were feds. He had called this meeting on a Sunday afternoon after finally getting the chance to talk to Carly about Luke the night before.

"We may have a suspect," Michael announced.

"Who?" Matt asked.

"Luke McInnis."

Matt sat back in his chair and thought about it as he tapped a pen on the table. "Hmm."

"Remember what we said at the outset?" Michael asked him. "That it was going to be someone we knew?"

"Yeah, wow," Matt said, looking intrigued. "Why haven't we thought of him before?"

"What've you got, Mike?" Nate asked.

He told them about the odd encounter Brian had had with Luke in the cemetery. "He fits the physical description—

he's six-three, about 220. Big feet. Last night I sat down with Carly and asked her what she knows about him. She said there's no way it's him, that she's known him since kindergarten and always thought of him as a friend."

"Is that how he thought of her?" Jeff asked.

"She thinks so. She can't recall anything outside the bounds of normal friendship with him. Except recently."

"How's that?" Nate asked.

"He asked her to go with him to their class reunion over Fourth of July weekend. But she saw that as a mercy thing more than a date. He was trying to help her feel better about going, since she still wasn't talking then. She got the feeling he was just doing her a favor."

"Was he disappointed when she said no?" Nate asked.

"She said he seemed to be for a moment, but then he was fine about it. He was a regular customer of hers at Miss Molly's, along with two other guys she's known all her life. The three of them work for the father of one of the others."

"If he fits the description, why haven't we taken a look at him before?" Jeff asked. "Especially since he went to school with Carly and Brian. Was his name on the shoe store list of special orders?"

"Nope," Matt said. "But he could get shoes anywhere—online, out of town. Who the hell knows? He hasn't been on our radar at all."

"Earlier, I rechecked the videotape from the candlelight vigil when Alicia Perry was missing, but there was no sign of him in the crowd," Michael said. "You know how sometimes perps like to turn out for gatherings like that because they get off on witnessing the suffering."

"We know what this guy gets off on," Jeff mumbled.

"What did Carly and Brian say about his social standing in school?" Nate asked.

"Interestingly, in separate interviews they both used the

same words to describe him. They said he was always just *there*, but neither of them was close to him. Carly said she's been friendlier with him at Miss Molly's than she ever was in school."

"And neither of them got the sense he wanted to be closer to them when they were still in school?" Nate asked.

"No," Michael said.

"I say we pick him up and have a talk with him," Nate said. "I'll also see about getting a warrant to search his house."

"Isn't that premature?" Jeff asked. "I mean, we have one odd conversation in a cemetery—and isn't every conversation in a cemetery odd? That's not enough to bring him in. Not to mention if it *is* him, we'd be tipping our hand that we're on to him."

"While I hear what you're saying, Jeff, we've got three murders and multiple aggravated sexual assaults on our hands here," Nate said. "And this is as close as we've come to a suspect. I want to talk to him." To Michael, he added, "Pick him up."

"Sorry, Jeff, but I agree with Nate," Michael said.

"For what it's worth," Matt said, "I've been rereading the reports and interviews with the victims and their families. I noticed something interesting."

"What's that?" Jeff asked.

"Well, I kept asking myself—why would he kill two of the girls, and the boyfriend of one of them, and not kill the other girls? So I started looking at common characteristics between Alicia and Kelly Graves, the girl from the carjacking. Both their mothers used similar words to describe them— one said firecracker, and the other said spark plug."

"So what're you thinking?" Nate asked.

"That they fought him and pissed him off, so he killed them."

Michael sat back in his chair to think about that. "And the other girls, the ones who lived to tell, didn't fight him."

"That's right," Matt said. "Tanya Lewis told us that she kept quiet and let him do what he was going to do. She said she was too petrified to say a word, which is apparently how he likes them, nice and docile. Alicia's mother said she would've fought him like a tomcat."

"Tanya also said he seemed to like it when she cried out in pain," Michael recalled.

"The others said that, too," Nate added. "So the secret to staying alive is to lie there and take it?"

"Apparently," Matt said grimly. "The autopsies on the carjacking victims indicated Kelly died an hour or so after the boyfriend, which I take to mean he made her watch him kill her boyfriend."

"Among other things," Jeff said.

"Most likely," Matt concurred.

"So we know he likes to be respected," Nate concluded. "Even by girls he's about to rape. This guy just gets sicker by the minute, doesn't he?" To Michael, he said, "Have you gotten anywhere with Brian about letting us set something up using Carly as bait?"

Michael shook his head. "I think that's a dead end."

"Well, let's pick up this Luke McInnis and see where that takes us," Nate said.

THE LATE AFTERNOON sun was warm as Brian rested facedown next to Carly on the blanket they had spread on the beach in Falmouth, Massachusetts. Zoë had wandered down to the water's edge to collect some shells to take home to her brother and sister.

Carly reached across the blanket to hold his hand. "How are you feeling?"

"Content—something I haven't experienced very often."

"She likes you."

Brian couldn't believe how much that pleased him. "You think so?"

"I know so."

"She's fabulous. I feel like I need a bigger word, though, because even that one doesn't do her justice."

"I know what you mean. Did you talk to your mother?"

"Just for a few minutes, when you and Zoë were swimming."

"How's she doing?"

"Okay, I guess." He pushed himself up on one elbow. "It's a lot for her to absorb. Maybe I shouldn't have told them. I don't know."

"You were right to tell them. She'll see that eventually."

"I guess we can only hope so. I called my dad, too. He said they're bringing Luke in for questioning."

Carly frowned. "They're barking up the wrong tree there."

"What if they aren't? What if it *is* him?"

"I just can't imagine a guy I've known all my life—someone I've thought of as a friend—being capable of the kind of things they're saying this man has done. That Luke McInnis could be the one who caused the accident, who killed Sam and the others . . ."

"I know, hon. It boggles my mind, too."

"He came to my defense." Carly sat up as she remembered. "I was so rattled last night by your dad suggesting it could be Luke, I forgot to tell him."

Brian sat up, too. "What do you mean 'came to your defense'?"

"There was a guy in the coffee shop giving me a hard time because I couldn't talk. He was obnoxious. Luke got in his face and said, 'No one treats Carly that way.' He was quite intimidating. What do you suppose that means in light of everything?"

"I don't know, but it's interesting. My dad would want to know about it." Brian reached into Carly's beach bag for his cell, pressed number one on his speed dial, and waited. "Dad? Hey, Carly remembered something else about Luke. I'll let her tell you." As he handed the phone to Carly, Zoë returned to the blanket.

Carly got up and walked away with the phone.

"What did you find?" Brian asked Zoë.

She held the hem of her T-shirt, which she had filled with shells. "This scallop shell is the best one. Lilly will love it." She glanced at Carly. "Who's she talking to?"

"My dad. Something about the case."

He watched as a shadow descended over Zoë's sunny disposition. Just like Carly, Zoë's every emotion showed on her face.

"Sit down. Let's see what else you've got there."

She did as he asked, but her enthusiasm for the shells was gone. "I hope they catch him. Soon."

Brian wished he could hug her. "I do, too."

She turned to him. "He killed your brother, right?"

"We think so."

"What was his name? Your brother?"

"Sam."

"You miss him."

Touched by her sensitivity, he said, "Always."

"Does it ever stop hurting so bad you think you're going to die, too?"

This time he didn't resist the urge to take her hand and hold it between his. "Yes, it does. You think it won't, but eventually you'll be surprised when you get through a whole day without the hurt."

"Carly said the same thing. That's good to know. The other people in the car with your brother, they were your friends, too?"

He nodded. "Other than your Aunt Carly, my very best friends."

"I'm sorry. That's an awful lot to lose all at once."

"Yes," Brian said, surprised by the pain. He couldn't believe it was still possible to feel it so acutely. "It was a terrible time for everyone."

"My mom said you were Auntie Carly's boyfriend in high school."

"That's right. Four and a half years, in fact."

"So why didn't you two get married before now?"

What to say? "We went through a bad time after the wreck, and circumstances kind of came between us. I had to leave for college, and Carly wasn't able to come with me like we'd planned." He shrugged. "We never saw each other again until recently."

"Do you wish you'd gotten married back then?"

Brian smiled. "You have no idea how much I wish we had. But you can't undo the past. All any of us has is right now, and you've got to do the best you can with today."

She nodded in agreement.

"I'm very sorry you lost your friend in such an awful way," he said.

"Thank you. I'm sorry for you, too."

Brian looked up to find Carly staring at their intertwined hands. He released Zoë and made room for Carly on the blanket.

"Everything okay?" she asked tentatively as she sat next to him and returned his phone to her bag.

"Zoë and I were just having a very nice chat," he said with a wink for the girl.

"That's right." Zoë's face lit up with a smile that was in sharp contrast to the sadness of a few minutes earlier. "I was just making sure he's worthy of you."

Carly laughed. "And?"

Brian waited breathlessly for Zoë's reply.

With an impish sideways glance at him, she said, "He'll do."

CHAPTER 25

*B*rian was almost asleep when the door between their adjoining rooms opened and Carly tiptoed in. Amused, he whispered, "What are you doing?"

"I thought you were sleeping." She slid into bed with him. "Zoë kicked me out."

Brian laughed softly as he pulled her tight against him. "Why? Did she find out you snore?"

Carly poked him. "I do *not*!"

He laughed and nibbled on her neck. "I was missing you anyway."

She wrapped her arms around him. "Oh, yeah?"

"Uh huh. I've gotten used to sleeping with you."

"I know," Carly said as she kissed him. "Me, too. She told me to go sleep with my fiancé. She guaranteed me—and I'm quoting here—that her morality won't go to hell in a hand-basket, and she won't tell her mother we slept together on the trip."

Brian's laughter echoed through both of them. "She's so funny."

"She also said she never gets a hotel bed all to herself. Apparently, she has to share with Lilly when they travel."

"I always had to share a bed with Sam. He used to kick the shit out of me—I think on purpose." He paused before he added, "Jeez, I haven't thought about that in years."

Carly caressed his face. "It's amazing how it can still hurt so badly, isn't it?"

"Yeah. Like I told Zoë today, it doesn't hurt every day anymore. But when it does . . ."

"It takes you by surprise."

"Yes." He worked a hand under the T-shirt she had worn to sleep in and rubbed her back. "I had the best time with her today. With both of you."

"I used to imagine spending a day with the two of you. I've wondered how it would feel to see you with her, but when I came upon the two of you holding hands . . . It was overwhelming."

"I felt an immediate bond with her."

"I think it's safe to say the feeling is mutual. She said, and again I'm quoting, that you're a 'hottie.'"

He snorted with laughter. "She has great taste in men, just like her Auntie Carly."

"Mmm," Carly said, getting into the back rub. "Lower."

He tugged at her shirt, eased it over her head, and tossed it on the floor. "That's better."

He felt her relax under his hands as he worked out the kinks that had gathered in her neck and shoulders over the last few stressful days.

"Go to sleep," he said, leaning over to kiss her cheek.

"Brian?"

"What, honey?"

"Will you make love with me?"

"Anytime you want."

"How about now?"

"With Zoë right next door?"

Carly turned over and reached for him. "I can be quiet. I've had a lot of practice."

Brian smiled, and the feel of her breasts against his chest made him tremble with desire, just as it had when he was eighteen. "That's very funny."

She clutched his shoulders. "We haven't made love in days. Do I need to be worried?"

"Of course not." He smoothed the curls off her face. "I'm sorry, honey. I've just had so much on my mind. This thing with Zoë and everything with the case."

"I know. And even though you've been so great about it, I'm still afraid it's put up a wall between us. There's a crazy man after me, but I wasn't truly afraid until the other night when I had a couple of hours to wonder what I'd do if you never came home again. After you found out."

He touched his lips to hers. "Where else would I have gone? You're home for me, Carly. It took me half my life to realize that, so you won't be getting rid of me any time soon."

Combing her fingers through his hair, she devoured him with a kiss that left him weak with need. "Love me, Brian."

"I do. You know I do."

"Show me."

"Turn over," he whispered.

"Why?" she asked nervously.

He nudged her onto her belly. "Just do it."

She glanced at him over her shoulder. "What are you going to do?"

He brushed his lips over her ear and dragged a finger slowly down her backbone. "Trust me?"

She trembled. "Of course I do."

"Then let me show you something new."

"There's *more*?"

His laughter was soft and easy, just like the movement of

his hands on her back. He massaged her shoulders until he felt her tension drain away.

"Feels good," she whispered.

"Yes, you do," he said as he worked his way to her lower back. Hooking his fingers into the waistband of her bikini panties, he pulled them down slowly. When he reached her feet, he tossed the panties and his boxers to the floor. He started the massage again with her feet and then moved to her calves.

"Brian."

"Yeah?"

"When do we get to the sex part?"

He laughed. "In a minute. I promise."

Inhaling a deep, frustrated breath, she rested her face on the pillow but watched him out of the corner of one eye.

His fingers coasted over her inner thighs, causing her to tense. "Relax, honey."

"I'm trying, but you're making me nuts."

"Good," he whispered against her ear, sending a shiver through her. "That's the point." Only his weight partially on top of her kept her from launching off the bed when he buried his fingers in her wet heat.

She groaned and pushed back against his hand.

He kept it up until her thighs began to tremble and she clutched him from within. Moving swiftly, he withdrew his fingers, raised her to her knees, and entered her from behind just as she climaxed with a restrained cry. He gripped her hips and pumped hard all the while biting his lip to keep from coming too soon.

When he felt her spasms begin to subside, he reached around to coax her up again.

"*Oh*," she gasped as he continued the relentless pace. "*Brian*."

His lips were pressed to her back, his fingers sliding over

her most sensitive place, and his concentration was so intense he didn't dare try to speak for fear of losing control. Instead, he pushed harder and deeper and was soon rewarded by another soft cry of completion. Cupping her breasts, he went deep one last time and lost himself in her. "*Carly.*"

As he landed half on her, half off, he was panting, sweaty, and so depleted he could only rest his head on her back and gulp for air. "Everything okay down there?" he finally asked.

"Mmm," she purred.

"Was that a good mmm?"

"*Mmm.*"

He smiled. "So we agree new things are good?"

This time she added a nod to go with her "Mmm hmm."

He reached up to lace his fingers through hers.

"Bri?"

Taking a page from her book, he said, "Hmm?"

"Can we do that again sometime when I don't have to be quiet?"

With his cheek pressed to her back, he laughed. "Definitely."

MICHAEL GOT HOME after midnight and moved quietly through the house so he wouldn't disturb Mary Ann. She hadn't slept much since they found out about Zoë. He hadn't slept so well himself, but it wasn't just because of Zoë. The pressure to solve this case sat on his shoulders like a thousand-pound weight he carried with him twenty-four hours a day.

They had spent three hours grilling Luke McInnis and had searched every inch of his house without finding a thing that tied him to any of the crimes. Either Luke was one cool customer, or he was innocent. They'd had no choice but to release him when they had failed to crack him. Michael hated that he was so desperate to solve this case that he had actually begun to hope it was Luke—a kid his sons had grown up with.

He opened a beer and sat in the dark living room. So many thoughts spiraled through his mind. No wonder he couldn't sleep. Not only was he obsessed with the case, but he was also worried about Brian and Carly, concerned about Mary Ann, curious about his granddaughter, and missing Sam more than he had in a long time. And that Zoë had been born on Sam's birthday. Incredible.

A sniffling sound came from the end of the hallway. His poor Mary Ann. She was heartbroken—again—and that bothered him more than anything else. With one big swallow he downed the rest of the beer and got up. He left the empty bottle in the kitchen and picked up the 9 millimeter handgun he kept close to him at all times these days. Tugging off his tie, he unbuttoned his white uniform shirt on his way down the hall.

"Hey, babe," he said from the doorway. He left the light on in the hallway so he could see her.

She pushed the hair from her face and sat up against the headboard. "You're so late."

He put the gun in the bedside table drawer, sat on the edge of the bed, and kicked off his shoes. "I left you a message earlier that it was going to be a long night. Did you get it?"

"When I got home from dinner with Carol."

"How'd that go?"

Mary Ann shrugged. "She feels terrible, of course. She said she begged Carly to tell Brian she was pregnant, but when Carly chose not to, she and Steve had to respect her decision. We should be two mothers focused on throwing together a wedding that's fifteen years overdue. Instead, we spent the whole night talking about the granddaughter we share—a granddaughter she's gotten to love and care for, and I never knew I had. It's hard not to resent Carol for that. I keep telling myself it wasn't her fault, but that doesn't make it any easier to hear what a great kid Zoë is."

He wiped the tears from her face and brought her hand to his lips. "I hate to see you so upset. What can I do for you?"

"You're doing it."

"Oh, I can do better than that." He quickly shed the rest of his uniform into a pile on the floor and got in bed. "Come here."

She curled up against him and released a deep rattling breath. "I want to be so mad with Carly, but I can't quite seem to get there."

"She's crazy about that boy of ours, and her devotion to him has never wavered, even during all the years he was gone," Michael reminded her. "She made a huge sacrifice for him. Maybe it wasn't what was best for us, but it *was* best for him. You have to know that."

"I *do* know that, Michael. I think that's why I can't seem to stay mad with her. She suffered as much as anyone after the accident."

"Maybe even more so."

"Maybe," she conceded. "When I think about the empty lives she and Brian have led when they should've been raising their daughter together, and then add to it everything Sam and the others were denied, that's when I really get mad. Whoever this monster is, the list of things he's taken from us and so many others just gets longer and longer. I blame *him* for the fact I don't know my granddaughter. It's *his* fault."

"You're absolutely right."

"You have to find him, Michael. You have to stop him."

He kissed her forehead. "I'm going to get him, babe, or die trying. I promise you that."

"Don't you dare die trying, because when you get him, you're going to retire."

"Yes, ma'am."

Startled, she looked up at him. "That was far too easy."

"If you want me to retire, I'll retire. Whatever you want."

Her laughter touched his heart. "You're so full of it. You'd already decided."

"I haven't given it a thought."

"Yeah, right. This case is kicking your butt, and you've had enough."

He could fool a lot of people but not his wife of thirty-five years. "If you say so."

"I don't care how it happens, as long as you mean it."

"I do. You might've heard my son is moving back to Rhode Island and marrying a girl we both love. He's promised me some grandkids before much longer, so it seems like a good time to hang up my hat."

"It's the perfect time. Besides, Matt's ready for his shot at being chief."

"Yes, he is, but I've got one loose end I need to sew up before I put in my papers."

"Just hurry up, will you?"

"I'm going as fast as I can, believe me."

"Michael?"

He was so tired. He couldn't remember ever being more tired. "Hmm?"

"Don't let him take you from me, too. Do you hear me?"

"I won't."

"Do you promise?"

Where the burst of energy came from he couldn't have said, but he rolled her under him and kissed her as if his life depended on it. Maybe it did. "I promise," he whispered and then went back for more.

~

CARLY AND BRIAN had just returned from Cape Cod and were unloading the Jeep in front of Carson's two days later when Luke McInnis pulled up behind them in his company truck. He got out and walked over to them. Carly squeezed Brian's arm to tell him to turn around.

"Hey, you guys," Luke said.

Brian stepped in front of Carly. "What do you want, Luke?"

"*What are you doing?*" Luke cried when he noticed Brian's protective gesture. "Do you think I'd *hurt* her? I've known her all my life! Why would I want to hurt her?"

Carly moved from behind Brian. "I don't think it's you, Luke. I told Chief Westbury and the others that. I said you were my friend, that you stuck up for me with that rude guy at Miss Molly's."

With his eyes still trained on Brian, Luke said, "Thank you."

"What were you doing in the cemetery the other night?" Brian asked him.

"The same thing as you! Visiting a dead relative. I was very close to my grandfather, and I go all the time."

"Interesting that we were there at the same time."

Luke snorted with disbelief. "So that coincidence was enough for you to go running to daddy and turn my whole life upside down? I always knew you could be an arrogant prick, Westbury, but I never thought you were malicious."

"Think whatever you want about me. All I care about is keeping Carly safe."

"And that makes you different from anyone else in this

town? Who do you think was keeping an eye out for her while you were off becoming a fancy lawyer?"

"I'm sorry you got dragged into this, Luke." Carly rested her hand on Luke's arm. "I never suspected for a minute that you'd be capable of the kind of things this man has done."

Luke looked at Brian. "He did, though, and so did his father. What I don't get is how *could you*, Brian? We were in freaking Cub Scouts together, for Christ sakes. You *know* me."

"No, I don't," Brian said. "I haven't seen you in fifteen years. And even before, I didn't know you that well."

Luke shook his head, his expression full of disdain. "I appreciate your support, Carly. I hope they catch this guy soon, so you can breathe easier—so we all can. I guess I'll see you at the concert."

"What concert?" she asked.

"A bunch of Rhode Island bands are doing a free concert on the town common tomorrow night. A show of support for the people of Granville."

"That's nice of them," Carly said. "We'll definitely be there."

"Be careful, Carly. Just like your *fiancé*," he said with a pointed look at Brian, "I don't want to see anything bad happen to you. Not after everything you've already been through."

"Thanks, Luke."

With a final glare for Brian, Luke turned and walked away. They watched him until he ducked into Miss Molly's.

Carly's eyes were focused on Miss Molly's. "It's not him. I'd know if I had anything to fear from him."

Brian tilted his head to study her. "And how would you know that?"

"When you lose something, like the ability to speak, it sharpens your senses, and you have to rely on your gut much more than the average person. I get these *feelings* about people. It's hard to explain. It's not him. I just know it isn't."

Brian put his arms around her. "I appreciate what you're saying, hon, but a gut feeling isn't forensic evidence."

"In the absence of evidence, it may be all we have."

He pulled back to look down at her, his face twisted into an amused expression. "Well, listen to you. You already sound like a prosecutor's wife."

She smiled. "A prosecutor's wife. I like the sound of that."

"Good, because in nine days, that's what you'll be."

"I just want to be Brian Westbury's wife. That's all I've ever wanted."

He kissed her, right there in the middle of Main Street, without a care in the world as to who might be watching. "You'll be that, too."

CHAPTER 26

"*I* like that one." Carly pointed to a plain gold band.

"That's nice." She looked over at Brian. "Don't you think?"

"It's boring."

"It's classic," Carly argued.

"We can do better." To the saleslady, who watched their exchange with amusement, he said, "Can we see that one?" He pointed to a circle of diamonds that glittered under the store's bright lights.

The lady reached inside the case, withdrew the ring, and handed it to Brian.

"Now that's more like it. Let me see it on you."

"I don't need this, Brian," Carly said as he reached for her hand and slid on the ring.

"It looks lovely with your engagement ring," the lady said. Reaching for Carly's hand, she asked, "May I?"

Carly nodded.

The woman bent to take a closer look. "It's exquisite. Is it antique?"

"It was my grandmother's," Brian said.

"The stone is beautiful. Two carats?"

"Just over."

"Well, I'll let you two talk about it. Give me a holler when you decide." She walked away.

Brian took Carly's hand and brought it to his lips. "It's perfect. That's the one I want you to have."

"It's too much, Brian."

"No, it's not."

Carly looked down at the sparkling combination.

With a finger to her chin, he brought her eyes back to his. "What's on your mind, honey?"

"We have to buy a house and cars. We've got the wedding and the honeymoon. We don't need to be spending money on something like this. The plain gold one is fine with me. That's what I want."

He smiled. "Carly, honey, we don't have to worry about money. We'll make a killing on my loft in New York. And I told you, I've worked so much over the last eight years that I didn't have time to spend even half of what I made. I invested most of it and forgot about it. I want you to have this ring. It's important to me."

"Why?"

"We've both had so little for so long. Don't we owe it to ourselves to live it up now?"

Touched, she said, "I guess so."

"Now what? You've got that look."

"I didn't spend much of the money I made, either. I'm sure it's nothing like what you managed to stockpile, but I've got about twenty-five thousand in CDs in the Granville Credit Union."

His face lit up with delight and what might've been pride. "Get out of here! You mean to tell me I'm marrying money?"

She rolled her eyes. "Whatever. I'm sure it's nothing compared to what you've got."

"It sure is something when you consider how hard you had to work for it."

She shrugged. "I guess."

"So no worries about money? Will you please let me buy you the ring I want you to have?"

"On one condition."

He smiled. "What's that?"

"I can buy *you* the one I want you to have."

His smile faded. "I don't know. I'm not a big jewelry person. You know that. Plain gold is about all you'll catch me wearing."

"Oh, so we're going to have a double standard in this marriage? Is that how it's going to work?"

"I'm starting to see there were benefits to you not being able to talk back to me," he grumbled.

Her grin lit up her face as she signaled to the saleslady. "Can you show us what you've got in wedding bling for men? I'm looking for something *really* flashy."

Michael paced the short length of his office, resisting the urge to sweep the piles off his cluttered desk. So great was his frustration, so overwhelming his sense of impotence, it was all he could do not to chuck the paperweight Brian had made for him in grade school right through the window. Only the knowledge that none of these urges would make anything better stopped him from acting on them.

A twinge of pain in his chest reminded him of the consequences of internalizing the stress. He dropped into the desk chair and did the breathing exercises they had taught him in the hospital.

"Bunch of voodoo science," he grumbled, even as the pain seemed to recede.

Matt burst into the room without knocking, his blue eyes bright with excitement. "We might have a break."

Michael sat up straighter in his chair. "What?"

"Remember a kid named Randy Lowell?"

"No, should I?"

"He was in Sam's class, Granville High class of 1996."

Michael racked his brain but couldn't come up with a face to go with that name. Shaking his head, he said, "What've we got on him?"

"Woonsocket police stopped him on suspicion of DUI. When they ran him through the system, they discovered an outstanding warrant for a parole violation in Missouri."

"What was he in for?"

"Attempted rape and second-degree sexual assault—on a high school cheerleader in Jefferson City."

Michael stood and made for the door. "Call Nate. Tell him to meet us there."

∽

AFTER A FULL DAY IN PROVIDENCE, Brian and Carly rode home to Granville in northbound rush-hour traffic leaving Rhode Island's capital city.

"When did they say you can pick up your suit?" Carly asked as she perused her wedding to-do list in the passenger seat.

"Three or four days."

"I know, I know. You've got twenty of them hanging in your closet in New York. But wasn't it easier to buy a new one than go to New York between now and the wedding?"

"Yes, dear."

Carly shot him a victorious smile. "Since I plan on being right most of the time, you'll need to get used to saying that."

His scowl made her laugh. "We'll have to get down to the

287

city eventually and clean out my place before I put it on the market—not that there's much to clean out."

"After the honeymoon," she said, filled with delight and anticipation. "Ten days in Jamaica. I can't wait."

"Are you sure you don't mind leaving the morning after the wedding? We can push it back a day or two if you want to rest up."

She arched an eyebrow. "Rest up for what?"

"The honeymoon, of course. You'll need to be *very* well rested."

"I don't know what you've got in mind, but I plan to sleep and lie on the beach."

Full of mock outrage, he said, "That's not a honeymoon! That's a vacation."

Carly smiled. She loved pushing his buttons. After a few weeks back together, it was as if they'd never been apart. Everything between them was as comfortable and easy as it had ever been.

They tuned into the radio when the concert planned for Granville led the newscast at the top of the hour. "Local bands from all over Rhode Island will come together tonight in a show of support for tiny Granville, which has been rocked by the recent rape and murder of a fifteen-year-old high school student and the aggravated sexual assault of another teen earlier this year. Granville Mayor Bob Simon joins us in the studio. Mayor, the entire state has been riveted by the events in your town. How are your citizens holding up?"

"It's been a difficult year, there's no doubt about that. But the people of Granville are resilient. We'll get through this."

"Are the police any closer to naming a suspect?"

"I'm not at liberty to discuss the investigation. All I can say is local, state, and federal authorities are doing every-thing they can to catch the person who has been terrorizing our town as well as young people in other parts of the state."

"Your police chief, Michael Westbury, was briefly hospitalized. The chatter on local talk radio has been trending toward a loss of support for the chief's leadership. Are you confident in Chief Westbury's ability to lead the department during this difficult time?"

"The chief and his men and women are working around the clock to bring this investigation to a successful conclusion."

"But does he have your full support?"

"I'd like to see an arrest—and soon. That's all I'll say."

"*Goddamn him!*" Brian slapped his hand on the steering wheel. "That's just what my dad needs—some limp-dick politician twenty years younger than him taking a shot at him on the radio."

Carly reached for his hand. "Try not to let it bother you, Bri. Your dad doesn't listen to stuff like that."

"He's working himself to death, and people *still* have the nerve to say he's not doing enough? He's not a miracle worker, for Christ sakes. Don't they think he wants to get this guy as much as anyone? His own *son* is one of the victims."

Carly had heard the rumblings in town since Alicia's murder. People were frustrated by the lack of progress in the investigation and looking for someone to blame. Unfortunately, Chief Westbury was the most readily available target. "Hopefully it'll all be over soon," she said.

"I don't know how much more of this my dad can take. I'm afraid he's going to drop dead one of these days from the stress."

"He'll be fine. He won't let gossip distract him."

Carly's cell phone rang, and when she reached into her purse for it, she noticed a scrap of white paper tucked into her phone. Puzzled, she flipped open the phone, and the paper fluttered onto her lap. She gasped when she looked down to find the word "SOON" in bright red letters. "Oh my God," she whispered.

Brian looked over and startled, causing the car to swerve. A horn blared from the lane next to them. "Don't touch it," he said, his eyes darting back and forth between the note on Carly's lap and the interstate.

"How did he get a note into my purse?" she whispered.

"Who was it that called?"

Her hands shaking, Carly checked her phone to find the number unavailable. "I can't tell."

Brian's knuckles turned white from the grip he had on the steering wheel.

They both jolted when the phone rang again.

"Who is it?" Brian asked.

Carly glanced at the caller ID. "It's an out-of-state number." She took a deep breath before she answered the call. "Hello?"

"Carly! It's Mrs. Townsend. I was so delighted to receive the invitation to your wedding and to get your mother's note that you're talking again. I'm just thrilled for you and Brian."

"Thank you," Carly said, relieved. "I hope you'll be able to make it to the wedding."

"That's why I'm calling—to tell you I wouldn't miss it for the world. I booked my flight from Baltimore just this morning. Mr. Townsend is living in Phoenix now, so I don't think he'll make it."

The reminder that Michelle's parents had divorced a few years after the accident saddened Carly. Their marriage hadn't survived the loss of their only daughter. "Well, I can't wait to see you. It's been too long."

"Yes, honey," Mrs. Townsend said. "Yes, it has. Michelle would be delighted to know you're finally marrying Brian."

"I think so, too. You didn't call before, did you? A few minutes ago?"

"No, why?"

"I had another call that I missed."

"No, it wasn't me. Listen, I've got to run, but I'll see you very soon."

"Looking forward to it." Carly closed the phone and sat perfectly still with the note staring up at her.

"It wasn't her before?" Brian asked as he flipped open his own cell phone to call his father.

"No."

"Hang on, honey. We're almost there."

THEY MET Michael at a park-and-ride lot in the south end of town. When they pulled in, he got out of his car and approached the passenger side of the SUV.

Opening the door, he stared at the note for a long moment before he used tweezers to put it in an evidence bag. "You didn't touch it?" he asked Carly.

"No. It fell from my cell when I opened it."

"I'd like to also take your purse to be analyzed for prints. We'll do it as fast as we can." When Carly nodded in agreement, he slipped the small purse into a larger evidence bag.

"What about her phone?" Brian asked.

"That, too," Michael said, holding open another bag for Carly to drop the phone into. "Has your purse been unattended recently?"

"Not that I can think of, but my mind is racing right now."

Michael reached out to put his large hand over both of hers. "Take a breath, honey, and try to think. Were you in a restaurant and left it at the table to go to the restroom, or in a store—"

"I went to Miss Molly's this morning to get coffee," she said as she suddenly remembered. "I took money with me but left my purse at home."

"Where were you?" Michael asked his son.

"In the shower."

The statement hung over them.

"Jesus Christ," Brian muttered. "He was in the apartment while I was in the shower?"

Carly whimpered as she looked at Brian. "I didn't even think to lock the door because I was coming right back. What if he had hurt you?"

Brian rested his hand on her arm.

"Did you see anyone you knew between your place and Miss Molly's?" Michael asked.

Carly thought about it, began to shake her head to say no, but then froze.

"What?" Brian asked. "Who did you see?"

"I saw . . . I saw Luke. He had just left Miss Molly's."

Michael's mouth tightened with tension as he exchanged glances with his son.

"It's not him!" Carly cried. "I *know* it isn't!"

"Carly, I know you don't *want* it to be him," Michael said. "Hell, I don't, either."

Brian explained to his father about the gut feelings Carly had relied upon during her years of silence. "She thinks if she had something to fear from him, she'd know it."

"It's not him," Carly said again.

"We might have another possibility. Did either of you know a kid named Randy Lowell in school? He was in Sam's class."

"I knew him," Brian said. "But just to say hi to."

"I don't remember him," Carly said.

"We were so sure this was about you, Carly, that we never

really looked at Sam's class. I could kick myself for being so stupid. If it turns out to be him..."

"What've you got so far?" Brian asked.

Michael brought them up to speed on the DUI arrest and the warrant. "They caught him late morning, so he could've been in Granville earlier and put the note in your purse. We spent most of the day questioning him, and when I left to come here, Matt and Nate were trying to put together a timeline of his whereabouts for the last few years. Lowell claims he just moved back to Rhode Island in April."

"If that's true, he wasn't the one who attacked Tanya Lewis in January," Brian said.

"I know," Michael said, sounding dejected. "He claims he was in Missouri and moved back here to be closer to his parents. However, he never registered as a sex offender, and he says the whole thing with the parole violation was a misunderstanding." Michael frowned as he added, "The other thing that's bugging me is he doesn't fit the physical description the girls have provided. He's tall, but not unusually tall like they all said."

"Still," Brian said, "it could be a break. There's a tie to all of us going back to high school and a record of similar crimes."

"Right," Michael said. "But there're still way too many ifs to say for sure that it's him. So we have to operate under the assumption that our guy is still out there. Until this is over, you two are together every minute of every day, you got me? No more trips to Miss Molly's or anywhere else alone. He's much less likely to go after you if Brian is with you."

Carly nodded. "I know." She took another deep breath in an attempt to calm her frazzled nerves.

"He's waiting for his chance, so you can't give him any opportunity," Michael added. "And make sure you always have your phone with you, son. You still have the pepper spray, right, Carly?"

She patted the pocket of her skirt. "With me every minute."

"We need about thirty minutes at your place to work up the door—not that we'll find anything," Michael said. "Can I borrow your key?"

Brian gave him his. "God, Dad, how much longer are we supposed to live this way?"

The strain showed on Michael's face. "I hope not much longer." He gestured to the evidence bags on the floor. "He's getting more brazen, which is a sign that he thinks he's invincible. He'll screw up, and when he does, we'll be waiting."

"Did you hear the stuff on the radio earlier?" Brian asked.

Michael shrugged with indifference. "The mayor's a putz. I've been ignoring his calls, so he's pissed with me. He doesn't bother me."

"You can't let it get to you," Carly said, resting her hand on Michael's arm. "You have to think about your health."

Michael smiled and squeezed her hand. "Don't worry about me. I need to get back to town. This concert was a nice idea, but it's causing us some major security and traffic headaches. Oh, I talked to Mom while I was waiting for you. She said to tell you she'll get a ride into town with Steve and Carol, and she'll meet you there."

"Okay," Brian said.

"You two be careful, you hear?"

"We will," Brian assured him. "I won't let Carly out of my sight."

"Good. I'll try to come by the common tonight to find you all if I can break loose for a bit." Michael picked up the three plastic bags and left them with a wave.

Brian and Carly watched him get into his car and drive away.

"I can't believe he was in our apartment," she said. "If anything had happened to you . . . What was I *thinking* leaving the door unlocked?"

"Hey." He brought her into his arms. "Nothing's going to happen to me—or you. I won't let it."

She rested her head on his shoulder. "I've been so focused on the wedding that I've let myself be lulled into a false sense of security. I guess I thought if I didn't think about him, he might go away."

Brian pressed his lips to her forehead. "There might be a way to bring this whole thing to a quick end."

She lifted her head to look at him. A muscle in his cheek pulsed with tension. "What do you mean?"

"Remember how they wanted to set something up with you as bait?"

She nodded. "You wouldn't hear of it. Have you changed your mind?"

"Not really. But I'm starting to realize this could go on indefinitely, and that's no way for either of us to live."

"So what're you saying?"

"I might be willing to hear what they have in mind—if you're still up for it, that is."

"I'd be up for anything that would help catch this guy."

"Even if it meant putting yourself in danger? Real danger, Carly."

She swallowed hard. "I'd do it, if for no other reason than to get the guy who killed Sam and the others. He all but ruined our lives, Brian. I want him to pay for what he took from us and so many other people."

"Tomorrow we'll talk to my dad and Agent Barclay. I'll need to be 100 percent certain they've thought of every possible scenario before I agree to it."

"I'll leave it up to you. You'll know better than me if it can be done or not."

He started the car. "I can't believe I'm even considering this."

"You were right when you said this is no way for us to live. If we can do something to end it before he hurts someone else, why wouldn't we?"

"Because if something went wrong, you could be raped . . . or worse. Dangling the woman he loves in front of a psychopath is not something a man does lightly."

"Let's put it out of our minds for tonight and try to enjoy the concert. Can you do that?"

He snorted. "Um, yeah. Sure. No problem."

Carly laughed and leaned over to kiss his cheek.

CHAPTER 27

*B*y the time Brian and Carly pulled onto Main Street, the Granville town common had been taken over by concert preparations. A makeshift stage had been erected at one end. Behind it, a huge generator truck provided power to the stage and several elaborate light towers. In front of the stage, a cluster of curious teens watched the setup. On the grass, families had claimed their spots with plaid blankets and stadium chairs.

Brian found a parking space on Main Street, six blocks past Carson's. "Looks like we got back just in time."

Carly looked around with amazement at the hubbub of activity in the usually tranquil downtown. "And the concert doesn't even start for an hour. I can see what your dad was saying about traffic and security."

Carrying the bags from their Providence shopping trip, they walked toward the center of town.

At the apartment, the police were just finishing their work. One of the detectives returned Brian's key. "We'll be out of your way in just a minute."

Carly and Brian waited on her deck until the police

cleared the scene a few minutes later. After they were gone, Carly stepped into the home that had been her sanctuary for so many years. That he had been in here, that he had invaded this place . . . She shuddered.

Brian must have sensed how she was feeling. He crossed the room, flipped the deadbolt on the door, and put his arms around her. "Don't let him in, honey. Don't let him touch us."

"I hate that he was here," she whispered. "In our home."

"He's not here now. It's just us." Brian dipped his head and pressed his lips to hers. He skimmed his tongue over her bottom lip, trying to cajole her into participating. "Kiss me, Carly. Let me help you forget."

She looped her arms around his neck and leaned into him.

He combed his fingers into her curls and tilted her face to receive a deep, passionate kiss.

Carly felt all her worries and fears slip away, allowing her to concentrate on the rush of feelings he'd always aroused in her. It took only the simplest of kisses, the barest of caresses, and she was his—completely and totally his. Only his. She gasped when he scooped her up to carry her to the bedroom. On the way, she rested her head on his shoulder.

He put her down next to the bed and kissed her neck as he unbuttoned her sleeveless blouse. "Sometimes," he whispered, "I still can't believe I can hold you and kiss you and make love with you anytime I want to."

His soft words accompanied by the feel of his lips on her sensitized skin made Carly's legs tremble with desire. When she reached for the button on his shorts, he stopped her.

"But—"

He silenced her with a kiss.

Carly didn't protest when she felt her bra slip away or when her skirt slid down over her legs.

He was still fully dressed when he urged her onto the bed and came down on top of her.

She put her arms around him.

Kissing her softly, he cradled her face with his hands.

Carly arched into him, wanting more. But he was apparently in no hurry. She ran her hands over his back and under his shirt. Needing to feel his skin against hers, she worked his shirt up.

He pulled away from her long enough to tug it over his head.

"Brian . . ."

"What, baby?" His lips made a path to her breasts.

"Do you think you'll still want me this much when we're married ten years?"

His tongue slid across her nipple. "I've wanted you this much since I was old enough to know what want was. I'll always want you. Always." He moved on to her other breast. "I love you so much. So very, very much."

Her heart raced with joy and relief and hope. There was so much to hope for. She had forgotten what it felt like to have hope during all the long years they'd spent apart. "Brian," she gasped as he made her crazy with what he was doing to her breasts.

"Tell me."

She tugged on his shorts. "I want you."

"Soon."

"Now."

He raised his head and found her eyes in the twilight.

"Please?"

His face softened into a smile. "Will you always know just how to get what you want from me?"

"I hope so," she said, running her fingers through his hair.

He got rid of his shorts and brought her to the edge of the bed. "How about another first?"

"There can't still be more! You're making this stuff up."

Laughing softly, he bent to lay a trail of kisses along her inner thigh.

"Brian. . ."

"Shh," he said, blowing lightly on the hair that covered her. He urged her legs further apart and knelt before her.

"What're you. . . *Oh my God*." Carly's mind went blank with shock as he parted her with his fingers and licked her *there*. Almost as if they had a mind of their own, her hips lifted into the intimate caress.

He slid two fingers into her and focused on the spot that pulsed with desire, drawing it into his mouth and sucking hard.

Carly came suddenly and explosively, crying out from the sensations that rocked her.

Brian stayed with her until the last spasm had passed. Standing, he hooked his arms under her legs and entered her.

The position gave him complete control, so she closed her eyes and gave herself over to the pleasure.

"Good?" he asked.

Carly could barely breathe let alone talk. "So good," she managed to say.

He kept up a steady pace for several minutes before he dipped his head and rolled her nipple between his teeth, making her come again with a cry that took them both by surprise.

"*Carly*," he groaned, pushing hard against her one last time before he released her legs and collapsed on top of her.

She held him close, sifting her fingers through his hair over and over again.

"Scoot up," he whispered.

They moved into a more comfortable position on the bed.

He tightened his arms around her and smoothed his foot down over her calf.

"That was amazing. Thank you."

"For what?"

"For taking care of me, for knowing I was letting him invade our home, and for not letting that happen." She felt her face heat with embarrassment. "And for showing me all the stuff we'd missed out on."

He brushed the hair back off her face. "I've never been happier in my life than I've been with you these last few weeks, Carly. Even the stuff with Zoë . . . It's been so much more than I've had since we were together before. And that we can make love *in a bed*, any time we want, without having to worry about getting caught. If this was all I ever had, if *you* were all I ever had, it would be enough."

"How did I ever stand to be without you for so long?"

"You'll never be without me again. I promise you that."

As the sheer over the bedroom window fluttered in the soft summer breeze, they listened to the noise coming from the street below. One of the bands ran a sound check, and the music echoed through the room.

"Imagine you're a Main Street resident who was planning to sleep tonight," Carly said.

"You're shit out of luck."

"We should get going."

"Do we have to?"

Surprised, she looked up at him. "You don't want to?"

"I'd much rather stay here with you and listen to it." He ran a hand up to cup her breast, telling her what else he had in mind.

Amazed to realize she already wanted him again, she said, "I'd have to call my mom and tell her we aren't coming."

"Is, um, will Zoë be there?"

Touched by the wistful tone of his voice, she caressed his face. "I think so. Cate and Tom aren't letting her run around with her friends the way she used to."

"I suppose we can go."

"Because Zoë will be there?" Carly asked, raising an eyebrow.

He replied with a sheepish grin. "Maybe. Is that all right?"

"Sure it is."

"How about a shower?"

"Together?"

"Why not?"

"I've never done that."

He brushed a light kiss over her lips. "No, I don't suppose you have."

"Have you?"

"Never with anyone I love. Come on." He tugged her out of bed and led her into the bathroom to turn on the shower.

Carly stepped in after him and was hit with a sudden wave of shyness, which was odd considering the intimacy they had shared only minutes earlier.

Turning to her, he moved to the side to share the water with her. "I used to wonder all the time why we didn't shower together in the hotel in Michigan."

"We never thought of it."

"There were so many things we didn't know then."

"I still don't know most of them." She once again felt a twinge of embarrassment as he watched the water sluice over her breasts with hot, hungry eyes.

"Oh, you will." He held her long hair under the water. "Ten days in Jamaica should get you all caught up."

"I'm concerned about what you've got planned for this honeymoon."

His grin lit up his face. "Be very afraid." He reached around her, lifted her, and pressed her against the wall.

She gasped from the chill of the tile against her back. "What're you doing?"

"Making sure you'll remember the first shower we ever took together."

"*Oh,*" she moaned, clutching his broad shoulders. "*Ohhhh.*"

THE FIRST BAND was well into its set by the time Brian and Carly found her family and his mother clustered together on four blankets. They were greeted with hugs, kisses, and teasing questions about why they were so late.

"We were, ah, busy," Carly said, grateful for the dark so her sisters wouldn't see her face turn bright red.

"Busy," Caren said with a wistful grin. "Remember when we had time to be 'busy,' Neil?"

Her husband, who had Justin in one arm and Julia in the other, laughed. "Busy got us this armload of trouble."

Zoë dashed across the blankets to hug and kiss Carly.

Brian seemed startled when he received the same effusive greeting—as if Zoë had known him all her life.

"I was wondering when you guys were going to get here. Did you bring the cookies?"

Carly smiled and produced a large container. "Yes, ma'am. As requested."

"Nice," Zoë said.

"Did you meet my mom?" Brian asked.

"Sure did." Zoë turned to Mary Ann, who seemed to be having trouble taking her eyes off the girl. "I think I remember now where I've met you before. Did you ever substitute at Granville Elementary?"

"Yes," Mary Ann said. "For years."

Zoë snapped her fingers. "That's it! I think I had you!"

"Oh," Mary Ann stammered.

Brian slipped his hand around his mother's.

"I was well behaved," Zoë added. "So you probably don't remember me."

Mary Ann laughed.

"Mom!" Zoë called. "Can I go to that blanket right over there to see Gretchen?"

"Right there and nowhere else," Cate said.

Zoë bolted.

Brian folded his mother into a hug. "Isn't she something?"

"She's amazing," Mary Ann agreed. "And I can see why you recognized her right away. It's like looking at Carly when she was that age." Mary Ann reached out to include Carly in their embrace. "I can't believe she was in a class of mine, and I had no idea who she was."

"I'm so sorry," Carly said. "The words sound so insignificant, but I'm truly sorry."

"It was a terrible time." Mary Ann kissed Carly's cheek. "For everyone. That's all that ever needs to be said."

Realizing Mary Ann had found a way to forgive her made Carly weak with relief as she hugged her future mother-in-law.

Brian kept an arm around both of them as they listened to the music. After a while, Carly's niece Lilly wandered over and climbed into her aunt's lap. Julia and Justin were right behind her, and when Carly reached capacity, they overflowed onto Brian's lap.

He looked over at Carly, and the delight on his face stopped her heart. With a squeeze of affection for the girls, Carly said a silent thank you to her nieces and nephew for accepting Brian into their family.

Michael took one look at Nathan Barclay's frustrated face and knew their latest lead had vaporized. "It's not him."

Nathan shook his head. "He produced bank statements that prove he made a deposit in Jefferson City on the same day Tanya Lewis was attacked. There was an ATM withdrawal in New York City on the day Alicia Perry disappeared."

"Tanya couldn't pick him out of a photo lineup, either."

Nathan punched the wall. "We just *cannot* catch a fucking break on this one."

"I've started sifting through Sam's class. I can't believe I didn't think to do that sooner. I was just so sure this was about Carly and Brian."

"Don't beat yourself up, Mike. Nothing about this case has been routine."

"What's happening with Lowell?"

"His parents got him a lawyer, and Woonsocket is sorting out the details with the warrant."

"I wanted it to be him," Michael said, rubbing at the stubble on his jaw. "I *need* to know who took my son from me and why." He glanced at the FBI agent who had become his friend. "I think I could kill whoever it is without blinking an eye. Does that make me a bad cop?"

"No. It makes you a father. Anyone who'd been through what you have would feel the same way."

Michael expelled a deep, rattling breath.

Nate squeezed his shoulder. "You look beat, man. You ought to go home and get some sleep."

"Not until I've run a check on every male member of Sam's class."

"How about I take half the alphabet?"

With a grateful smile, Michael handed him a yearbook. "Thanks."

IN BETWEEN BANDS, Alicia Perry's father was called up to the stage. The crowd fell silent as they waited for him to get himself together.

"I want to thank you all for the overwhelming love and support you've shown my family over these last few difficult weeks. Alicia was a special girl, and we were blessed to have had fifteen years with her. When you think of Alicia, don't remember how she died. Remember how she lived—with enthusiasm and humor and delight in everything she did. And if you have a young person in your life, give them an extra hug tonight." His voice broke. "You never know when it'll be the last time. Thank you all again for reminding us why we chose to raise our family in Granville."

Carly looked over to find Zoë had returned to her family's blanket. Her face was pressed against Tom's chest, and her shoulders shook with sobs.

Brian watched intently as another man cared for his daughter.

Carly squeezed his hand.

He forced a smile for her, but she could feel the struggle that gripped him.

"It'll take some time," he said softly.

She nodded, knowing exactly what he meant. Reclining against his chest, she tried to clear her mind and enjoy the rest of the concert. When the final band had completed its set, a lone guitarist took the stage and sang Bruce Springsteen's "My Hometown."

The song gave Carly chills. She realized that while they could live anywhere in the state and be close enough for Brian to commute to Providence, she wanted to stay in Granville and raise her children in the same small-town environment she and Brian had grown up in. Even though she had the freedom now to go anywhere she wanted, there was nowhere else she wanted to be. This was *their* hometown. It was where they belonged—and it was where their daughter lived, too. Caren had mentioned a house for sale on her street. Tomorrow Carly would ask Brian if they could go take a look.

By the time the song ended, the crowd was on its feet applauding. Floodlights lit up the common as people gathered their belongings and began walking home or to their cars.

Carly was saying goodnight to her parents when Matt Collins joined them.

"Hey, Matt." Mary Ann kissed his cheek. "Did you get to hear any of the concert?"

"Some," he said. "It's been a busy night."

"Take these cookies back to the station," Carly said, handing him a paper plate.

"Thanks. The guys will appreciate that." He turned to Brian. "Your dad asked me to bring you and Carly to meet him."

"Where?" Brian asked.

"At the place where Randy Lowell had been hiding out. The chief wants to see if you can ID any of the items we found. He thinks it's possible some of it was taken from your place earlier today."

"So you've decided it's him?" Brian asked.

Matt glowed with excitement as he nodded. "We've got him nailed."

"I didn't notice anything missing from the apartment," Carly said.

"We didn't exactly look, though," Brian said with a meaningful glance at Carly.

"Do you mind coming?" Matt asked. "It shouldn't take long."

"No problem. We're happy to help if we can." Brian put his arm around Carly. "Let's go."

They said good night to the others and followed Matt to his squad car, which was double-parked on Main Street. He held the back door for them and then used his flashing lights to get around the traffic leaving downtown.

Sitting close to Brian, Carly looked through the cage that separated the front seat from the back. Just as she realized there were no handles on the back doors, alarms began to go off in her gut. She vividly remembered what Chief Westbury had said when he gave her the pepper spray: if you feel like you're in danger, you probably are. She reached into the pocket of her shorts and wrapped her hand around the pepper spray she carried with her all the time. Her heart beat hard as she looked up at Brian.

He raised a questioning eyebrow that she could barely see in the dark.

She put her lips right up to his ear and said, "I don't like this."

His face twisted into a perplexed expression, and she knew he was wondering what she didn't like about being with a police officer he had known since he was a kid.

She shook her head and pointed to her stomach.

Brian cleared his throat. "So, Matt, where's this place you found?"

"Up by the Massachusetts border. A hunter called it in." When he looked back at them in the mirror, his eyes burned with excitement. "You wouldn't believe the stuff we found there."

Brian looked over at Carly, and she could see he no longer liked it, either.

"Matt, I want you to stop the car and let us out. I'll talk to my dad when he gets home, and we can go out there tomorrow."

"Sorry, Brian," Matt said, glancing in the mirror again. "I'm just following orders."

Brian clutched Carly's hand.

Looking at him, she pushed her free hand against the cell phone in his pocket.

He nodded, slowly withdrew the phone, put it on silent mode, and dialed 911. Then he jammed it into the space between the seats.

They drove for twenty tense minutes before Matt pulled onto a rutted dirt road.

The night was so dark Carly had been unable to follow the route they had taken.

At least a mile later, if not more, he parked in front of a cabin. In the dark, Carly couldn't see much, but she noticed right away there were no other cars nor were any lights on in the cabin.

"I wonder where they went," Matt said as he got out of the car and shut the door.

"*Fuck!*" Brian cried the moment they were alone. "No *fucking* way!" He retrieved the phone from between the seats. "This is Brian Westbury. Patch me into Chief Westbury. *Right now!*"

"I need your location, Mr. Westbury," the operator replied.

"Get my father on the line, *this minute.*"

Carly watched the cabin, saw a flicker of light in the darkness, and then nothing.

"I'm sorry, I can't reach Chief Westbury."

"Tell him this—are you listening?"

"Yes, sir."

"Tell him Brian called, the perp is Deputy Chief Collins, and he has Brian and Carly twenty minutes north of downtown by the Mass line—maybe even into Massachusetts. I'm calling from a cell phone, and I'm leaving the line open. Two lives depend on you getting this right. This is an emergency —treat it accordingly."

"Can you text your dad?" Carly asked.

"Not with the line open. I called 911 because I wanted to be sure the phone put out a signal."

"He's coming back," Carly cried.

Brian pushed the phone between the seats. "They'll follow the signal. They'll find us, honey."

Matt opened the back door and pointed his gun at them. "Let's go."

Brian pushed Carly behind him. "Matt, for God's sakes, what are you doing? My father is your good friend. How could you be the guy who killed my brother?"

"Get the fuck out of the car before I blow your head off. Believe me, it would give me great pleasure."

Brian took Carly's hand and got out of the car with her following right behind him.

Matt flipped the gun toward the cabin. "Move it."

As they walked the short distance across the gravel driveway, Carly felt a strange sense of calm come over her. Whatever was about to happen, she would withstand it as best she could. Staying alive—and keeping Brian alive—was all that mattered.

CHAPTER 28

*M*ichael arrived home about thirty minutes after the concert ended, ready to drop after yet another sixteen-hour day that had yielded nothing new or useful to the investigation. He couldn't keep up this pace for much longer. Even his usual end-of-the-day beer held no appeal tonight. All he cared about was his bed and six uninterrupted hours of sleep.

As he was untying his shoes at the kitchen table, Mary Ann came out from the bedroom. She squinted as her eyes adjusted to the light.

"Hey." He raised his cheek to receive her kiss. "Did I wake you?"

"No, I was waiting for you. Did you get everything taken care of with Brian and Carly?"

"Before the concert?"

"No, after. Matt said you were waiting for them."

"What do you mean?"

"He said you needed them for something to do with the case."

Michael looked up at her, confounded. "I have no idea what you're talking about. Tell me exactly what he said."

"Just that you'd found the place where Randy someone had been hiding out and you needed the kids to identify some things he'd taken from Carly's apartment. He said you wanted him to bring them there to meet you."

Michael stood, all his senses on full alert. "I have no idea what he's talking about. I never asked him—"

"Michael? What? What is it?"

The whole thing was so suddenly and painfully obvious that Michael wondered how he could've missed it—not a shred of evidence left behind, a tall, hulking man with big feet. *I buy my shoes at Gleason's.* On vacation and out of touch when Alicia Perry went missing. "Oh my God. It's Matt."

"No, Michael. No. It can't be."

Michael reached for his cell phone as it began to ring in concert with the home phone and the police radio he had left on the counter. The dispatcher relayed the message the 911 operator had received from Brian.

"He has them!" Mary Ann shrieked. *"He has my son!"*

MATT PUSHED them ahead of him into the cabin, which glowed with candlelight.

Carly took a step back.

Brian realized she was afraid of the fire and rested his hands on her shoulders to offer what comfort he could.

She stiffened when she saw the wall of photos devoted to her. "Oh," she gasped. "Oh God."

"Jesus," Brian whispered on a long exhale.

"Give me your cell phones," Matt said.

"We didn't bring them with us tonight because we

wouldn't have been able to hear them over the music," she said.

Brian was impressed by the calm tenor of her voice when she had every reason to be hysterical.

Matt tucked the gun under his arm and quickly frisked Carly to make sure she wasn't lying about the phone.

Watching his hands move over Carly's body was more than Brian could bear. He eyed the gun, trying to gauge whether he had a prayer of wrestling it away from Matt. But though Matt was ten years older than Brian, he was taller by four inches and outweighed him by at least twenty pounds. If Brian was going to lunge for the gun, he'd better be damned sure he would come away with it. The alternative was unimaginable.

When Matt was satisfied Carly didn't have her phone, he ordered her to sit on the big brass bed.

Ropes were attached to elaborate head- and footboards, and Brian felt his mouth go dry with fear when he imagined Carly tied to the bed at the mercy of a madman.

Matt frisked Brian next, looking for his phone. When he didn't find it, he pushed Brian into a wooden chair and tied his ankles to the legs of the chair.

As Matt tied him, Brian kept his eyes on Carly, willing her to stay strong no matter what. He winced when Matt pulled his arms straight back and tightened a rope around his wrists. "Why are you doing this? My dad thinks of you as one of his closest friends."

"Your *dad* is an idiot who would've lost that lofty job of his years ago without me. I've spent my whole career making him look good."

"He would never deny that."

Matt snorted with disgust. "So then why is he the chief and I'm just a peon?"

"You would've been the next chief. You know that."

"He'll never retire. They'll have to cart him out of there in a pine box. By then I'll be too old to give a shit."

"Why did you kill Sam and the others?"

Matt's smile was affable, almost friendly. "I never intended to kill him. I just wanted to make one of you perfect Westbury boys look bad. I was so sick and tired of listening to your father go on and on about how great the two of you were. It was enough to make me puke. Brian this, Sam that. Who the fuck cares?"

"You were in the road," Brian said. "I saw you."

"I guess you were a better driver than your brother. I wanted one of you to crash the car so your old man would shut the fuck up about the two of you. The car bursting into flames with all those jocks and cheerleaders inside was a bonus. I was only sorry the golden boy and his whore weren't with them."

Carly whimpered.

The blast of rage had Brian wishing he could lash out. He had no doubt he could beat this man to death if he hadn't been tied to a fucking chair.

Forcing himself to think like a prosecutor, Brian pressed on, knowing his father would need the answers. "Why every five years?"

"People forget a lot in five years' time. I have to give your old man credit, though. He figured out the pattern."

"I guess he's not as much of an idiot as you give him credit for being."

Matt took a fistful of Brian's hair and pulled hard. "Stay quiet or I'll gag you, got me?"

Brian nodded and had to bite back a scream when Matt turned and approached Carly. She inched back on the bed.

Matt tugged roughly on her arm. "Get up."

"If it's Chief Westbury you hate so much, then what do you want with me?" she asked.

Matt's eyes glittered, and Brian realized he was staring at true evil. The shock of it was almost debilitating.

"What do you *think* I want with you?" He ran his hands over Carly's bare arms and cupped her breasts. "Take off your clothes."

"No!" Brian cried.

"*Shut the fuck up!* The only reason you're still alive is so you can watch your whore get it on with a real man. *So shut up!*" He turned back to Carly. "I said to take off your clothes, and hurry up about it, or I'll tie you to the bed and cut them off like I did with the others. Is that how you want it?"

Carly shook her head and reached for the top button to her blouse.

"When was the last time you did him?" Matt asked, nodding at Brian.

"Earlier tonight."

"How did you do it? Was he on top or were you? I know you like to be on top. I used to watch you under the willow."

Brian strained against the rope, which cut into his wrists. It was tied so tight, there was no way he could free himself. As he watched Carly's hands shake as she unbuttoned her blouse, Brian wished Matt had shot him. He'd rather be dead than have to watch this.

"He was on top," she said.

"Did you do it just once?"

"Twice. The second time in the shower."

He grabbed her hair and pulled hard to tip her face up. "You're as much of a whore as you always were, aren't you?"

"I'm not a whore. He's the only man I've ever made love with."

"He *was* the only man. Tonight you're finally going to have a *real* man." Kneading her bottom with a bruising grip, he lifted her against his enormous erection.

Carly swallowed hard. "Why are you doing this? What do you have against me?"

"You remind me of someone I used to know. A long time ago."

"Who was she?"

That's the way, Carly, Brian thought. *Keep him talking.*

"Someone just like you—a pretty cheerleader who went around acting like her shit didn't stink and giving it up to a jock in the back of his daddy's car."

"You loved her," Carly said.

"*I hated her.* She was the first person I ever killed. Melissa Spellman back in Milwaukee. Funny how she became a whore when she figured out I'd kill her if she didn't give me what I wanted. She looked just like you—right down to the curls. It was a great pleasure to take what I wanted from her and then kill her."

"Why did you kill Alicia?"

"Just like Melissa and that girl in Pawtucket, she didn't respect me, so I didn't have any choice. The others respected me, so I let them live."

All Brian could think about as he watched Matt Collins's hands roam all over Carly was *where the fuck are the cops?*

Matt squeezed her breasts. Hard.

Tears filled Carly's eyes. "Why do you have to hurt me? I'm not fighting you or disrespecting you."

"You will. They all do eventually."

"Is that why you became a police officer? For the respect?"

Matt seemed startled by her insight. "That's exactly why. You'd be surprised how people fall into line when it's a cop telling them what to do." He unbuttoned his white uniform shirt and pulled it loose from his pants. After putting his service revolver and handcuffs on the bedside table, Matt unbuckled his pants. He caught Carly staring at his rampant erection. "Feel it."

She reached out to put her hand on him.

"How does that measure up to the jock over there?"

"It's impressive." Her voice was dull and impassive. "I'm sure you've left many women well satisfied."

"A few." He started to ease the top off her shoulders.

Carly stiffened. "Don't. Please."

Tears blinded Brian. *Where the fuck are the cops?*

Matt stared at her breasts. "Nice, perky tits. Bigger than I remember from the willow, but I like them this way. Melissa had great big tits she let that asshole jock suck on for hours." Matt licked his lips in anticipation.

She finally looked over at Brian, and the pleading in her eyes tore at his soul.

"Matt!" Brian cried. "They're going to find us. Why don't you just stop this and get the hell out of here before you get caught?"

Matt turned eyes filled with hate toward Brian. "They won't catch me. They're too fucking stupid to realize only someone on the inside would know how to commit the perfect crime—over and over and over again. They've got nothing on me." With his eyes still fixed on Brian, Matt gripped Carly's arms.

When she cried out in pain, Brian had no choice but to look away.

Matt's laughter echoed through the small room. "Look at the golden boy now. The great and powerful prosecutor can't even take care of his own fiancée. Must be a terrible disappointment to find out that despite what your asshole father thinks of you, you're as human as the next guy, huh?"

As Brian fought against the ropes, a warm trickle of blood pooled in the palm of his hand.

"How do you like it?" Carly asked.

Brian's head whipped up to find her focused on Matt, running her finger through his thick chest hair. The only sign of the tension that must have been coursing through her was her other hand, which was curled into a fist behind her back. His heart racing, he strained for a better look at her hand. *Holy shit! She's got the pepper spray!*

"Do you like to be on the bottom or the top?" she asked Matt.

"The bottom," Matt said, all but panting for her.

"Then get on the bed."

Oh God. Carly! Do it now! Spray him! Brian struggled fiercely against the ropes and almost passed out from the pain of them ripping into his bloody wrists.

With her top hanging open, Carly crawled onto the bed and straddled Matt.

His eyes lit up with unrestrained lust. "You're not what I expected," he rasped.

"I'm a whore," she said in a low, throaty voice. "Isn't that what you said?"

Good, baby. That's good. Distract him.

Matt reached up to cup her breasts, and Brian fought back the urge to howl. "All you cheerleader types are whores. There's not one of you who's different."

"Then why are you surprised I want it as much as you do?" she asked, positioning a hand on either side of his head.

"What about him?" Matt asked.

"Don't worry about him. I'll take care of him."

"I don't want to have to kill you, Missy."

Brian almost stopped breathing.

Matt's cheeks were wet with tears as he combed his fingers through Carly's long hair. "I want you to love me. *Why can't you love me?* Why do you have to give yourself to someone who doesn't care about you? He only wants your body." He pulled at the Carly's shorts. "Take them off so I can make love to you. Let me love you, Missy."

Carly brought her hands back to do as he asked.

In the next instant, Matt let out a wild shriek.

Carly leaped off the bed and grabbed Matt's handcuffs, her hands shaking wildly as she secured one end to his wrist and the other around the brass bedpost.

With his free hand, Matt clawed at his eyes. "*You fucking whore!*"

Glancing over her shoulder to make sure Matt wasn't going anywhere, Carly dashed to Brian, knelt before him, and went to work on the knots at his ankles. Her hands were trembling so hard that she was all thumbs.

"*Hurry*, honey."

"I'm *trying*," she cried, "but they're so tight!" She looked around the cabin in desperate need of something to cut the ropes. "I don't know if I can do it."

Matt's screams faded into sobs.

A burst of adrenaline made Brian's heart pound so hard he was certain it would explode.

Carly grabbed a candle and rushed to a dark corner of the cabin. "There's a kitchen over here!"

He heard her rattling around before she came running back, carrying a butcher knife.

She put down the candle, quickly cut his legs loose, and then scooted behind him. "Oh, Bri. Oh, God, look at your arms!"

"I'm fine." He grabbed her hand. "Let's get the hell out of here."

"*You fucking whore!*" Matt screamed, the handcuffs clanking against the brass headboard. "*Just like all the others!*" He dissolved into tears. "Just like all the others."

Brian and Carly dashed into the darkness.

She screamed when strong arms embraced her.

"It's okay," Nathan Barclay said, holding her tight against him. "The place is surrounded by SWAT. You're safe."

"Brian needs medical care. His wrists are bleeding."

"What I need first is this." Brian reached for her. "You saved our lives, Carly. You were so incredible in there. So incredibly brave."

Carly clung to him and finally fell apart.

They stood like that for a long time, both trying to absorb that their long nightmare was over. The monster had been caught, Sam's name would be cleared, and there was nothing —and no one—left to fear.

"Where's my dad?" Brian asked Nate.

"He was right here a second ago." Nate turned on a large flashlight and shined it at the cabin.

Michael stood in the doorway, his back to them.

Nate bolted toward the cabin. "Mike! Wait! *Don't!*"

A gunshot pierced the night.

CHAPTER 29

*C*arly rested her head on Brian's shoulder.

"Do you think it's over for now?" He ran a damp paper towel over her forehead. "We can take a later flight if you don't feel up to going."

"That should be it for today," she said, weak and depleted after a vicious bout of vomiting.

"How long did you say this went on with Zoë?"

"Three full months."

"You've got to be kidding."

"I wish I was."

"*I feel so bad,*" he groaned. "I wish there was something I could do for you."

"Just hold me, Bri. That's what I need."

He tightened his arm around her and ran his other thumb over her sparkling new wedding ring. "What you need is ten days in Jamaica."

"Are we really married or was yesterday a dream?"

"Married, pregnant, the whole nine yards."

She reached for his hand to study his new—plain white gold—ring. "It's a dream come true."

"Even the vomiting?" he asked with a chuckle.

Running her fingers gently over the bandage on his wrist, she said, "I'd rather be sick for ninety straight days than spend one more minute of my life wishing for all the things I have now."

He brushed his lips over her curls.

"I meant to tell you," she said. "It was nice of you to apologize to Luke and invite him to the wedding."

Brian shrugged. "When I'm wrong, I say so. He was a good friend to you when I wasn't here."

"Yes, he was."

The TV in the gate area was tuned to one of the network news programs, which had run nonstop coverage of the events in Granville over the last week. Carly and Brian watched, transfixed, as a broken-looking Matt Collins was led into his arraignment wearing an orange jumpsuit, a bulletproof vest, leg chains, and handcuffs.

Eventually, they would have to testify against him. But the trial was months away, and they had agreed not to spend their time thinking about him or the realization that the only reason he had told them everything he did was because he'd planned to kill them and skip town.

"I look at him, even all these days later, and I still can't believe it," Brian said, his eyes fixed on the television. "That my brother is dead because of him."

"I wonder if your dad will ever be able to get past it."

"He was telling me how Matt went out of his way during the investigation to 'discover' things about the perp that made them all sick—like his need for respect from his victims, for one thing. With hindsight, Dad can see he was showing off—he wanted them to know why he killed some of them and let the others live. He wanted to be sure they knew he did that carjacking, too."

Carly shuddered. She had trembled for three full days

after the encounter with Matt. When she thought about what those other poor girls had withstood at his hands . . . Well, it was better not to think about it, because when she did, the trembling returned.

"It's a bitter pill for Dad to swallow, that's for sure. All those years he spent working with and confiding in a psychopath. Oh, look, there he is now."

Michael appeared on the courthouse steps, still wearing a sling over his left arm.

The reporters chased him down, and he stopped to answer a few of their questions.

Carly winced when she saw the chief's face pinched with pain that she knew was both physical and emotional. "I still can't believe I didn't do something with Matt's gun when I had the chance," she said.

"Are you *serious*? You were like freaking Wonder Woman in there. Don't obsess about the gun, honey. He got off a lucky shot, considering he was still blinded by the pepper spray and fired erratically. We're lucky he didn't take Dad's head off."

"I just keep seeing it over and over again, the blood on your dad's back . . ." She shook her head to clear her mind of yet another image that would haunt her forever. "All I could think about in that moment was what am I going to do if we got through this nightmare only to lose him?"

"Fortunately, we don't have to think about any of it for a while. We can focus on each other, our baby, our new house, my new job."

"Yes, you're right." Carly smiled with contentment. "I don't know if I've mentioned recently that Carly Westbury loves Brian Westbury."

"And you said it wouldn't roll off the tongue as easily as the earlier version. I have to say I disagree."

She laughed, and when she looked up, an older heavyset

woman sitting across from them smiled at her. The woman wore a bright red Hawaiian shirt.

"You two are so cute," she said. "You *have* to be newlyweds."

Carly cringed as she lifted her head off Brian's shoulder. "Are we that obvious?"

The woman clapped her hands with delight. "I knew it! Tell me everything. How did you meet?"

"We, um, we went to high school together," Brian said.

"Oh, that's so wonderful, and now here you are, back together and married." She nudged her husband, who pretended to be bored by the whole thing. "Isn't that something, Lou?"

He grunted in agreement.

"Let me guess: You met up again at a reunion, and all the old sparks were still there. Am I right?"

Carly smiled as she looked up at her handsome husband. "Yes," she said. "That's exactly how it happened."

HAVE you read Marie's Fatal Series yet? If not, turn the page for a sneak peek at book 1, *Fatal Affair*...

FATAL AFFAIR

CHAPTER ONE

The smell hit him first.

"Ugh, what the hell is that?" Nick Cappuano dropped his keys into his coat pocket and stepped into the spacious, well-appointed Watergate apartment that his boss, Senator John O'Connor, had inherited from his father.

"Senator!" Nick tried to identify the foul metallic odor.

Making his way through the living room, he noticed parts and pieces of the suit John wore yesterday strewn over sofas and chairs, laying a path to the bedroom. He had called the night before to check in with Nick after a dinner meeting with Virginia's Democratic Party leadership, and said he was on his way home. Nick had reminded his thirty-six-year-old boss to set his alarm.

"Senator?" John hated when Nick called him that when they were alone, but Nick insisted the people in John's life afford him the respect of his title.

The odd stench permeating the apartment caused a tingle of anxiety to register on the back of Nick's neck. "John?"

He stepped into the bedroom and gasped. Drenched in blood, John sat up in bed, his eyes open but vacant. A knife spiked through his neck held him in place against the head-board. His hands rested in a pool of blood in his lap.

Gagging, the last thing Nick noticed before he bolted to the bathroom to vomit was that something was hanging out of John's mouth.

Once the violent retching finally stopped, Nick stood up on shaky legs, wiped his mouth with the back of his hand, and rested against the vanity, waiting to see if there would be more. His cell phone rang. When he didn't take the call, his pager vibrated. Nick couldn't find the wherewithal to answer, to say the words that would change everything. *The senator is dead. John's been murdered.* He wanted to go back to when he was still in his car, fuming and under the assumption that his biggest problem that day would be what to do about the man-child he worked for who had once again slept through his alarm.

Thoughts of John, dating back to their first meeting in a history class at Harvard freshman year, flashed through Nick's mind, hundreds of snippets spanning a nearly twenty-year friendship. As if to convince himself that his eyes had not deceived him, he leaned forward to glance into the bedroom, wincing at the sight of his best friend—the brother of his heart—stabbed through the neck and covered with blood.

Nick's eyes burned with tears, but he refused to give in to them. Not now. Later maybe, but not now. His phone rang again. This time he reached for it and saw it was Christina, his deputy chief of staff, but didn't take the call. Instead, he dialed 911.

Taking a deep breath to calm his racing heart and making a supreme effort to keep the hysteria out of his voice, he said, "I need to report a murder." He gave the address and stumbled into the living room to wait for the police, all the while trying to get his head around the image of his dead friend, a visual he already knew would haunt him forever.

Twenty long minutes later, two officers arrived, took a quick look in the bedroom and radioed for backup. Nick was certain neither of them recognized the victim.

He felt as if he was being sucked into a riptide, pulled further and further from the safety of shore, until drawing a breath became a laborious effort. He told the cops exactly what happened—his boss failed to show up for work, he came looking for him and found him dead.

"Your boss's name?"

"United States Senator John O'Connor." Nick watched the two young officers go pale in the instant before they made a second more urgent call for backup.

"Another scandal at the Watergate," Nick heard one of them mutter.

His cell phone rang yet again. This time he reached for it.

"Yeah," he said softly.

"Nick!" Christina cried. "Where the *hell* are you guys? Trevor's having a heart attack!" She referred to their communications director who had back-to-back interviews scheduled for the senator that morning.

"He's dead, Chris."

"Who's dead? What're you talking about?"

"John."

Her soft cry broke his heart. *"No."* That she was desperately in love with John was no secret to Nick. That she was also a consummate professional who would never act on those feelings was one of the many reasons Nick respected her.

"I'm sorry to just blurt it out like that."

"How?" she asked in a small voice.

"Stabbed in his bed."

Her ravaged moan echoed through the phone. "But who... I mean, *why?*"

"The cops are here, but I don't know anything yet. I need you to request a postponement on the vote."

"I can't," she said, adding in a whisper, "I can't think about that right now."

"You have to, Chris. That bill is his legacy. We can't let all his hard work be for nothing. Can you do it? For him?"

"Yes...okay."

"You have to pull yourself together for the staff, but don't tell them yet. Not until his parents are notified."

"Oh, God, his poor parents. You should go, Nick. It'd be better coming from you than cops they don't know."

"I don't know if I can. How do I tell people I love that their son's been murdered?"

"He'd want it to come from you."

"I suppose you're right. I'll see if the cops will let me."

"What're we going to do without him, Nick?" She posed a question he'd been grappling with himself. "I just can't imagine this world, this *life,* without him."

"I can't either," Nick said, knowing it would be a much different life without John O'Connor at the center of it.

"He's really dead?" she asked as if to convince herself it wasn't a cruel joke. "Someone killed him?"

"Yes."

Outside the chief's office suite, Detective Sergeant Sam Holland smoothed her hands over the toffee-colored hair she corralled into a clip for work, pinched some color into cheeks that hadn't seen the light of day in weeks, and adjusted her gray suit jacket over a red scoop-neck top.

Taking a deep breath to calm her nerves and settle her chronically upset stomach, she pushed open the door and stepped inside. Chief Farnsworth's receptionist greeted her with a smile. "Go right in, Sergeant Holland. He's waiting for you."

Great, Sam thought as she left the receptionist with a weak smile. Before she could give into the urge to turn tail and run, she erased the grimace from her face and went in.

"Sergeant." The chief, a man she'd once called Uncle Joe, stood up and came around the big desk to greet her with a firm handshake. His gray eyes skirted over her with concern and sympathy, both of which were new since "the incident." She despised being the reason for either. "You look well."

"I feel well."

"Glad to hear it." He gestured for her to have a seat. "Coffee?"

"No, thanks."

Pouring himself a cup, he glanced over his shoulder. "I've been worried about you, Sam."

"I'm sorry for causing you worry and for disgracing the department." This was the first chance she'd had to speak directly to him since she returned from a month of administrative leave, during which she'd practiced the sentence over and over. She thought she'd delivered it with convincing sincerity.

"Sam," he sighed as he sat across from her, cradling his mug between big hands. "You've done nothing to disgrace yourself or the department. Everyone makes mistakes."

"Not everyone makes mistakes that result in a dead child, Chief."

He studied her for a long, intense moment as if he was making some sort of decision. "Senator John O'Connor was found murdered in his apartment this morning."

"Jesus," she gasped. "How?"

"I don't have all the details, but from what I've been told so far, it appears he was dismembered and stabbed through the neck. Apparently, his chief of staff found him."

"Nick," she said softly.

"Excuse me?"

"Nick Cappuano is O'Connor's chief of staff."

"You know him?"

"*Knew* him. Years ago," she added, surprised and unsettled to discover the memory of him still had power over her, that just the sound of his name rolling off her lips could make her heart race.

"I'm assigning the case to you."

Surprised at being thrust so forcefully back into the real work she had craved since her return to duty, she couldn't help but ask, "Why me?"

"Because you need this, and so do I. We both need a win."

The press had been relentless in its criticism of him, of her, of the department, but to hear him acknowledge it made her ache. Her father had come up through the ranks with Farnsworth, which was probably the number one reason why she still had a job. "Is this a test? Find out who killed the senator and my previous sins are forgiven?"

He put down his coffee cup and leaned forward, elbows resting on knees. "The only person who needs to forgive you, Sam, is you."

Infuriated by the surge of emotion brought on by his softly spoken words, Sam cleared her throat and stood up. "Where does O'Connor live?"

"The Watergate. Two uniforms are already there. Crime scene is on its way." He handed her a slip of paper with the address. "I don't have to tell you that this needs to be handled with the utmost discretion."

He also didn't have to tell her that this was the only chance she'd get at redemption.

"Won't the Feds want in on this?"

"They might, but they don't have jurisdiction, and they know it. They'll be breathing down my neck, though, so report directly to me. I want to know everything ten minutes after you do. I'll smooth it with Stahl," he added, referring to the lieutenant she usually answered to.

Heading for the door, she said, "I won't let you down.

"You never have before."

With her hand resting on the door handle, she turned back to him. "Are you saying that as the chief of police or as my Uncle Joe?"

His face lifted into a small but sincere smile. "Both."

Fatal Affair is available in print from *Amazon.com* and other online retailers, or you can purchase a signed copy from Marie's store at *shop.marieforce.com*.

ALSO BY MARIE FORCE

Contemporary Romances Available from Marie Force

The Gansett Island Series

Book 1: Maid for Love (*Mac & Maddie*)

Book 2: Fool for Love (*Joe & Janey*)

Book 3: Ready for Love (*Luke & Sydney*)

Book 4: Falling for Love (*Grant & Stephanie*)

Book 5: Hoping for Love (*Evan & Grace*)

Book 6: Season for Love (*Owen & Laura*)

Book 7: Longing for Love (*Blaine & Tiffany*)

Book 8: Waiting for Love (*Adam & Abby*)

Book 9: Time for Love (*David & Daisy*)

Book 10: Meant for Love (*Jenny & Alex*)

Book 10.5: Chance for Love, *A Gansett Island Novella (Jared & Lizzie)*

Book 11: Gansett After Dark (*Owen & Laura*)

Book 12: Kisses After Dark (*Shane & Katie*)

Book 13: Love After Dark (*Paul & Hope*)

Book 14: Celebration After Dark (*Big Mac & Linda*)

Book 15: Desire After Dark (*Slim & Erin*)

Book 16: Light After Dark (*Mallory & Quinn*)

Book 17: Victoria & Shannon (Episode 1)

Book 18: Kevin & Chelsea (Episode 2)

A Gansett Island Christmas Novella (*Appears in Mine After Dark*)

Book 19: Mine After Dark (*Riley & Nikki*)

Book 20: Yours After Dark (*Finn & Chloe*)

Book 21: Trouble After Dark *(Deacon & Julia)*

Book 22: Rescue After Dark *(Mason & Jordan)*

Book 23: Blackout After Dark *(Full Cast)*

Book 24: Temptation After Dark *(Gigi & Cooper)*

Book 25: Resilience After Dark *(Jace & Cindy)*

Book 26: Hurricane After Dark *(Full Cast)*

Book 27: Renewal After Dark *(Coming 2024)*

The Green Mountain Series

Book 1: All You Need Is Love *(Will & Cameron)*

Book 2: I Want to Hold Your Hand *(Nolan & Hannah)*

Book 3: I Saw Her Standing There *(Colton & Lucy)*

Book 4: And I Love Her *(Hunter & Megan)*

Novella: You'll Be Mine *(Will & Cam's Wedding)*

Book 5: It's Only Love *(Gavin & Ella)*

Book 6: Ain't She Sweet *(Tyler & Charlotte)*

The Butler, Vermont Series

(Continuation of Green Mountain)

Book 1: Every Little Thing *(Grayson & Emma)*

Book 2: Can't Buy Me Love *(Mary & Patrick)*

Book 3: Here Comes the Sun *(Wade & Mia)*

Book 4: Till There Was You *(Lucas & Dani)*

Book 5: All My Loving *(Landon & Amanda)*

Book 6: Let It Be *(Lincoln & Molly)*

Book 7: Come Together *(Noah & Brianna)*

Book 8: Here, There & Everywhere *(Izzy & Cabot)*

Book 9: The Long and Winding Road *(Max & Lexi)*

Romantic Suspense Novels Available from Marie Force

The Fatal Series

One Night With You, *A Fatal Series Prequel Novella*

Book 1: Fatal Affair

Book 2: Fatal Justice

Book 3: Fatal Consequences

Book 3.5: Fatal Destiny, *the Wedding Novella*

Book 4: Fatal Flaw

Book 5: Fatal Deception

Book 6: Fatal Mistake

Book 7: Fatal Jeopardy

Book 8: Fatal Scandal

Book 9: Fatal Frenzy

Book 10: Fatal Identity

Book 11: Fatal Threat

Book 12: Fatal Chaos

Book 13: Fatal Invasion

Book 14: Fatal Reckoning

Book 15: Fatal Accusation

Book 16: Fatal Fraud

Sam and Nick's story continues...

Book 1: State of Affairs

Book 2: State of Grace

Book 3: State of the Union

Book 4: State of Shock

Book 5: State of Denial

Book 6: State of Bliss (Dec. 2023)

Book 7: State of Suspense (Coming 2024)

Single Titles

Five Years Gone

One Year Home

Sex Machine

Sex God

Georgia on My Mind

True North

The Fall

The Wreck

Love at First Flight

Everyone Loves a Hero

Line of Scrimmage

Historical Romance Available from Marie Force

The Gilded Series

Book 1: Duchess by Deception

Book 2: Deceived by Desire

ABOUT THE AUTHOR

Marie Force is the #1 *Wall Street Journal*
bestselling author of more than 100
contemporary romance, romantic
suspense and erotic romance novels.
Her series include Fatal, First Family,
Gansett Island, Butler Vermont, Quan-
tum, Treading Water, Miami Nights and Wild Widows.

Her books have sold more than 13 million copies world-
wide, have been translated into more than a dozen languages
and have appeared on the *New York Times* bestseller list more
than 30 times. She is also a *USA Today* bestseller, as well as a
Spiegel bestseller in Germany.

Her goals in life are simple—to spend as much time as she
can with her "kids" who are now adults, to keep writing
books for as long as she possibly can and to never be on a
flight that makes the news.

Join Marie's mailing list on her website at *marieforce.com*
for news about new books and upcoming appearances in
your area. Follow her on Facebook at *www.Facebook.-
com/MarieForceAuthor*, Instagram at *www.instagram.-
com/marieforceauthor/* and TikTok at *https://www.tiktok.com/@
marieforceauthor?*. Contact Marie at *marie@marieforce.com*.

Made in United States
North Haven, CT
18 October 2024

59090527R10205